DISCARDED

The

of

Eyton Forest

The Hermit
of
Eyton Forest

The Fourteenth Chronicle
of Brother Cadfael

Ellis Peters

General
— PAPERBACKS —
Toronto, Canada

Chapter One

IT WAS on the eighteenth day of October of that year 1142 that Richard Ludel, hereditary tenant of the manor of Eaton, died of a debilitating weakness, left after wounds received at the battle of Lincoln, in the service of King Stephen.

The news was duly brought to Hugh Beringar in Shrewsbury castle, since Eaton was one of the many manors in the shire which had been expropriated from William FitzAlan, after that powerful nobleman took arms on the wrong side in the struggle for the throne, held Shrewsbury for the Empress Maud, and took to flight when Stephen besieged and captured the town. His wide lands, forfeited to the crown, had been placed in the sheriff's care as overlord, but their tenants of long standing had been left undisturbed, once it was clear that they had wisely accepted the judgement of battle, and pledged their allegiance to the king. Ludel, indeed, had done more than declare his loyalty, he had proved it in arms at Lincoln, and now, it seemed, paid a high price for his fealty, for he was no more than thirty-five years old at his death.

Hugh received the news with the mild regret natural to one who had barely known the man, and whose duties were unlikely to be complicated by any closer contact with the death. There was an heir, and no second son to cloud the issue of inheritance, certainly no need to interfere with the smooth succession. The Ludels were Stephen's men, and loyal, even if the new incumbent was hardly likely to take arms for his king for many years to come, being, Hugh recalled, about ten years old. The boy was in school at the abbey, placed there by his father when the mother died, most likely, so rumour said, to get him out of the hands of a domineering grand-mother, rather than simply to ensure that he learned his letters.

It seemed, therefore, that the abbey, if not the castle, had some unenviable responsibility in the matter, for someone would have to tell young Richard that his father was dead. The funeral rites would not fall to the abbey, Eaton having its own church and parish priest, but the custody of the heir was a matter of importance. And as for me, thought Hugh, I had better make certain how competent a steward Ludel has left to manage the boy's estate, while he's not yet of age to manage it himself.

'You have not taken this word to the lord abbot yet?' he asked the groom who had brought the message.

'No, my lord, I came first to you.'

'And have you orders from the lady to speak with the heir himself?'

'No, my lord, and would as soon leave that to those who have the daily care of him.'

'You may well be right there,' Hugh agreed. 'I'll go myself and speak with Abbot Radulfus. He'll know best how to deal. As to the succession, Dame Dionisia need have no concern, the boy's title is secure enough.'

In times full of trouble, with cousins contending bitterly for the throne, and opportunist lords changing their coats according to the pendulum fortunes of this desultory war, Hugh was only too glad to be guardian of a shire which had changed hands but once, and settled down doggedly thereafter to keep King Stephen's title unchallenged and the tide of unrest at bay from its borders, whether the threat came from the empress's forces, the unpredictable cantrips of the wild Welshmen of Powys to the west, or the calculating ambition of the earl of Chester in the north. Hugh had balanced his relationships with all these perilous neighbours for some years now with fair success, it would have been folly to consider handing over Eaton to another tenant, whatever the possible drawbacks of allowing the succession to pass unbroken to a child. Why upset a family which had remained submissive and loyal, and dug in its heels sturdily to await events when its overlord fled to France? Recent rumour had it that William FitzAlan was back in England, and had joined the empress in Oxford, and the sense of his presence, even at that distance, might stir older loyalties among his former tenants, but that was a risk to be met when it showed signs of arising. To give Eaton to another tenant might well be to rouse the old allegiance needlessly from its prudent slumber. No, Ludel's son should have his rights. But it would be well to have a look at the steward, and make sure he could be trusted, both to keep to his late lord's policies and to take good care of his new lord's interests and lands.

Hugh rode out unhurriedly through the town, in the fine mid-morning after the early mist had lifted, gently uphill to the High Cross, steeply downhill again by the winding Wyle to the eastward gate, and across the stone bridge towards the Foregate, where the crossing tower of the abbey church loomed solidly against a pale blue sky. The Severn ran rapid but tranquil under the arches of the bridge, still at its mild summer level, its two small, grassy islands rimmed with a narrow edging of bleached brown which would be covered again when the first heavy rain brought storm-water down from Wales. To the left, where the highroad opened before him, the clustering bushes and trees rising from the riverside just

7

touched the dusty rim of the road, before the small houses and yards and gardens of the Foregate began. To the right the mill-pool stretched away between its grassy banks, a faint bloom of lingering mist blurring its silver surface, and beyond, the wall of the abbey enclave arose, and the arch of the gatehouse.

Hugh dismounted as the porter came out to take his bridle. He was as well known here as any who wore the Benedictine habit and belonged within the walls.

'If you're wanting Brother Cadfael, my lord,' offered the porter helpfully, 'he's away to Saint Giles to replenish their medicine cupboard. But he's been gone an hour or so now, he left after chapter. He'll be back soon, surely, if you're minded to wait for him.'

'My business is with the lord abbot first,' said Hugh, acknowledging without protest the assumption that his every visit here must inevitably be in search of one close crony. 'Though no doubt Cadfael will hear the same word afterwards, if he hasn't heard it in advance! The winds always seem to blow news his way before they trouble about the rest of us.'

'His duties take him forth, more than most of us ever get the chance,' said the porter good-humouredly. 'Come to that, how do the poor afflicted souls at Saint Giles ever come to hear so much of what goes on in the wide world? For he seldom comes back without some piece of gossip that's amazement to everybody this end of the Foregate. Father Abbot's down in his own garden. He's been closeted over accounts with the sacristan for an hour or more, but I saw Brother Benedict leave him a little while ago.' He reached a veined brown hand to caress the horse's neck, very respectfully, for Hugh's big, raw-boned grey, as cross-grained as he was strong, had little but contempt for all things human except his master, and even he was regarded rather as an equal, to be respected but kept in his place. 'There's no news from Oxford yet?'

Even within the cloister they could not choose but keep one ear cocked for news of the siege. Success there now might well see the empress a prisoner, and force an end at last to this dissension that tore the land apart.

'Not since the king got his armies through the ford and into the town. We may hear something soon, if some who had time to get out of the city drift up this way. But the garrison will have made sure the castle larders were well filled. I doubt it will drag on for many weeks yet.'

Siege is slow strangulation, and King Stephen had never been noted for patience and tenacity, and might yet find it tedious to sit waiting for his enemies to reach starvation, and take himself off to find brisker action elsewhere. It had happened before, and could happen again.

Hugh shrugged off his liege lord's shortcomings, and set off down the great court to the abbot's lodging, to distract Father Radulfus from his cherished if slightly jaded roses.

Brother Cadfael was back from the hospital of Saint Giles and busy in his workshop, sorting beans for next year's seed, when Hugh came back from the abbot's lodging and made his way to the herbarium. Recognising the swift, light tread on the gravel, Cadfael greeted him without turning his head.

'Brother Porter told me you'd be here. Business with Father Abbot, he says. What's in the wind? Nothing new from Oxford?'

'No,' said Hugh, seating himself comfortably on the bench against the timber wall, 'nearer home. This is from no farther off than Eaton. Richard Ludel is dead. The dowager sent a groom with the news this morning. You've got the boy here at school.'

Cadfael turned then, with one of the clay saucers, full of seed dried on the vine, in his hand. 'So we have. Well, so his sire's gone, is he? We heard he was dwindling. The youngster was no more than five when he was sent here, and they fetch him home very seldom. I think his father thought the child was better here with a few fellows near his own age than kept around a sick man's bed.'

'And under the rule of a strong-willed grandmother, from all I hear. I don't know the lady,' said Hugh thoughtfully, 'except by reputation. I did know the man, though I've seen nothing of him since we got our wounded back from Lincoln. A good fighter and a decent soul, but dour, no talker. What's the boy like?'

'Sharp – venturesome . . . A very fetching imp, truth to tell, but as often in trouble as out of it. Bright at his letters, but he'd rather be out at play. Paul will have the task of telling him his father's dead, and himself master of a manor. It may trouble Paul more than it does the boy. He hardly knows his sire. I suppose there's no question about his tenure?'

'None in the world! I'm all for letting well alone, and Ludel earned his immunity. It's a good property, too, fat land, and much of it under the plough. Good grazing, water-meadows and woodland, and it's been well tended, seemingly, for it's valued higher now than ten years since. But I must get to know the steward, and make sure he'll do the boy right.'

'John of Longwood,' said Cadfael promptly. 'He's a good man and a good husbandman. We know him well, we've had dealings with him, and always found him reasonable and fair. That land falls between the abbey holdings of Eyton-by-Severn on the one side, and Aston-under-Wrekin on the other, and John has always given our forester free access between the two woodlands whenever needed, to save him time and labour. We bring wood out from our part of the Wrekin forest that way. It suits us both very well. Ludel's part of Eyton forest bites into ours there, it would be folly to fall out. Ludel had left everything to John these last two years, you'll have no trouble there.'

'The abbot tells me,' said Hugh, nodding satisfaction with this good-neighbourliness, 'that Ludel gave the boy as ward into his hands, four years ago, should he himself not live to see his son grown to manhood. It seems he made all possible provision for the future, as if he saw his own death coming towards him.' And he added, somewhat grimly: 'As well most of us have no such clear sight, or there'd be some hundreds in Oxford now hurrying to buy Masses for their souls. By this time the king must hold the town. It would fall into his hands of itself once he was over the ford. But the castle could hold out to the year's end, at a pinch, and there's no cheap way in there, it's a matter of starving them out. And if Robert of Gloucester in Normandy has not had word of all this by now, then his intelligencers are less able than I gave them credit for. If he knows how his sister's pressed, he'll be on his way home in haste. I've known the besiegers become the besieged before now, it could as well happen again.'

'It will take him some time to get back,' Cadfael pointed out comfortably. 'And by all accounts no better provided than when he went.'

The empress's half-brother and best soldier had been sent overseas, much against his inclination, to ask help for the lady from her less than loving husband, but Count Geoffrey of Anjou was credibly reported to be much more interested in his own ambitions in Normandy than in his wife's in England, and had been astute enough to inveigle Earl Robert into helping him pick off castle after castle in the duchy, instead of rushing to his wife's side to assist her to the crown of England. As early as June Robert had sailed from Wareham, against his own best judgement but at his sister's urgent entreaty, and Geoffrey's insistence, if he was to entertain any ambassador from her at all. And here was September ended, Wareham back in King Stephen's hands, and Robert still detained in Geoffrey's thankless service in Normandy. No, it would not be any quick or easy matter for him to come to his sister's rescue. The iron grip of siege tightened steadily round Oxford castle, and for once Stephen showed no sign of abandoning his purpose. Never yet had he come so close to making his cousin and rival his prisoner, and forcing her acceptance of his sovereignty.

'Does he realise,' wondered Cadfael, closing the lid of a stone jar on his selected seed, 'how near he's come to getting her into his power at last? How would you feel, Hugh, if you were in his shoes, and truly got your hands on her?'

'Heaven forefend!' said Hugh fervently, and grinned at the very thought. 'For I shouldn't know what to do with her! And the devil of it is, neither will Stephen, if ever it comes to that. He could have kept her tight shut into Arundel the day she landed, if he'd had the sense. And what did he do? Gave her an escort, and sent her off to Bristol to join her brother! But if the queen ever gets the lady into her power, that will be another story. If he's a grand fighter, she's the better general, and knows how to hold on to her advantages.'

Hugh rose and stretched, and a rising breeze from the open door ruffled his smooth black hair, and rustled the dangling bunches of dried herbs hanging from the roof beams. 'Well, there's no hurrying the siege to an end, we must wait and see. I hear they've finally given you a lad to help you in the herb garden, is it true? I noticed your hedge has had a second clipping, was that his work?'

'It was.' Cadfael went out with him along the gravel path between the patterned beds of herbs, grown a little wiry at this end of the growing season. The box hedge at one side had indeed been neatly trimmed of the straggling shoots that come late in the summer. 'Brother Winfrid you'll see him busy in the patch where we've cleared the bean vines, digging in the holms. A big, gangling lad all elbows and knees. Not long out of his novitiate. Willing, but slow. But he'll do. They sent him to me, I fancy,

12

because he turned out fumble-fisted with either pen or brush, but give him a spade, and that's more his measure. He'll do!'

Outside the walled herb garden the vegetable plots extended, and beyond the slight rise on their right the harvested pease fields ran down to the Meole Brook, which was the rear border of the abbey enclave. And there was Brother Winfrid in full vigorous action, a big, loose-jointed youth with a shock-head of wiry hair hedging in his shaven crown, his habit kilted to brawny knees, and a broad foot shod in a wooden clog driving the steel-edged spade through the fibrous tangle of bean holms as through blades of grass. He gave them one beaming glance as they passed, and returned to his work without breaking the rhythm. Hugh had one glimpse of a weather-browned country face and round, guileless blue eyes.

'Yes, I should think he might do very well,' he said, impressed and amused, 'whether with a spade or a battle-axe. I could do with a dozen such at the castle whenever they care to offer their services.'

'He'd be no use to you,' said Cadfael with certainty. 'Like most big men, the gentlest soul breathing. He'd throw his sword away to pick up the man he'd flattened. It's the little, shrill terriers that bare their teeth.'

They emerged into the band of flowerbeds beyond the kitchen garden, where the rose bushes had grown leggy and begun to shed their leaves. Rounding the corner of the box hedge, they came out into the great court, at this working hour of the morning almost deserted but for one or two travellers coming and going about the guest hall, and a stir of movement down in the stables. Just as they rounded the tall hedge to step into the court, a small figure shot out of the gate of the grange court, where the barns and storage lofts lined three sides of a compact yard, and made off at a run across the narrows of the court into the cloister, to emerge a minute later at the

13

other end at a decorous walk, with eyes lowered in seemly fashion, and plump, childish hands devoutly linked at his belt, the image of innocence. Cadfael halted considerately, with a hand on Hugh's arm, to avoid confronting the boy too obviously.

The child reached the corner of the infirmary, rounded it, and vanished. There was a distinct impression that as he quit the sight of any watchers in the great court he broke into a run again, for a bare heel flashed suddenly and was gone. Hugh was grinning. Cadfael caught his friend's eye, and said nothing.

'Let me hazard!' said Hugh, twinkling. 'You picked your apples yesterday, and they're not yet laid up in the trays in the loft. Lucky it was not Prior Robert who saw him at it, and he with the breast of his cotte bulging like a portly dame!'

'Oh, there are some of us have a sort of silent understanding. He'll have taken the biggest, but only four. He thieves in moderation. Partly from decent obligation, partly because half the sport is to tempt providence again and again.'

Hugh's agile black eyebrow signalled amused enquiry. 'Why four?'

'Because we have but four boys still in school, and if he thieves at all, he thieves *for* all. There are several novices not very much older, but to them he has no obligation. They must do their own thieving, or go without. And do you know,' asked Cadfael complacently, 'who that young limb is?'

'I do not, but you are about to astonish me.'

'I doubt if I am. That is Master Richard Ludel, the new lord of Eaton. Though plainly,' said Cadfael, wryly contemplating shadowed innocence, 'he does not yet know it.'

Richard was sitting cross-legged on the grassy bank above the mill-pond, thoughtfully nibbling out the last shreds of white flesh from round his apple core, when one of the novices came looking for him.

'Brother Paul wants you,' announced the messenger, with the austerely complacent face of one aware of his own virtue, and delivering a probably ominous summons to another. 'He's in the parlour. You'd best hurry.'

'Me?' said Richard, round-eyed, looking up from his enjoyment of the stolen apple. No one had any great cause to be afraid of Brother Paul, the master of the novices and the children, who was the gentlest and most patient of men, but even a reproof from him was to be evaded if possible. 'What does he want me for?'

'You should best know that,' said the novice, with mildly malicious intent. 'It was not likely he'd tell me. Go and find out for yourself, if you truly have no notion.'

Richard committed his denuded core to the pond, and rose slowly from the grass. 'In the parlour, you say?' The use of so private and ceremonial a place argued something grave, and though he was unaware of any but the most venial of misdeeds that could be laid to his account during the past weeks, it behoved him to be wary. He went off slowly and thoughtfully, trailing his bare feet in the coolness of the grass, deliberately scuffing hard little soles along the cobbles of the court, and duly presented himself in the small, dim parlour, where visitors from the outside world might occasionally talk in private with their cloistered sons.

Brother Paul was standing with his back to the single window, rendering the small room even dimmer than it need have been. The straight, close-shorn ring of hair round his polished crown was still black and thick at fifty, and he habitually stood, as indeed he also sat, stooped a little forward, from so many years of dealing with creatures half his size, and desiring to reassure them rather than awe them with his stature and bearing. A

15

kindly, scholarly, indulgent man, but a good teacher for all that, and one who could keep his chicks in order without having to keep them in terror. The oldest remaining *oblatus*, given to God when he was five years old, and now approaching fifteen and his novitiate, told awful stories of Brother Paul's predecessor, who had ruled with the rod, and been possessed of an eye that could freeze the blood.

Richard made his small obligatory obeisance, and stood squarely before his master, lifting to the light an impenetrable countenance, lit by two blue-green eyes of radiant innocence. A thin, active child, small for his years but agile and supple as a cat, with a thick, curly crest of light brown hair, and a band of golden freckles over both cheekbones and the bridge of his neat, straight nose. He stood with feet braced sturdily apart, toes gripping the floorboards, and stared up into Brother Paul's face, dutiful and guileless. Paul was well acquainted with that unblinking gaze.

'Richard,' he said gently, 'come, sit down with me. I have something I must tell you.'

That in itself was enough to discount one slight childish unease, only to replace it with another and graver, for the tone was so considerate and indulgent as to prophesy the need for comfort. But what Richard's sudden flickering frown expressed was simple bewilderment. He allowed himself to be drawn to the bench and seated there within the circle of Brother Paul's arm, bare toes just touching the floor, and braced there hard. He could be prepared for scolding, but here was surely something for which he was not prepared, and had no idea how to confront.

'You know that your father fought at Lincoln for the king, and was wounded? And that he has since been in poor health.' Secure in robust, well-fed and well-tended youth, Richard hardly knew what poor health might be, except that it was something that happened to the old.

16

But he said: 'Yes, Brother Paul!' in a small, accommodating voice, since it was expected of him.

'Your grandmother sent a groom to the lord sheriff this morning. He has brought a sad message, Richard. Your father has made his last confession and received his Saviour. He is dead, my child. You are his heir, and you must be worthy of him. In life and in death,' said Brother Paul, 'he is in the hand of God. So are we all.'

The look of thoughtful bewilderment had not changed. Richard's toes shoved hard against the floor, and his hands gripped the edge of the bench on which he was perched.

'My father is dead?' he repeated carefully.

'Yes, Richard. Soon or late, it touches us all. Every son must one day step into his father's place and take up his father's duties.'

'Then I shall be the lord of Eaton now?'

Brother Paul did not make the mistake of taking this for a simple expression of self-congratulation on a personal gain, rather as an intelligent acceptance of what he himself had just said. The heir must take up the burden and the privilege his sire had laid down.

'Yes, you are the lord of Eaton, or you will be as soon as you are of fit age. You must study to get wisdom, and manage your lands and people well. Your father would expect that of you.'

Still struggling with the practicalities of his new situation, Richard probed back into his memory for a clear vision of this father who was now challenging him to be worthy. In his rare recent visits home at Christmas and Easter he had been admitted on arrival and departure to a sick-room that smelled of herbs and premature aging, and allowed to kiss a grey, austere face and listen to a deep voice, indifferent with weakness, calling him son and exhorting him to study and be virtuous. But there was little more, and even the face had grown dim in his memory. Of what he did remember he went in awe.

They had never been close enough for anything more intimate.

'You loved your father, and did your best to please him, did you not, Richard?' Brother Paul prompted gently. 'You must still do what is pleasing to him. And you may say prayers for his soul, which will be a comfort also to you.'

'Shall I have to go home now?' asked Richard, whose mind was on the need for information rather than comfort.

'To your father's burial, certainly. But not to remain there, not yet. It was your father's wish that you should learn to read and write, and be properly instructed in figures. And you're young yet, your steward will take good care of your manor until you come to manhood.'

'My grandmother,' said Richard by way of explanation, 'sees no sense in my learning my letters. She was angry when my father sent me here. She says a lettered clerk is all any manor needs, and books are no fit employment for a nobleman.'

'Surely she will comply with your father's wishes. All the more is that a sacred trust, now that he is dead.'

Richard jutted a doubtful lip. 'But my grandmother has other plans for me. She wants to marry me to our neighbour's daughter, because Hiltrude has no brother, and will be the heiress to both Leighton and Wroxeter. Grandmother will want that more than ever now,' said Richard simply, and looked up ingenuously into Brother Paul's slightly startled face.

It took a few moments to assimilate this news, and relate it to the boy's entry into the abbey school when he was barely five years old. The manors of Leighton and Wroxeter lay one on either side of Eaton, and might well be a tempting prospect, but plainly Richard Ludel had not concurred in his mother's ambitious plans for her grandson, since he had taken steps to place the boy out of the lady's reach, and a year later had made Abbot

Radulfus Richard's guardian, should he himself have to relinquish the charge too soon. Father Abbot had better know what's in the wind, thought Brother Paul. For of such a misuse of his ward, thus almost in infancy, he would certainly not approve.

Very warily he said, fronting the boy's unwavering stare with a grave face: 'Your father said nothing of what his plans for you might be, some day when you are fully grown. Such matters must wait their proper time, and that is not yet. You need not trouble your head about any such match for years yet. You are in Father Abbot's charge, and he will do what is best for you.' And he added cautiously, giving way to natural human curiosity: 'Do you know this child – this neighbour's daughter?'

'She isn't a child,' Richard stated scornfully. 'She's quite old. She was betrothed once, but her bridegroom died. My grandmother was pleased, because after waiting some years for him, Hiltrude wouldn't have many suitors, not being even pretty, so she would be left for me.'

Brother Paul's blood chilled at the implications. 'Quite old' probably meant no more than a few years past twenty, but even that was an unacceptable difference. Such marriages, of course, were a commonplace, where there was property and land to be won, but they were certainly not to be encouraged. Abbot Radulfus had long had qualms of conscience about accepting infants committed by their fathers to the cloister, and had resolved to admit no more boys until they were of an age to make the choice for themselves. He would certainly look no more favourably on committing a child to the equally grave and binding discipline of matrimony.

'Well, you may put all such matters out of your mind,' he said very firmly. 'Your only concern now and for some years to come must be with your lessons and the pastimes proper to your years. Now you may go back to your fellows, if you wish, or stay here quietly for a while, as you prefer.'

Richard slid out of the supporting arm readily and stood up sturdily from the bench, willing to face the world and his curious fellow pupils at once, and seeing no reason why he should shun the meeting even for a moment. He had yet to comprehend the thing that had happened to him. The fact he could grasp, the implications were slow to reach beyond his intelligence into his heart.

'If there is anything more you wish to ask,' said Brother Paul, eyeing him anxiously, 'or if you feel the need for comfort or counsel, come back to me, and we'll go to Father Abbot. He is wiser than I, and abler to help you through this time.'

So he might be, but a boy in school was hardly likely to submit himself voluntarily to an interview with so awesome a personage. Richard's solemn face had settled into the brooding frown of one making his way through unfamiliar and thorny paths. He made his parting reverence and went out briskly enough, and Brother Paul, having watched him out of sight from the window, and seen no signs of imminent distress, went to report to the abbot what Dame Dionisia Ludel was said to be planning for her grandson.

Radulfus heard him out with alert attention and a thoughtful frown. To unite Eaton with both its neighbouring manors was an understandable ambition. The resulting property would be a power in the shire, and no doubt the formidable lady considered herself more than capable of ruling it, over the heads of bride, bride's father and infant bridegroom. Land greed was a strong driving force, and children were possessions expendable for so desirable a profit.

'But we trouble needlessly,' said Radulfus, shaking the matter resolutely from his shoulders. 'The boy is in my care, and here he stays. Whatever she may intend, she will

20

not be able to touch him. We can forget the matter. She is no threat to Richard or to us.'

Wise as he might be, this was one occasion when Abbot Radulfus was to find his predictions going far astray.

Chapter Two

THEY were all at chapter, on the twentieth morning of October, when the steward of the manor of Eaton presented himself, requesting a hearing with a message from his mistress.

John of Longwood was a burly, bearded man of fifty, with a balding crown and neat, deliberate movements. He made a respectful obeisance to the abbot, and delivered his errand bluntly and practically, as one performing a duty but without committing himself to approval or disapproval.

'My lord, Dame Dionisia Ludel sends me to you with her devout greetings, and asks that you will send back to her, in my charge, her grandson Richard, to take up his rightful place as lord of the manor of Eaton in his father's room.'

Abbot Radulfus leaned back in his stall and regarded the messenger with an impassive face. 'Certainly Richard shall attend his father's funeral. When is that to be?'

'Tomorrow, my lord, before High Mass. But that is not my mistress's meaning. She wants the young lord to leave his studies here and come to take his proper place as lord of Eaton. I'm to say that Dame Dionisia feels herself to be the proper person to have charge of him, now that he's come into his inheritance, as she's assured he shall do, without delay or hindrance. I have orders to bring him back with me.'

'I fear, master steward,' said the abbot with deliberation, 'that you may not be able to carry out your orders. Richard Ludel committed the care of his son to me, should he himself die before the boy came to manhood. It was his wish that his son should be properly educated, the better to manage his estate when he came to inherit. I intend to fulfil what I undertook. Richard remains in my care until he comes of age and takes control of his own affairs. Until which time, I am sure, you will serve him as well as you have served his father, and keep his lands in good heart.'

'Very surely I will, my lord,' said John of Longwood, with more warmth than he had shown in delivering his mistress's message. 'My lord Richard has left all to me since Lincoln, and he never had cause to find fault, and neither shall his son ever be the loser by me. On that you may rely.'

'So I do. And therefore we may continue here with easy minds, and take as good care of Richard's schooling and wellbeing as you do of his estates.'

'And what reply am I to take back to Dame Dionisia?' asked John, without any apparent disappointment or reluctance.

'Say to your lady that I greet her reverently in Christ, and that Richard shall come tomorrow, as is due, properly escorted,' said the abbot with a slightly admonitory emphasis, 'but that I have his father's sacred charge to hold him in wardship myself until he is a man, and by his father's wishes I shall abide.'

'I will say so, my lord,' said John with a straight, wide stare and a deep reverence, and walked jauntily out of the chapterhouse.

Brother Cadfael and Brother Edmund the infirmarer emerged into the great court just in time to see the messenger from Eaton mount his stocky Welsh cob at the gatehouse and ride unhurriedly out into the Foregate.

'There goes a man, unless I'm much mistaken,' remarked Brother Cadfael sagely, 'no way seriously displeased at taking back a flat refusal. Nor at all afraid of delivering it. A man might almost think he'll savour the moment.'

'He is not dependent on the dame's good will,' said Brother Edmund. 'Only the sheriff as overlord can threaten his tenure, until the boy is his own master, and John knows his worth. And so does she, for that matter, having a shrewd head and proper appreciation of good management. For the sake of peace he'll do her bidding, he does not have to relish the task, only to keep his mouth shut.'

And John of Longwood was a man of few words at the best of times, it would probably be no hardship to him to contain his dissent and keep a wooden face.

'But this will not be the end of it,' Cadfael warned. 'If she has a greedy eye on Wroxeter and Leighton she'll not give up so easily, and the boy's her only means of getting her hands on them. We shall yet hear more from Dame Dionisia Ludel.'

Abbot Radulfus had taken the warning seriously. Young Richard was accompanied to Eaton by Brother Paul, Brother Anselm and Brother Cadfael, a bodyguard stout enough to fend off even an attempt at abduction by force, which was unlikely in the extreme. Far more probable that the lady would try using the fond persuasions of affection and the ties of blood to work upon the boy with tears and blandishments, and turn him into a homesick ally in the enemy camp. If she had any such ideas, Cadfael reflected, studying Richard's face along the way, she was under-estimating the innocent shrewdness of children. The boy was quite capable of weighing up his own interests and making the most of what advantages he had. He was happy enough at school, he had companions of

24

his own age, he would not lightly abandon a known and pleasant life for one as yet strange, devoid of brothers, and threatened with a bride already old in his eyes. No doubt he valued and longed for his inheritance, but his it was, and safe, and whether he stayed at school or came home, he would not yet be allowed to rule it as he wished. No, it would take more than grandmotherly tears and embraces to secure Richard's alliance, especially tears and embraces from a source never before known to be demonstratively fond.

It was a matter of seven miles or more from the abbey to the manor of Eaton, and for the honour and dignity of the monastery of Saint Peter and Saint Paul, in attendance on so solemn an occasion, they were sent forth mounted. Dame Dionisia had sent a groom with a stout Welsh pony for her grandson, perhaps as a first move in a campaign to enlist him as her ally, and the gift had been received with greedy pleasure, but it would not therefore necessarily produce a return in kind. A gift is a gift, and children are shrewd enough, and have a sharp enough perception of the motives of their elders, to take what is offered unsolicited, without the least intention of paying for it in the fashion expected of them. Richard sat his new pony proudly and happily, and in the fine, dewy autumn morning and the pleasure of being loosed from school for the day, almost forgot the sombre reason for the ride. The groom, a long-legged boy of sixteen, loped cheerfully beside him, and led the pony as they splashed through the ford at Wroxeter, where centuries back the Romans had crossed the Severn before them. Nothing remained of their sojourn now but a gaunt, broken wall standing russet against the green fields, and a scattering of stones long ago plundered by the villagers for their own building purposes. In the place of what some said had been a city and a fortress there was now a flourishing manor blessed with fat, productive land, and a prosperous church that maintained four canons.

Cadfael viewed it with some interest as they passed, for this was one of the two manors which Dame Dionisia hoped to secure to the Ludel estate by marrying off Richard to the girl Hiltrude Astley. So fine a property was certainly tempting. All this stretch of country on the northern side of the river extended before them in rich water meadows and undulating fields, rising here and there into a gentle hill, and starred with clusters of trees just melting into the first gold of their autumn foliage. The land rose on the skyline into the forested ridge of the Wrekin, a great heaving fleece of woodland that spread downhill to the Severn, and cast a great tress of its dark mane across Ludel land and into the abbey's woods of Eyton-by-Severn. There was barely a mile between the grange of Eyton, close beside the river, and Richard Ludel's manor house at Eaton. The very names sprang from the same root, though time had prised them apart, and the Norman passion for order and formulation had fixed and ratified the differences.

As they rode nearer, their view of the long hog-back of forest changed and foreshortened. By the time they reached the manor they were viewing it from its end, and the hill had grown into an abrupt mountain, with a few sheer faces of rock just breaking the dark fell of the trees near the summit. The village sat serenely in the meadows, just short of the foothills, the manor within its long stockade raised over an undercroft, and the small church close beside it. Originally it had been a dependent chapel of the church at its neighbour Leighton, down-river by a couple of miles.

They dismounted within the stockade, and Brother Paul took Richard firmly by the hand as soon as the boy's foot touched ground, as Dame Dionisia came sweeping down the steps from the hall to meet them, advanced with authority upon her grandson, and stooped to kiss him. Richard lifted his face somewhat warily, and submitted to the salute, but he kept fast hold of Paul's hand. With one power bidding for his custody he knew where he stood, with the other he could not be sure of his standing.

Cadfael eyed the lady with interest, for though her reputation was known to him, he had never before been in her presence. Dionisia was tall and erect, certainly no more than fifty-five years old, and in vigorous health. She was, moreover, a handsome woman, if in a somewhat daunting fashion, with sharp, clear features and cool grey eyes. But their coolness showed one warning flash of fire as they swept over Richard's escort, recording the strength of the enemy. The household had come out at her back, the parish priest was at her side. There would be no engagement here. Later, perhaps, when Richard Ludel was safely entombed, and she could open the house in funeral hospitality, she might make a first move. The heir could hardly be kept from his grandmother's society on this day of all days.

The solemn rites for Richard Ludel took their appointed course. Brother Cadfael made good use of the time to survey the dead man's household, from John of Longwood to the youngest villein herdsman. There was every indication that the place had thrived well under John's stewardship, and his men were well content with their lot. Hugh would have good reason to let well alone. There were neighbours present, too, Fulke Astley among them, keeping a weather eye on what he himself might have to gain if the proposed match ever took place. Cadfael had seen him once or twice in Shrewsbury, a gross, self-important man in his late forties, running to fat, ponderous of movement, and surely no match for that restless, active, high-tempered woman standing grim-faced over her son's bier. She had Richard beside her, a hand possessively rather than protectively on his shoulder. The boy's eyes had dilated to engulf half his face, solemn as the grave that had been opened for his father, and was now about to be sealed. Distant death is one thing, its actual presence quite another. Not until

27

this minute had Richard fully realised the finality of this deprivation and severance.

The grandmotherly hand did not leave his shoulder as the cortège of mourners wound its way back to the manor, and the funeral meats spread for them in the hall. The long, lean, aging fingers had a firm grip on the cloth of the boy's best coat, and she guided him with her among guests and neighbours, properly but with notable emphasis making him the man of the house, and presiding figure at his father's obsequies. That did no harm at all. Richard was fully aware of his position, and well able to resent any infringement of his privilege. Brother Paul watched with some anxiety, and whispered to Cadfael that they had best get the boy away before all the guests departed, or they might fail to get him away at all, for want of witnesses. While the priest was still present, and those few others not of the household, he could hardly be retained by force.

Cadfael had been observing those of the company not well known to him. There were two grey-habited monks from the Savigniac house of Buildwas, a few miles away down-river, to which Ludel had been a generous patron on occasion, and with them, though withdrawn modestly throughout into the background, was a personage less easily identifiable. He wore a monastic gown, rusty black and well worn at the hems, but a head of unshorn dark hair showed within his cowl, and a gleam of reflected light picked out two or three metallic gleams from his shoulder that looked like the medals of more than one pilgrimage. Perhaps a wandering religious about to settle for the cloister. Savigny had been at Buildwas now for some forty years, a foundation of Roger de Clinton, bishop of Lichfield. Good, detached observers surely, these three. Before such reverend guests no violence could be attempted.

Brother Paul approached Dionisia courteously to take a discreet leave and reclaim his charge, but the lady took

28

the wind from his sails with a brief, steely flash of her eyes and a voice deceptively sweet: 'Brother, let me plead with you to let me keep Richard overnight. He has had a tiring day and begins to be weary now. He should not leave until tomorrow.' But she did not say that she would send him back on the morrow, and her hand retained its grip on his shoulder. She had spoken loudly enough to be heard by all, a solicitous matron anxious for her young.

'Madam,' said Brother Paul, making the best of a disadvantaged position, 'I was about to tell you, sadly, that we must be going. I have no authority to let Richard stay here with you, we are expected back for Vespers. I pray you pardon us.'

The lady's smile was honey, but her eyes were sharp and cold as knives. She made one more assay, perhaps to establish her own case with those who overheard, rather than with any hope of achieving anything immediately, for she knew the occasion rendered her helpless.

'Surely Abbot Radulfus would understand my desire to have the child to myself one more day. My own flesh and blood, the only one left to me, and I have seen so little of him these last years. You leave me uncomforted if you take him from me so soon.'

'Madam,' said Brother Paul, firm but uneasy, 'I grieve to withstand your wish, but I have no choice. I am bound in obedience to my abbot to bring Richard back with me before evening. Come, Richard, we must be going.'

There was an instant while she kept and tightened her hold, tempted to act even thus publicly, but she thought better of it. This was no time to put herself in the wrong, rather to recruit sympathy. She opened her hand, and Richard crept doubtfully away from her to Paul's side.

'Tell the lord abbot,' said Dionisia, her eyes daggers, but her voice still mellow and sweet, 'that I shall seek a meeting with him very soon.'

'Madam, I will tell him so,' said Brother Paul.

*　　*　　*

She was as good as her word. She rode into the abbey enclave the next day, well attended, bravely mounted, and in her impressive best, to ask audience of the abbot. She was closeted with him for almost an hour, but came forth in a cold blaze of resentment and rage, stormed across the great court like a sudden gale, scattering unoffending novices like blown leaves, and rode away again for home at a pace her staid jennet did not relish, with her grooms trailing mute and awed well in the rear.

'There goes a lady who is used to getting her own way,' remarked Brother Anselm, 'but for once, I fancy, she's met her match.'

'We have not heard the last of it, however,' said Brother Cadfael drily, watching the dust settle after her going.

'I don't doubt her will,' agreed Anselm, 'but what can she do?'

'That,' said Cadfael, not without quickening interest, 'no doubt we shall see, all in good time.'

They had but two days to wait. Dame Dionisia's man of law announced himself ceremoniously at chapter, requesting a hearing. An elderly clerk, meagre of person but brisk of bearing and irascible of feature, bustled into the chapterhouse with a bundle of parchments under his arm, and addressed the assembly with chill, reproachful dignity, in sorrow rather than in anger. He marvelled that a cleric and scholar of the abbot's known uprightness and benevolence should deny the ties of blood, and refuse to return Richard Ludel to the custody and loving care of his only surviving close kinswoman, now left quite bereft of all her other menfolk, and anxious to help, guide and advise her grandson in his new lordship. A great wrong was being done to both grandmother and child, in the denial of their natural need and the frustration of their mutual affection. And yet once more the clerk put forth the solemn request that the wrong should be set right, and Richard Ludel sent back with him to his manor of Eaton.

Abbot Radulfus sat with a patient and unmoved face and listened to the end of this studied speech very courteously. 'I thank you for your errand,' he said then mildly, 'it was well done. I cannot well change the answer I gave to your lady. Richard Ludel who is dead committed the care of his son to me, by letter properly drawn and witnessed. I accepted that charge, and I cannot renounce it now. It was the father's wish that the son should be educated here until he comes to manhood, and takes command of his own life and affairs. That I promised, and that I shall fulfil. The death of the father only makes my obligation the more sacred and binding. Tell your mistress so.'

'My lord,' said the clerk, plainly having expected no other answer, and ready with the next step in his embassage, 'in changed circumstances such a private legal document need not be the only argument valid in a court of law. The king's justices would listen no less to the plea of a matron of rank, widowed and now bereaved of her son, and fully able to provide all her grandson's needs, besides the natural need she has of the comfort of his presence. My mistress desires to inform you that if you do not give up the boy, she intends to bring suit at law to regain him.'

'Then I can but approve her intention,' said the abbot serenely. 'A judicial decision in the king's court must be satisfying to us both, since it lifts the burden of choice from us. Tell her so, and say that I await the hearing with due submission. But until such a judgement is made, I must hold to my own sworn undertaking. I am glad,' he said with a dry and private smile, 'that we are thus agreed.'

There was nothing left for the clerk to do but accept this unexpectedly pliant response at its face value, and bow himself out as gracefully as he could. A slight rustle

31

and stir of curiosity and wonder had rippled round the chapterhouse stalls, but Abbot Radulfus suppressed it with a look, and it was not until the brothers emerged into the great court and dispersed to their work that comment and speculation could break out openly.

'Was he wise to encourage her?' marvelled Brother Edmund, crossing towards the infirmary with Cadfael at his side. 'How if she does indeed take us to law? A judge might very well take the part of a lone lady who wants her grandchild home.'

'Be easy,' said Cadfael placidly. 'It's but an empty threat. She knows as well as any that the law is slow and costs dear, at the best of times, and this is none of the best, with the king far away and busy with more urgent matters, and half his kingdom cut off from any manner of justice at all. No, she hoped to make the lord abbot think again and yield ground for fear of long vexation. She had the wrong man. He knows she has no intention of going to law. Far more likely to take law into her own hands and try to steal the boy away. It would take slow law or swift action to snatch him back again, once she had him, and force is further out of the abbot's reach than it is out of hers.'

'It is to be hoped,' said Brother Edmund, aghast at the suggestion, 'that she has not yet used up all her persuasions, if the last resort is to be violence.'

No one could quite determine exactly how young Richard came to know every twist and turn of the contention over his future. He could not have overheard anything of what went on at chapter, nor were the novices present at the daily gatherings, and there was none among the brothers likely to gossip about the matter to the child at the centre of the conflict. Yet it was clear that Richard did know all that went on, and took perverse pleasure in it. Mischief made life more interesting, and here within the enclave he felt quite safe from any real danger, while he could enjoy being fought over.

'He watches the comings and goings from Eaton,' said Brother Paul, confiding his mild anxiety to Cadfael in the peace of the herb garden, 'and is sharp enough to be very well aware what they mean. And he understood all too well what went on at his father's funeral. I could wish him less acute, for his own sake.'

'As well he should have his wits about him,' said Cadfael comfortably. 'It's the knowing innocents that avoid the snares. And the lady's made no move now for ten days. Maybe she's grown resigned, and given up the struggle.' But he was by no means convinced of that. Dame Dionisia was not used to being thwarted.

'It may be so,' agreed Paul hopefully, 'for I hear she's taken in some reverend pilgrim, and refurbished the old hermitage in her woodland for his use. She wants his prayers daily for her son's soul. Eilmund was telling us about it when he brought our allowance of venison. We saw the man, Cadfael, at the funeral. He was there with the two brothers from Buildwas. He'd been lodged with them a week, they give him a very saintly report.'

Cadfael straightened up with a grunt from his bed of mint, grown wiry and thin of leaf now in late October. 'The fellow who wore the scallop shell? And the medal of Saint James? Yes, I remember noticing him. So he's settling among us, is he? And chooses a cell and a little square of garden in the woods rather than a grey habit at Buildwas! I never was drawn to the solitary life myself, but I've known those who can think and pray the better that way. It's a long time since that cell was lived in.'

He knew the place, though he seldom passed that way, the abbey's forester having excellent health, and very little need of herbal remedies. The hermitage, disused now for many years, lay in a thickly wooded dell, a stone-built hut with a square of ground once fenced and cultivated, now overgrown and wild. Here the belt of forest embraced both Eaton ground and the abbey's woodland of Eyton, and the hermitage occupied a spot where the Ludel border jutted into neighbour territory, close to the forester's cherished coppice. 'He'll be quiet enough there,' said Cadfael, 'if he means to stay. By what name are we to know him?'

'They call him Cuthred. A neighbour saint is a fine thing to have, and it seems they're already beginning to bring their troubles to him to sort. It may be,' ventured Brother Paul optimistically, 'that it's he who has tamed the lady. He must have a strong influence over her, or she'd never have entreated him to stay. And there's been no move from her these ten days. It may be we're all in his debt.'

And indeed, as the soft October days slid away tranquilly one after another, in dim, misty dawns, noon-days bright but veiled, and moist green twilights magically still, it seemed that there was to be no further combat over young Richard, that Dame Dionisia had thought better of the threat of law, and resigned herself to submission. She even sent, by her parish priest, a gift of money to pay for Masses in the Lady Chapel for her son's soul, a gesture which could only be interpreted as a move towards reconciliation. So, at least, Brother Francis, the new custodian of Saint Mary's altar, con-sidered it.

'Father Andrew tells me,' he reported after the visitor had departed, 'that since the Savigniac brothers from Buildwas brought this Cuthred into her house she sets great store by his counsel, and rules herself by his advice and example. The man has won a great report for holiness already. They say he's taken strict vows in the old way, and never leaves his cell and garden now. But he never refuses help or prayers to any who ask. Father Andrew thinks very highly of him. The anchorite way is not our way,' said Brother Francis with great earnest-ness, 'but it's no bad thing to have such a holy man living so close, on a neighbouring manor. It cannot but bring a blessing.'

So thought all the countryside, for the possession of so devout a hermit brought great lustre to the manor of Eaton, and the one criticism that ever came to Cadfael's ears concerning Cuthred was that he was too modest, and at first deprecated, and later forbade, the too lavish sounding of his praises abroad. No matter what minor prodigy he brought about, averting by his prayers a threatened cattle murrain, after one of Dionisia's herd sickened, sending out his boy to give warning of a coming storm, which by favour of his intercessions passed off without damage, whatever the act of grace, he would not allow any of the merit for it to be ascribed to him, and grew stern and awesomely angry if the attempt was made, threatening the wrath of God on any who disobeyed his ban. Within a month of his coming his discipline counted for more in the manor of Eaton than did either Dionisia's or Father Andrew's, and his fame, banned from being spread openly, went about by neighbourly whispers, like a prized secret to be exulted in privately but hidden from the world.

Chapter Three

EILMUND, the forester of Eyton, came now and then to chapter at the abbey to report on work done, or on any difficulties he might have encountered, and extra help he might need. It was not often he had anything but placid progress to report, but in the second week of November he came one morning with a puzzled frown fixed on his brow, and a glum face. It seemed that a curious blight of misfortune had settled upon his woodland.

Eilmund was a thickset, dark, shaggy man past forty, very powerful of body, and sharp enough of mind. He stood squarely in the midst at chapter, solidly braced on his sturdy legs like a wrestler confronting his opponent, and made few words of what he had to tell.

'My lord abbot, there are things happening in my charge that I cannot fathom. A week ago, in that great rainstorm we had, the brook that runs between our coppice and the open forest washed down some loose bushes, and built up such a dam that it overflowed and changed its course, and flooded my newest planting. And no sooner had I cleared the block than I found the flood-water had undercut part of the bank of my ditch, a small way upstream, and the fall of soil had bridged the ditch. By the time I found it the deer had got into the coppice. They've eaten off all the young growth from the plot we cropped two years ago. I doubt some of the trees may die, and all will be held back a couple more years at least before they get their growth. It spoils my planning,' complained Eilmund, outraged for the ruin of his cycle of culling, 'besides the present loss.'

Cadfael knew the place, Eilmund's pride, the farmed part of Eyton forest, as neat and well-ditched a coppice as any in the shire, where the regular cutting of six- or seven-year-old wood let in the light at every cropping, so that the wealth of ground cover and wild flowers was always rich and varied. Some trees, like ash, spring anew from the stool of the original trunk, just below the cut. Some, like elm or aspen, from below the ground all round the stump. Some of the stools in Eilmund's care, several times cropped afresh, had grown into groves of their own, their open centres two good paces across. No grave natural disaster had ever before upset his pride in his skills. No wonder he was so deeply aggrieved. And the loss to the abbey was itself serious, for coppice wood for fuel, charcoal, hafts of tools, carpentry and all manner of uses brought in good income.

'Nor is that the end of it,' went on Eilmund grimly, 'for yesterday when I made my rounds on the other side of the copse, where the ditch is dry but deep enough and the bank steep, what should have happened but the sheep from Eaton had broke out of their field by a loose pale, just where Eaton ground touches ours, and sheep, as you know, my lord, make nothing of a bank that will keep out deer, and there's nothing they like better for grazing than the first tender seedlings of ash. They've made short work of much of the new growth before I could get them out. And neither I nor John of Longwood can tell how they got through so narrow a gap, but you know if the matron ewe takes a notion into her head there's no stopping her, and the others will follow. It seems to me my forest is bewitched.'

'Far more like,' suggested Prior Robert, looking

severely down his long nose, 'that there has been plain human negligence, either on your part or your neighbour's.'

'Father Prior,' said Eilmund, with the bluntness of one who knows his value, and knows that it is equally well known to the only superior he needs to satisfy here, 'in all my years in the abbey's service there has never yet been complaint of my work. I have made my rounds daily, yes, and often nightly, too, but I cannot command the rain not to fall, nor can I be everywhere at once. Such a spate of misfortunes in so short a time I've never before known. Nor can I blame John of Longwood, who has always been as good a neighbour as any man needs.'

'That is the truth,' said Abbot Radulfus with authority. 'We have had cause to be thankful for his good will, and do not doubt it now. Nor do I question your skill and devotion. There has never been need before, and I see none now. Reverses are sent to us so that we may overcome them, and no man can presume to escape such testings for ever. The loss can be borne. Do what you can, Master Eilmund, and if you should feel in need of another helper, you shall have one.'

Eilmund, who had always been equal to his tasks and was proud of his self-sufficiency, said thanks for that somewhat grudgingly, but declined the offer for the time being, and promised to send word if anything further should happen to change his mind. And off he went as briskly as he had come, back to his cottage in the forest, his daughter, and his grievance against fate, since he could not honestly find a human agency to blame.

By some mysterious means young Richard got to know of the unusual purport of Eilmund's visit, and anything to do with his grandmother, and all those people who had their labour and living about the manor of Eaton, was of absorbing interest to him. However wise and watchful his guardian the abbot might be, however competent his

38

steward, it behoved him to keep an eye on his estate for himself. If there was mischief afoot near Eaton, he itched to know the reason, and he was far more likely than was the Abbot Radulfus to attribute mischief, however incomprehensibly procured, to the perversity or malice of humanity, having so often found himself arraigned as the half-innocent agent of misrule.

If the sheep of Eaton had made their way into the ash coppice of Eyton not by some obscure act of God, but because someone had opened the way for them and started them towards their welcome feast, then Richard wanted to know who, and why. They were, after all, his sheep.

Accordingly, he kept a sharp eye open for any new comings and goings about the hour of chapter each morning, and was curious when he observed, two days after Eilmund's visit, the arrival at the gatehouse of a young man he had seen but once before, who asked very civilly for permission to appear at chapter with an embassage from his master, Cuthred. He was early, and had to wait, which he did serenely. That suited Richard very well, for he could not play truant from school, but by the time the chapter ended he would be at liberty, and could ambush the visitor and satisfy his curiosity.

Every hermit worth his salt, having taken vows of stability which enjoin him to remain thenceforth within his own cell and closed garden, and having gifts of foresight and a sacred duty to use them for his neighbours' good, must have a resident boy to run his errands and deliver his admonitions and reproofs. Cuthred's boy, it seemed, had arrived already in his service, accompanying him in his recent wanderings in search of the place of retirement appointed for him by God. He came into the chapterhouse of the abbey with demure assurance, and stood to be examined by all the curious brothers, not at all

39

discomposed by such an assault of bright, inquisitive eyes.

From the retired stall which he preferred, Cadfael studied the messenger with interest. A more unlikely servitor for an anchorite and popular saint, in the old Celtic sense that took no account of canonisation, he could not well have imagined, though he could not have said on the instant where the incongruity lay. A young fellow of about twenty years, in a rough tunic and hose of brown cloth, patched and faded – nothing exceptional there. He was built on the same light, wiry lines as Hugh Beringar, but stood a hand's breadth taller, and he was lean and brown and graceful as a fawn, managing his long limbs with the same angular, animal beauty. Even his composed stillness held implications of sudden, fierce movement, like a wild creature motionless in ambush. His running would be swift and silent, his leaping long and lofty as that of a hare. And his face had a similar slightly ominous composure and awareness, under a thick, close-fitted cap of waving hair the colour of copper beeches. A long oval of a face, tall-browed, with a long, straight nose flared at the nostrils, again like a wild thing sensitive to every scent the breeze brought him, a supple, crooked mouth that almost smiled even in repose, as if in secret and slightly disturbing amusement, and long amber eyes that tilted upwards at the outer corners, under oblique copper brows. The burning glow of those eyes he shaded, but did not dim or conceal, beneath round-arched lids and copper lashes long and rich as a woman's.

What was an antique saint doing with an unnerving fairy thing in his employ?

But the boy, having waited a long moment to be inspected thoroughly, lifted his eyelids and showed to Abott Radulfus a face of candid and childlike innocence, and made him a very charming and respectful reverence.

He would not speak until he was spoken to, but waited to be questioned.

'You come from the hermit of Eyton?' asked the abbot mildly, studying the young, calm, almost smiling face attentively.

'Yes, my lord. The holy Cuthred sends a message by me.' His voice was quiet and clear, pitched a little high, so that it rang bell-like under the vault.

'What is your name?' Radulfus questioned.

'Hyacinth, my lord.'

'I have known a bishop of that name,' said the abbot, and briefly smiled, for the sleek brown creature before him had certainly nothing of the bishop about him. 'Were you named for him?'

'No, my lord. I have never heard of him. I was told, once, that there was a youth of that name in an old story, and two gods fell out over him, and the loser killed him. They say flowers grew from his blood. It was a priest who told me,' said the boy innocently, and slanted a sudden brief smile round the chapterhouse, well aware of the slight stir of disquiet he had aroused in these cloistered breasts, though the abbot continued unruffled.

Into that old story, thought Cadfael, studying him with pleasure and interest, you, my lad, fit far better than into the ambit of bishops, and well you know it. Or hermits either, for that matter. Now where in the world did he discover you, and how did he tame you?

'May I speak my message?' asked the boy ingenuously, golden eyes wide and clear and fixed upon the abbot.

'You have learned it by heart?' enquired Radulfus, smiling.

'I must, my lord. There must be no word out of place.'

'A very faithful messenger! Yes, you may speak.'

'I must be my master's voice, not my own,' said the boy by way of introduction, and forthwith sank his voice several tones below its normal ringing lightness, in a startling piece of mimicry that made Cadfael, at least, look at him more warily and searchingly than ever. 'I have heard with much distress,' said the proxy hermit

41

gravely, 'both from the steward of Eaton and the forester of Eyton, of the misfortunes suddenly troubling the woodland. I have prayed and meditated, and greatly dread that these are but the warnings of worse to come, unless some false balance or jarring discord between right and wrong can be amended. I know of no such offence hanging over us, unless it be the denial of right to Dame Dionisia Ludel, in witholding her grandchild from her. The father's wish must indeed be regarded, but the grief of the widow for her young cannot be put away out of mind, and she bereaved and alone. I pray you, my lord abbot, for the love of God, consider whether what you do is well done, for I feel the shadow of evil heavy over us all.'

All this the surprising young man delivered in the sombre and weighty voice which was not his own, and undeniably the trick was impressive, and caused some of the more superstitious young brothers to shift and gape and mutter in awed concern. And having ended his recital, the messenger again raised his amber eyes and smiled, as if the purport of his embassage concerned him not at all.

Abbot Radulfus sat in silence for a long moment, closely eyeing the young man, who gazed back at him unwinking and serene, satisfied at having completed his errand.

'Your master's own words?'

'Every one, my lord, just as he taught them to me.'

'And he did not commission you to argue further in the matter on his behalf? You do not want to add anything?'

The eyes opened still wider in astonishment. 'I, my lord? How could I? I only run his errands.'

Prior Robert said superciliously into the abbot's ear: 'It is not unknown for an anchorite to give shelter and employment to a simpleton. It is an act of charity. This is clearly one such.' His voice was low, but not low enough to escape ears as sharp, and almost as pointed, as those of a fox, for the boy Hyacinth gleamed, and flashed a crooked smile. Cadfael, who had also caught the drift of this comment, doubted very much whether the abbot would agree with it. There seemed to him to be a very sharp intelligence behind the brown faun's face, even if it suited him to play the fool with it.

'Well,' said Radulfus, 'you may go back to your master, Hyacinth, and carry him my thanks for his concern and care, and for his prayers, which I hope he will continue on behalf of us all. Say that I have considered and do consider every side of Dame Dionisia's complaint against me, and have done and will continue to do what I see to be right. And for the natural misfortunes that give him so much anxiety, mere men cannot control or command them, though faith may overcome them. What we cannot change we must abide. That is all.'

Without another word the boy made him a deep and graceful obeisance, turned, and walked without haste from the chapterhouse, lean and light-footed, and moving with a cat's almost insolent elegance.

In the great court, almost empty at this hour when all the brothers were at chapter, the visitor was in no hurry to set out back to his master, but lingered to look about him curiously, from the abbot's lodging in its small rose garden to the guest halls and the infirmary, and so round the circle of buildings to the gatehouse and the long expanse of the south range of the cloister. Richard, who had been lying in wait for him for some minutes, emerged confidently from the arched southern doorway, and advanced into the stranger's path.

Since the intent was clearly to halt him, Hyacinth obligingly halted, looking down with interest at the solemn, freckled face that studied him just as ardently. 'Good morrow, young sir!' he said civilly. 'And what might you want with me?'

'I know who you are,' said Richard. 'You are the

serving-man the hermit brought with him. I heard you say you came with a message from him. Was it about me?'

'That I might better answer,' said Hyacinth reasonably, 'if I knew who your lordship might be, and why my master should be concerning himself with such small fry.'

'I am not small fry,' said Richard with dignity. 'I am Richard Ludel, the lord of Eaton, and your master's hermitage is on my land. And you know very well who I am, for you were there among the servants at my father's funeral. And if you did bring some message that concerns me, I think I have a right to know about it. That's only fair.' And Richard jutted his small, square chin and stood his ground with bare feet spread apart, challenging justice with unblinking blue-green eyes.

For a long moment Hyacinth returned his gaze with a bright, speculative stare. Then he said in a brisk, matter-of-fact tone, as man to man and quite without mockery: 'That's a true word, and I'm with you, Richard. Now, where can we two talk at ease?'

The middle of the great court was, perhaps, a little too conspicuous for lengthy confidences, and Richard was sufficiently taken with the unmistakably secular stranger to find him a pleasing novelty among these monastic surroundings, and meant to get to know all about him now that he had the opportunity. Moreover, very shortly chapter would be ending, and it would not do to invite Prior Robert's too close attention in such circumstances, or court Brother Jerome's busybody interference. With hasty confidence he caught Hyacinth by the hand, and towed him away up the court to the retired wicket that led through the enclave to the mill. There on the grass above the pool they were private, with the wall at their backs and the thick, springy turf under them, and the midday sun still faintly warm on them through the diaphanous veil of haze.

'Now!' said Richard, getting down sternly to the matter in hand. 'I need to have a friend who'll tell me truth, there are so many people ordering my life for me, and can't agree about it, and how can I take care of myself and be ready for them if there's no one to warn me what's in their minds? If you'll be on my side I shall know how to deal. Will you?'

Hyacinth leaned his back comfortably against the abbey wall, streched out before him shapely, sinewy legs, and half-closed his sunlit eyes. 'I tell you what, Richard, as you can best deal if you know all that's afoot, so can I be most helpful to you if I know the why and wherefore of it. Now I know the end of this story thus far, and you know the beginning. How if we put the two together, and see what's to be made of them?'

Richard clapped his hands. 'Agreed! So first tell me what was the message you brought from Cuthred today!'

Word for word as he had delivered it in chapter, but without the mimicry, Hyacinth told him.

'I knew it!' said the child, thumping a small fist into the thick grass. 'I knew it must be some way about me. So my grandmother has cozened or persuaded even her holy man into arguing her cause for her. I heard about these things that have been happening in the coppice, but such things do happen now and then, who can prevent? You'll need to warn your master not to be over-persuaded, even if she has made herself his patroness. Tell him the whole tale, for *she* won't.'

'So I will,' agreed Hyacinth heartily, 'when I know it myself.'

'No one has told you why she wants me home? Not a word from your master?'

'Lad, I just run his errands, he doesn't confide in me.' And it seemed that the unquestioning servitor was in no hurry about returning from this errand, for he settled his back more easily against the mosses of the wall, and crossed his slim ankles. Richard wriggled a little nearer,

45

and Hyacinth shifted good-naturedly to accommodate the sharp young bones that leaned into his side.

'She wants to marry me off,' said Richard, 'to get hold of the manors either side of mine. And not even to a proper bride. Hiltrude is old – at least twenty-two ...'

'A venerable age,' agreed Hyacinth gravely.

'But even if she was young and pretty I don't want her. I don't want any woman. I don't *like* women. I don't see any need for them.'

'You're in the right place to escape them, then,' suggested Hyacinth helpfully, and under his long copper lashes his amber eyes flashed a gleam of laughter. 'Become a novice, and be done with the world, you'll be safe enough here.'

'No, that's no sport, neither. Listen, I'll tell you all about it.' And the tale of his threatened marriage, and his grandmother's plans to enlarge her little palatine came tripping volubly from his tongue. 'So will you keep an eye open for me, and let me know what I must be ware of? I need someone who'll be honest with me, and not keep everything from me, as if I were still a child.'

'I will!' promised Hyacinth contentedly, smiling. 'I'll be your lordship's liege man in the camp at Eaton, and be eyes and ears for you.'

'And make plain my side of it to Cuthred? I shouldn't like him to think evil of Father Abbot, he's only doing what my father wanted for me. And you haven't told me your name. I must have a name for you.'

'My name is Hyacinth. I'm told there was a bishop so named, but I'm none. Your secrets are safer with a sinner than with a saint, and I'm closer than the confessional, never fear me.'

They had somehow become so content and familiar with each other that only the timely reminder of Richard's stomach, nudging him that it was time for his dinner, finally roused them to separate. Richard trotted beside his new friend along the path that skirted the

46

enclave wall as far as the Foregate, and there parted from him, and watched the light, erect figure as it swung away along the highroad, before he turned and went dancing gleefully back to the wicket in the enclave wall.

Hyacinth covered the first miles of his return journey at a springy, long-stepping lope, less out of any sense of haste or duty than for pure pleasure in the ease of his own gait, and the power and precision of his body. He crossed the river by the bridge at Attingham, waded the watery meadows of its tributary the Tern, and turned south from Wroxeter towards Eyton. When he came into the fringes of the forest land he slowed to a loitering walk, reluctant to arrive when the way was so pleasant. He had to cross abbey land to reach the hermitage which lay in the narrow, thrusting finger of Ludel land probing into its neighbour woods. He went merrily whistling along the track that skirted the brook, close round the northern rim of Eilmund's coppice. The bank that rose beyond, protecting the farmed woodland, was high and steep, but well kept and well turfed, never before had it subsided at any point, nor was the brook so large or rapid that it should have undercut the seasoned slope. But so it had, the raw soil showed in a steep dark scar well before he reached the place. He eyed it as he approached, gnawing a thoughtful lip, and then as suddenly shrugged and laughed. 'The more mischief the more sport!' he said half-aloud, and passed on to where the bank had been deeply undercut.

He was still some yards back from the worst, when he heard a muted cry that seemed to come from within the earth, and then an indrawn howl of struggle and pain, and a volley of muffled curses. Startled but quick in reaction, he broke into a leaping run, and pulled up as abruptly on the edge of the ditch, no more than placidly filled now with the still muddied stream, but visibly rising. On the other side of the water there had been a fresh fall, and a

47

solitary old willow, its roots partially stripped by the first slip, had heeled over and fallen athwart the brook. Its branches heaved and rustled with the struggles of someone pinned beneath, half in, half out of the water. An arm groped for a hold through the leaves, heaving to shift the incubus, and the effort fetched a great groan. Through the threshing leaves Hyacinth caught a glimpse of Eilmund's soiled and contorted face.

'Hold still! he shouted. 'I'm coming down!'

And down he went, thigh-deep, weaving under the first boughs to get his back beneath their weight and try to lift them enough for the imprisoned forester to drag himself clear. Eilmund, groaning and gasping, doubled both fists grimly into the soil at his back and hauled himself partially free of the bough that held him by the legs. The effort cost him a half-swallowed scream of pain.

'You're hurt!' Hyacinth took him under the armpits with both hands, arching his supple back strongly beneath the thickest bough, and the tree rocked ponderously. 'Now! Heave!'

Eilmund braced himself yet again, Hyacinth hauled with him, fresh slithers of soil rolled down on them both, but the willow shifted and rolled over with a splash, and the forester lay in the raw earth, gasping, his feet just washed by the rim of the brook. Hyacinth, muddy and streaked with green, went on his knees beside him.

'I'll need to go for help, I can't get you from here alone. And you'll not be going on your own two feet for a while. Can you rest so, till I fetch John of Longwood's men up from the fields? We'll need more than one, and a hurdle or a shutter to carry you. Is there worse than I can see?' But what he could see was enough, and his brown face was shaken and appalled under the mud stains.

'My leg's broke.' Eilmund let his great shoulders sink cautiously back into the soft earth, and drew long, deep breaths. 'Main lucky for me you came this way, I was pinned fast, and the brook's building again. I was trying to shore up the bank. Lad,' he said, and grinned ruefully round a groan, 'there's more strength in those shoulders of yours than anyone would think to look at you.'

'Can you bide like that for a little while?' Hyacinth looked up anxiously at the bank above, but only small clods shifted and slid harmlessly, and the rim of impacted turf, herbage and roots at the top looked secure enough. 'I'll run. I'll not be long.'

And run he did, fast and straight for the Eaton fields, and hailed the first Eaton men he sighted. They came in haste, with a hurdle borrowed from the sheep fold, and between them with care and with some suppressed and understandable cursing from the victim, lifted Eilmund on to it, and bore him the half-mile to his forest cottage. Mindful that the man had a daughter at home, Hyacinth took it upon himself to run on before to give her warning and reassurance, and time to prepare the injured man's couch.

The cottage lay in a cleared assart in the forest, with a neat garden about it, and when Hyacinth reached it the door was standing open, and within the house a girl was singing softly to herself as she worked. Strangely, having run his fastest to get to her, Hyacinth seemed almost reluctant to knock at the door, or enter without knocking, and while he was hesitating on the doorstone her singing ceased, and she came out to see whose fleet footsteps had stirred the small stones of the pathway.

She was small but sturdy, and very trimly made, with a straight blue gaze, the fresh colouring of a wild rose, and smoothly-braided hair of a light brown sheen like the grain of polished oak, and she looked him over with a candid curiosity and friendliness that for once silenced his ready silver tongue. It was she who had to speak first, for all the urgency of his errand.

'You're looking for my father? He's away to the coppice, you'll find him where the bank slid.' And the

49

blue eyes quickened with interest and approval, liking what they saw. 'You're the boy who came with the old dame's hermit, aren't you? I saw you working in his garden.'

Hyacinth owned to it, and recalled with a lurch of the heart what he had to tell. 'I am, mistress, and my name's Hyacinth. Your father's on his way back to you now, sorry I am to say it, after a mishap that will keep him to the house for a while, I fear. I came to let you know before they bring him. Oh, never fret, he's live and sound, he'll be his own man again, give him time. But his leg's broken. There was another slip, it brought down a tree on him in the ditch. He'll mend, though, no question.'

The quick alarm and blanching of her face had brought no outcry. She took in what he said, shook herself abruptly, and went to work at once setting wide the inner and the outer doors to open the way for the hurdle and its burden, and making ready the couch on which to lay him, and from that to setting on a pot of water at the fire. And as she went she talked to Hyacinth over her shoulder, very practically and calmly.

'Not the first time he's come by injuries, but never a broken leg before. A tree came down, you say? That old willow – I knew it leaned, but I never thought it could fall. It was you found him? And fetched help for him?' The blue eyes looked round and smiled on him.

'Some of the Eaton men were close, clearing a drainage ditch. They're carrying him in.' They were approaching the door by then, coming as fast as they could. She went out to meet them, with Hyacinth at her elbow. It seemed that he had something more, something different to say to her, and for the moment had lost his opportunity, for he hovered silently but purposefully on the edge of the scurry of activity, as Eilmund was carried into the house and laid on the couch, and stripped of his wet boots and hose, very carefully but to a muffled accompaniment of groans and curses. His left leg was misshapen below the

50

knee, but not so grossly that the bone had torn through the flesh.

'Above an hour lying there in the brook,' he got out, between gritting his teeth on the pain as they handled him, 'and if it hadn't been for this young fellow I should have been there yet, for I couldn't shift the weight, and there was no one within call. God's truth, there's more muscle in the lad than you'd believe. You should have seen him heft that tree off me.'

Very strangely, Hyacinth's spare, smooth cheeks flushed red beneath their dark gold sheen. It was a face certainly not given to blushing, but it had not lost the ability. He said with some constraint: 'Is there anything more I could be doing for you? I would, gladly! You'll be needing a skilled hand to set that bone. I'm no use there, but make use of me if you need an errand run. That's my calling, that I can do.'

The girl turned for an instant from the bed, her blue eyes wide and shining on his face. 'Why, so you can, if you'll be so good and add to our debt. Will you send to the abbey, and ask for Brother Cadfael to come?'

'I will well!' said Hyacinth, as heartily as if she had made him a most acceptable gift. But as she turned back from him he hesitated, and caught her by the sleeve for an instant, and breathed into her ear urgently: 'I must talk to you – alone, later, when he's cared for and resting easy.' And before she could say yes or no, though her eyes certainly were not refusing him, he was off and away through the trees, on the long run back to Shrewsbury.

Chapter Four

HUGH came looking for Brother Cadfael in mid-afternoon, with the first glimmers of news that had found their way out of Oxford since the siege began.

'Robert of Gloucester is back in England,' he said. 'I have it from an armourer who took thought in time to get out of the city. A few were lucky and took warning. He says Robert has landed at Wareham in spite of the king's garrison, brought in all his ships safely and taken the town. Not the castle, though, not yet, but he's settled down to siege. He got precious little out of Geoffrey, maybe a handful of knights, no more.'

'If he's safe ashore and holds the town,' said Cadfael reasonably, 'what does he want with the castle? I should have thought he'd be hotfoot for Oxford to hale his sister out of the trap.'

'He'd rather lure Stephen to come to him, and draw him off from his own siege. My man says the castle at Wareham's none too well garrisoned, and they've come to a truce agreement, and sent to the king to relieve them by a fixed date – a know-all, but truly well informed, though even he doesn't know the day appointed – or if he fails them they'll surrender. That suits Robert. He knows it's seldom any great feat to lure Stephen off a scent, but I fancy he'll hold fast this time. When will he get such a chance again? Even he can't throw it away, surely.

'There's no end to the follies any man can commit,' said Cadfael tolerantly. 'To give him his due, most of his idiocies are generous, which is more than can be said for the lady. But I could wish this siege at Oxford might be the end of it. If he does take castle and empress and all, she'll be safe enough of life and limb with him, it's rather he who may be in danger. What else is new from the south?'

'There's a tale he tells of a horse found straying not far from the city, in the woods close to the road to Wallingford. Some time ago, this was, about the time all roads out of Oxford were closed, and the town on fire. A horse dragging a blood-stained saddle, and saddlebags slit open and emptied. A groom who'd slipped out of the town before the ring closed recognised horse and harness as belonging to one Renaud Bourchier, a knight in the empress's service, and close in her confidence, too. My man says it's known she sent him out of the garrison to try and break through the king's lines and carry a message to Wallingford for her.'

Cadfael ceased to ply the hoe he was drawing leisurely between his herb beds, and turned his whole attention upon his friend. 'To Brian FitzCount, you mean?'

The lord of Wallingford was the empress's most faithful adherent and companion, next only to the earl, her brother, and had held his castle for her, the most easterly and exposed outpost of her territory, through campaign after campaign and through good fortune and bad, indomitably loyal.

'How comes it he's not with her in Oxford? He hardly ever leaves her side, or so they say.'

'The king moved so much faster than anyone thought for. And now he's cut off from her. Moreover, she needs him in Wallingford, for if that's ever lost she has nothing left but an isolated holding in the west country, and no way out towards London. She may well have sent out to him at the last moment, in so desperate a situation as she's in now. And rumour down there says, it seems, that Bouchier was carrying treasure to him, less in coin than in jewels. It may well be so, for he needs to pay his men. Loyal for love though they may be, they still have to live and eat, and he's beggared himself already in her service.'

'There's been talk, this autumn,' said Cadfael, thoughtfully frowning, 'that Bishop Henry of Winchester has been busy trying to lure away Brian to the king's side. Bishop Henry has money enough to buy whoever's for sale, but I doubt if even he could bid high enough to move FitzCount. All this time the man has shown as incorruptible. She had no need to try and outbid her enemies for Brian.'

'None. But she may well have thought, when the king's host closed round her, to send him an earnest of the value she sets on him, while the way was still open, or might at least be attempted by a single brave man. At such a pass, it may even have seemed to her the last chance for such a word ever to pass between them.'

Cadfael thought on that, and acknowledged its truth. King Stephen would never be a threat to his cousin's life, however bitter their rivalry had been, but if once she was made captive he would be forced to hold her in close ward for his crown's sake. Nor was she likely ever to relinquish her claim, even in prison, and agree to terms that would lightly release her. Friends and allies thus parted might, in very truth, never see each other again.

'And a single brave man did attempt it,' reflected Cadfael soberly. 'And his horse found straying, his harness awry, his saddlebags emptied, and blood on saddle and saddlecloth. So where is Renaud Bourchier? Murdered for what he carried, and buried somewhere in the woods or slung into the river?'

'What else can a man think? They have not found his body yet. Round Oxford men have other things to do

54

this autumn besides scour the woods for a dead man. There are dead men enough to bury after the looting and burning of Oxford town,' said Hugh with dry bitterness, almost resigned to the random slaughters of this capricious civil war.

'I wonder how many within the castle knew of his errand? She would hardly blazon abroad her intent, but someone surely got wind of it.'

'So it seems, and made very ill use of what he knew.' Hugh shook himself, heaving off from his shoulders the distant evils that were out of his writ. 'Thanks be to God, I am not sheriff of Oxfordshire! Our troubles here are mild enough, a little family bickering that leads to blows now and then, a bit of thieving, the customary poaching in season. Oh, and of course the bewitchment that seems to have fallen on your woodland of Eyton.' Cadfael had told him what the abbot, perhaps, had not thought important enough to tell, that Dionisia had somehow coaxed her hermit into her quarrel, and that good man had surely taken very seriously her impersonation of a grieving grandam cruelly deprived of the society of her only grandhild. 'And he fears worse to come, does he? I wonder what the next news from Eyton will be?'

As it so happened the next news from Eyton was just hurrying towards them round the corner of the tall box hedge, borne by a novice despatched in haste by Prior Robert from the gatehouse. He came at a run, the skirts of his habit billowing, and pulled up with just enough breath to get out his message without waiting to be asked.

'Brother Cadfael, you're wanted urgently. The hermit's boy's come back to say you're needed at Eilmund's assart, and Father Abbot says take a horse and go quickly, and bring him back word how the forester does. There's been another landslip, and a tree came down on him. His leg's broken.'

*　　　*　　　*

They offered Hyacinth rest and a good meal for his trouble, but he would not stay. As long as he could hold the pace he clung by Cadfael's stirrup leather and ran with him, and even when he was forced to slacken and let Cadfael ride on before at his best speed, the youth trotted doggedly and steadily behind, bent on getting back to the woodland cottage, it seemed, rather than to his master's cell. He had been a good friend to Eilmund, Cadfael reflected, but he might come in for a lashing with tongue or rod when he at last returned to his sworn duty. Though Cadfael could not, on consideration, picture that wild, unchancy creature submitting tamely to reproof, much less to punishment.

It was about the hour for Vespers when Cadfael dismounted within the low pale of Eilmund's garden, and the girl flung open the door and came out eagerly to meet him.

'Brother, I hardly expected you for a while yet. Cuthred's boy must have run like the wind, and all that way! And after he'd soaked himself in the brook getting my father clear! We've had good cause to be glad of him and his master this day, there might have been no one else by for hours.'

'How is he?' asked Cadfael, unslinging his scrip and making for the house.

'His leg's broken below the knee. I've made him lie still, and packed it round as well as I could, but it needs your hand to set it. And he lay half in the brook a long time before the young man found him, I fear he's taken a chill.'

Eilmund lay well covered, and by now grimly reconciled to his helplessness. He submitted stoically to Cadfael's handling, and gritted his teeth and made no other sound as his leg was straightened and the fractured ends of bone brought into line.

'You might have come off worse,' said Cadfael, relieved. 'A good clean break, and small damage to the flesh, though it's a pity they had to move you.'

'I might have drowned else,' growled Eilmund, 'the brook was building. And you'd best tell the lord abbot to get men out here and shift the tree, before we have a lake there again.'

'I will, I will! Now, hold fast! I don't want to leave you with one leg shorter than the other.' By heel and instep he drew out the broken leg steadily to match its fellow. 'Now, Annet, your hands where mine are, and hold it so.'

She had not wasted her time while waiting, but had hunted out straight spars of wood from Eilmund's store, and had ready sheep's wool for padding, and rolled linen for bindings. Between them they completed the work neatly, and Eilmund lay back on his brychan and heaved a great breath. His face, weatherbeaten always, none-theless had a fierce flush over the cheekbones. Cadfael was not quite easy about it.

'Now if you can rest and sleep, so much the better. Leave the lord abbot, and the tree, and everything else that needs to be dealt with here, to me, I'll see it cared for. I'll make you a draught that will ease the pain and help you to sleep.' He mixed it and administered it to Eilmund's scornful denial of the need, but it went down without protest nonetheless.

'And sleep he will,' said Cadfael to the girl, as they withdrew into the outer room. 'But make sure he keeps warm and covered through the night, for there may be a slight fever if he's taken cold. I'll make certain I get leave to go back and forth for a day or two, till I see all's well. If he gives you a hard time, bear with him, it will mean he's taken no great harm.'

She laughed softly, undisturbed. 'Oh, he's mild as milk for me. He growls, but never bites. I know how to manage him.'

It was already beginning to be twilight when she opened the house door. The sky above was still faintly golden with the moist, mysterious afterglow, dripping light between the dark branches of the trees that surrounded the garden. And there in the turf by the gate Hyacinth was sitting motionless, waiting with the timeless patience of the tree against which his straight, supple back was braced. Even so his stillness had the suggestion of a wild thing in ambush. Or perhaps, thought Cadfael, changing his mind, of a hunted wild thing trusting to silence and stillness to be invisible to the hunter.

As soon as he saw the door open he was on his feet in a single lissome movement, though he did not come within the pale.

Twilight or no, Cadfael saw the glance that locked and held fast between the youth and the girl. Hyacinth's face was still and mute as bronze, but a gleam of the fading light caught the amber brilliance of his eyes, fierce and secret as a cat's, and a sudden quickening and darkening in their depths that was reflected in the flush and brightness in Annet's startled countenance. It was no great surprise. The girl was pretty, and the boy undoubtedly attractive, all the more because he had been of invaluable service to her father. And it was natural and human, that that circumstance should endear father and daughter to him, no less than him to them. Nothing is more pleasing and engaging than the sense of having conferred benefits. Not even the gratification of receiving them.

'I'll be on my way, then,' said Cadfael to the unregarding air, and mounted softly, not to break the spell that held them still. But from the shelter of the trees he looked back, and saw them standing just as he had left them, and heard the boy's voice clear and solemn in the silence of the dusk, saying: 'I must speak to you!'

Annet did not say anything, but she closed the house door softly behind her, and came forward to meet him at the gate. And Cadfael rode back through the woods mildly aware that he was smiling, though he could not be

58

sure, on more sober reflection, that there was anything to smile about in so unlikely an encounter. For what common ground could there be, for those two to meet on, and hold fast for more than a moment: the abbey forester's daughter, a good match for any lively and promising young man this side the shire, and a beggarly, rootless stranger dependent on charitable patronage, with no land, no craft and no kin?

He went to tend and stable his horse before he sought out Abbot Radulfus to tell him how things stood in Eyton forest. There was a late stir within there, of new guests arrived, and their mounts being accommodated and cared for. Of late there had been little movement about the county; the business of the summer, when so many merchants and tradesmen were constantly on the move, had dwindled gently away into the autumn quiet. Later, as the Christmas feast drew near, the guest halls would again be full with travellers hastening home, and kinsmen visiting kinsmen, but at this easy stage between, there was time to note those who came, and feel the human curiosity that is felt by those who have sworn stability about those who ebb and flow with the tides and seasons.

And here just issuing from the stables and crossing the yard in long, lunging strides, the gait of a confident and choleric man, was someone undoubtedly of consequence in his own domain, richly dressed, elegantly booted, and wearing sword and dagger. He surged past Cadfael in the gateway, a big, burly, thrusting man, his face abruptly lit as he swung past the torch fixed at the gate, and then as abruptly darkened. A massive face, fleshy and yet hard, muscled like a wrestler's arms, handsome in a brutal fashion, the face of a man not in anger at this moment, but always ready to be angry. He was shaven clean, which made the smooth power of his features even more daunting, and the eyes that stared imperiously straight before him looked disproportionately small, though in reality they probably were not, because of the massy flesh in which they were but shallowly set. By the look of him, not a man to cross. He might have been fifty years old, give or take a few years, but time certainly had not softened what must have been granite from the start.

His horse was standing in the stable yard outside an open stall, stripped and gently steaming as if his saddle-cloth had only just been removed, and a groom was rubbing him down and hissing to him gently as he worked. A meagre but wiry fellow, turning grey, in faded homespun of a dull brown, and a rubbed leather coat. He slid one sidelong glance at Cadfael and nodded a silent greeting, so inured to being wary of all men that even a Benedictine brother was to be avoided rather than welcomed.

Cadfael gave him good-even cheerfully, and began his own unsaddling. 'You've ridden far? Was that your lord I met at the gate?'

'It was,' said the man without looking up, and spared no more words.

'A stranger to me. Where are you from? Guests are thin this time of year.'

'From Bosiet – it's a manor the far side of Northampton, some miles south-east of the town. He *is* Bosiet – Drogo Bosiet. He holds that and a fair bit of the county besides.'

'He's well away from his home ground,' said Cadfael with interest. 'Where's he bound? We see very few travellers from Northamptonshire in these parts.'

The groom straightened up to take a longer and narrower look at this inquisitive questioner, and visibly his manner eased a little, finding Cadfael amiable and harmless. But he did not on that account grow less morose, nor more voluble.

'He's hunting,' he said with a grim and private smile.

'But not for deer,' hazarded Cadfael, returning the

inspection and caught by the wryness of the smile. 'Nor, I dare say, for the beasts of the warren.'

'You dare say well. It's a man he's after.'

'A runaway?' Cadfael found it hard to believe. 'So far from home? Was a runaway villein worth so much time and expense to him?'

'This one is. He's valuable and skilled, but that's not the whole of it,' confided the groom, discarding his suspicion and reticence. 'He has a score to settle with this one. One report we got of him, setting out westwards and north, and *he*'s combed every village and town along all this way, dragging me one road while his son with another groom goes another, and he won't stop short of the Welsh border. Me? If I did clap eyes on the lad he's after, I'd be blind. I wouldn't give him back a dog that ran from him, let alone a man.' His dry voice had gathered sap and passion as he talked, and he turned fully for the first time, so that the torchlight fell on his face. One cheek was marked with a blackening bruise, the corner of his mouth torn and swollen, with the look of a festering infection about it.

'His mark?' asked Cadfael, eyeing the wound.

'His seal, sure enough, and done with a seal ring. I was not quick enough at his stirrup when he mounted, yesterday morning.'

'I can dress that for you,' said Cadfael, 'if you'll wait while I go and make report to my abbot about another matter. You'd best let me, it could take bad ways. By the same token,' he said quietly, 'you're far enough out of his country, and near enough to the border, to do some running of your own, if you're so minded.'

'Brother,' said the groom with the briefest and harshest of laughs, 'I have a wife and children in Bosiet, I'm manacled. But Brand was young and unwed, his heels are lighter than mine. And I'd best get this beast stalled, and be off to wait on my lord, or he'll be laying the other cheek open for me.'

61

'Then come out to the guest hall steps,' said Cadfael, recalled as sharply to his own duty, 'when he's in bed and snoring, and I'll clean that sore for you.'

Abbot Radulfus listened with concern, but also with relief, to Cadfael's report, promised to send at first light enough helpers to clear away the willow tree, clean out the brook and shore up the bank above, and nodded gravely at the suggestion that Eilmund's long wait in the water might complicate his recovery, even though the fracture itself was simple and clean.

'I should like,' said Cadfael, 'to visit him again tomorrow and make sure he stays in his bed, for there may be a degree of fever, and you know him, Father, it will take more than his daughter's scolding to keep him tamed. If he has your orders he may take heed. I'll take his measure for crutches, but not let them near him till I'm sure he's fit to rise.'

'You have my leave to go and come as you see fit,' said Radulfus, 'for as long as he needs your care. Best keep that horse for your use until then. The journey would be too slow on foot, and we shall need you here some part of the day, Brother Winfrid being new to the discipline.'

Cadfael smiled, remembering. 'It was no slow journey the young man Hyacinth made of it. Four times today he's run those miles, back and forth on his master's errand, and back and forth again for Eilmund. I only hope the hermit did not take it ill that his boy was gone so long.'

It was in Cadfael's mind that the groom from Bosiet might be too much in fear of his master to venture out by night, even when his lord was sleeping. But come he did, slipping out furtively just as the brothers came out from Compline. Cadfael led him out through the gardens to the workshop in the herbarium, and there kindled a lamp to examine the lacerated wound that marred the man's face.

The little brazier was turfed down for the night, but not extinguished, evidently Brother Winfrid had been careful to keep it alive in case of need. He was learning steadily, and strangely the delicacy of touch that eluded him with pen or brush showed signs of developing now that he came to deal with herbs and medicines. Cadfael uncovered the fire and blew it into a glow, and put on water to heat.

'He's safe asleep, is he, your lord? Not likely to wake? Though if he did, he should have no need of you at this hour. But I'll be as quick as I may.'

The groom sat docile and easy under the ministering hands, turning his face obediently to the light of the lamp. The bruised cheek was fading at the edges from black to yellow, but the tear at the corner of his mouth oozed blood and pus. Cadfael bathed away the encrusted exudations and cleaned the gash with a lotion of water betony and sanicle.

'He's free with his fists, your lord,' he said ruefully. 'I see two blows here.'

'He seldom stops at one,' said the groom grimly. 'He does after his kind. There are some worse than him, God help all those who serve them. His son's another made to the same pattern. What else could we look for, when he's lived so from birth? In a day or so he's to join us here, and if he has not got his hands on Brand by then – God forbid! – the hunt will go on.'

'Well, at least if you stay a day or so I can get this gash healed for you. What's your name, friend?'

'Warin. Yours I know, Brother, from the hospitaller. That feels cool and kind.'

'I should have thought,' said Cadfael, 'that your lord would have gone first to the sheriff, if he had a real complaint against this runaway of his. The guildsmen of the town would likely keep their mouths shut, even if they knew anything, a town stands to gain by taking in a good craftsman. But the king's officers are bound, willing or no, to help a man to his own property.'

'We got here too late, as you saw, to do much in that kind until the morrow. He knows, none so well, that Shrewsbury is a charter borough, and may cheat him of his prey if the lad has got this far. He does intend going to the sheriff. But since he's lodged here, and reckons the church as well as the law ought to help him to his own, he's asked to put his case at chapter tomorrow, and after that he'll be off into the town to seek out the sheriff. There's no stone he won't up-end to get at Brand's hide.'

Cadfael was thinking, though he did not say it, that there might be time in between to send word to Hugh to make himself very hard to find. 'What in the world,' he asked, 'has the man done, to make your master so vindictive against him?'

'Why, he was for ever on the edge of trouble, being a lad that would stand up for himself, yes, and for others, too, and that's crime enough for Drogo. I don't know the rights of what happened that last day, but however it was, I saw Bosiet's steward, who takes his style from his master, carried into the manor on a shutter, and he was laid up for days. Seemingly something had happened between them, and Brand had laid him flat, for the next we knew, Brand was nowhere, and they were hunting him along all the roads out of Northampton. But they never caught up with him, and here we are still hot on his trail. If ever Drogo lays hands on him he'll flay him, but he won't cripple him, he's too valuable to waste. But he'll have every morsel of his grudge out of the lad's skin, and then wring every penny of profit out of his skills lifelong, and make good sure he never gets the chance to run again.'

'Then he had better make a good job of it now,' agreed Cadfael wryly. 'If well-wishing can help him, he has it. Now hold still a moment – there! And this ointment you can take with you and use as often as you choose. It helps take out the sting and lower the swelling.'

Warin turned the little jar curiously in his hand, and touched a finger to his cheek. 'What's in it, to work such healing?'

'Saint John's wort and the small daisy, both good for wounds. And if chance offers tomorrow, let me see you again and hear how you do. And keep out of his reach!' said Cadfael warmly, and turned to bed down his brazier again with fresh turves, to smoulder quietly and safely until morning.

Drogo Bosiet duly appeared at chapter next morning, large, loud and authoritative in an assembly where a wiser man would have realised that authority lay with the abbot, and the abbot's grip on it was absolute, however calm and measured his voice and austere his face. So much the better, thought Cadfael, watching narrowly and somewhat anxiously from his retired stall, Radulfus will know how to weigh the man, and let nothing slip too soon.

'My lord abbot,' said Drogo, straddling the flags of the floor like a bull before the charge, 'I am here in search of a malefactor who attacked and injured my steward and fled my lands. He is known to have made for Northampton, my manor, to which he is tied, being several miles south-east of the town, and I have it in mind that he would make for the Welsh border. We have hunted for him all this way, and from Warwick I have taken this road from Shrewsbury, while my son goes on to Stafford, and will join me here from that place. All I ask here is whether any stranger of his years has lately come into these parts.'

'I take it,' said the abbot after a long and thoughtful pause, and steadily eyeing the powerful face and arrogant stance of his visitor, 'that this man is your villein.'

'He is.'

'And you do know,' pursued Radulfus mildly, 'that since it would seem you have failed to reclaim him within

65

four days, it will be necessary to apply to the courts to regain possession of him legally?'

'My lord,' said Drogo with impatient scorn, 'so I can well do, if I can but find him. The man is mine, and I mean to have him. He has been a cause of trouble to me, but he has skills which are valuable, and I do not mean to be robbed of what is mine. The law will give me my rights in the lands where the offence arose.' And so, no doubt, such a law as survived in his own shire would certainly do, at the mere nod of his head.

'If you will tell us what your fugitive is like,' said the abbot reasonably, 'Brother Denis can tell you at once whether we have had such a one as guest in our halls.'

'He goes by the name of Brand – twenty years old, dark of hair but reddish, lean and strong, beardless – '

'No,' said Brother Denis the hospitaller without hesitation, 'I have had no such young man lodged here, not for five or six weeks back certainly. If he had found work along the way with some trader or merchant carrying goods, such as come with three or four servants, then he might have passed this way. But a young man alone – no, none.'

'As to that,' said the abbot with authority, forestalling reply from any other, though indeed no one but Prior Robert would have ventured to speak before him, 'you would do well to take your question to the sheriff at the castle, for his officers are far more likely than we here within the enclave to know of any newcomers entering the town. The pursuit of criminals and offenders such as you describe is their business, and they are thorough and careful about it. The guildsmen of the town are also wary and jealous of their rights, and have good reason to keep their eyes open, and their wits about them. I recommend you to apply to them.'

'So I intend, my lord. But you will bear in mind what I have asked, and if any here should recall anything to the purpose, let me hear of it.'

'This house will do whatever is incumbent upon it in good conscience,' said the abbot with chilly emphasis, and watched with an unrevealing face as Drogo Bosiet, with only the curtest of nods by way of leavetaking, turned on his booted heel and strode out of the chapterhouse. Nor did Radulfus see fit to make any comment or signify any conclusion when the petitioner was gone, as if he felt no need to give any further instruction than he had given by the tone of his replies. And by the time they emerged from chapter, some time later, both Drogo and his groom had saddled and ridden forth, no doubt over the bridge and into the town, to seek out Hugh Beringar at the castle.

Brother Cadfael had intended to pay a quick visit to the herbarium and his workshop, to see all was in order there and set Brother Winfrid to work on what was safest and most suitable for his unsupervised attentions, and then set off at once for Eilmund's cottage, but events prevented. For there was a death that day among the old, retired brothers in the infirmary, and Brother Edmund, in need of a companion to watch out the time with him after the tired old man had whispered the few almost inaudible words of his last confession and received the final rites, turned first and confidently to his closest friend and associate among the sick. They had done the same service together many times in forty years of a vocation imposed from birth in Edmund's case, though willingly embraced later, but chosen after half a lifetime in the outer world by Cadfael. They stood at the opposite poles of *oblatus* and *conversus*, and they understood each other so well that few words ever needed to pass between them.

The old man's dying was painless and feather-light, all the substance of his once sharp and vigorous mind gone on before; but it was slow. The fading candle flame did not flicker, only dimmed in perfect stillness second by second, so mysteriously that they missed the moment when the last spark withdrew, and only knew he was gone when they began to realise that the prints of age were smoothing themselves out gently from his face.

'So pass all good men!' said Edmund fervently. 'A blessed death as ever I saw! I wonder will God deal as gently with me, when my time comes!'

They cared for the dead man together, and together emerged into the great court to arrange for his body to be carried to the mortuary chapel. And then there was a small matter of Brother Paul's youngest schoolboy, who had missed his footing in haste on the day stairs and rolled down half the flight, bloodying his knees on the cobbles of the court, and had to be picked up and bathed and bandaged, and despatched to his play with an apple by way of reward for his bravery in denying stoutly that he was hurt. Only then could Cadfael repair to the stable and saddle the horse assigned to him, and by then it was almost time for Vespers.

He was leading his horse across the court to the gatehouse when Drogo Bosiet rode in under the archway, his finery a little jaded and dusty from a day's frustration and exertion, his face blackly set, and the groom Warin a few yards behind him, warily attentive, alert to obey the least gesture, but anxious meantime to stay out of sight and out of mind. Clearly the hunt had drawn no quarry anywhere, and the hunters came back with the approach of evening empty-handed. Warin would have to stand clear of the length of that powerful arm tonight.

Cadfael went forth through the gate reassured and content, and made good speed towards his patient at Eyton.

Chapter Five

RICHARD had been out all afternoon with the other boys in the main abbey gardens beside the river, where the last pears were just being harvested. The children were allowed to help, and within reason to sample, though the fruit had still to ripen after gathering. But these, the last, had hung so long on the tree that they were already eatable. It had been a good day, with sun, and freedom, and some dabbling in the river where there were safe shallows, and he was reluctant to go indoors to Vespers at the end of it, and then to supper and bed. He loitered at the end of the procession winding its way along the riverside path, and up the green, bushy slope to the Foregate. In the stillness of late afternoon there were still clouds of midges dancing over the water, and fish rising to them lazily. Under the bridge the flow looked almost motionless though he knew it was fast and deep. There had been a boatmill moored there once, powered by the stream.

Nine-year-old Edwin, his devoted ally, loitered with him, but a little anxiously, casting a glance over his shoulder to see how the distance between them and the tailend of the procession lengthened. He had been praised for his stoicism after his fall, and was in no mind to lose the warm sense of virtue the incident had left with him by being late for Vespers. But neither could he lightly desert his bosom friend. He hovered, rubbing at a bandaged knee that still smarted a little.

'Richard, come on, we mustn't dawdle. Look, they're nearly at the highroad.'

'We can easily catch up with them,' said Richard, dabbling his toes in the shallows. 'But you go on, if you want to.'

'No, not without you. But I can't run as fast as you, my knee's stiff. Do come on, we shall be late.'

'*I* shan't, I can be there long before the bell goes, but I forgot you couldn't run as well as usual. You go on, I'll overtake you before you reach the gatehouse. I just want to see whose boat this is, coming down towards the bridge.'

Edwin hesitated, weighing his own virtuous peace of mind against desertion, and for once decided in accordance with his own wishes. The last black habit at the end of the procession was just climbing to the level of the highroad, to vanish from sight. No one had looked back to call the loiterers, or scold, they were left to their own consciences. Edwin turned and ran after his fellows as fast as he could for his stiffening knee. From the top of the slope he looked back, but Richard was ankle-deep in his tiny cove, skimming stones expertly across the surface of the water in a dotted line of silvery spray. Edwin decided on virtue, and abandoned him.

It had never been in Richard's mind to play truant, but his game seduced him as each cast bettered the previous one, and he began to hunt for smoother and flatter pebbles under the bank, ambitious to reach the opposite shore. And then one of the town boys who had been swimming under the green sweep of turf that climbed to the town wall took up the challenge, and began to return the shower of dancing stones, splashing naked in the shallows. So absorbed was Richard in the contest that he forgot all about Vespers, and only the small, distant chime of the bell startled him back to his duty. Then he did drop his stone, abandon the field to his rival, and scramble hastily ashore to snatch up his discarded shoes and run like a hart for the Foregate and the abbey. He had left it too late. The moment he arrived breathless at the gatehouse, and sidled in cautiously by the wicket to avoid notice, he heard the chanting of the first psalm from within the church.

Well, it was not so great a sin to miss a service, but for all that, he did not wish to add it to his score at this time, when he was preoccupied with grave family matters outside the cloister. By good fortune the children of the stewards and the lay servants were also accustomed to attend Vespers, which so conveniently augmented the numbers of the schoolboys that one small truant might not be missed, and if he could slip back into their enveloping ranks as they left the church afterwards it might be assumed that he had been among them all along. It was the best course he could think of. Accordingly he slipped into the cloister, and installed himself in the first carrel of the south walk, curled up in the corner, where he could see the south door of the church, by which brothers, guests and boys would all emerge when the service ended. Once the obedientiaries and choir monks had passed, it should not be difficult to worm his way in among the boys without being noticed.

And here they came at last, Abbot Radulfus, Prior Robert and all the brothers, passing decorously by, and out into the evening on their way to supper; and then the less orderly throng of the abbey young. Richard was sidling along the wall that concealed him, ready to slip out and mingle with them as they passed, when a familiar and censorious voice made itself heard just on the other side of the wall, in the very archway through which the children must pass.

'Silence, there! Let me hear no chattering so soon after divine worship! Is this how you were taught to leave the

71

holy place? Get into line, two and two, and behave with due reverence.'

Richard froze, his back pressed against the chill stone of the wall, and drew back stealthily into the darkest corner of the carrel. Now what had possessed Brother Jerome to let the procession of the choir monks pass by without him, and wait here to hector and scold the unoffending children? For there he stood immovable, harrying them into tidy ranks, and Richard was forced to crouch in hiding and let his best hope of escape dwindle away into the evening air in the great court, leaving him trapped. For of all the brothers, Jerome was the one before whom he would least willingly creep forth ignominiously to be arraigned and lectured. And now the boys were gone, a few abbey guests emerging at leisure from the church, and still Jerome stood there waiting, for Richard could see his meagre shadow on the flags of the floor.

And suddenly it appeared that he had been waiting for one of the guests, for the shadow intercepted and melted into a more substantial shadow. Richard had seen the substance pass, a big, muscular striding man with a face as solid and russet as a sandstone wall, and the rich gown of the middle nobility, short of the baronage or even their chief tenants, but still to be reckoned with.

'I have been waiting, sir,' said Brother Jerome, self-important but respectful, 'to speak a word to you. I have been thinking of what you told us at chapter this morning. Will you sit down with me in private for a few moments?'

Richard's young heart seemed to turn over within him, for there he was crouched on the stone bench by one of Brother Anselm's aumbries in the carrel right beside them, and he was in terror that they would immediately walk in upon him. But for his own reasons, it seemed, Brother Jerome preferred to be a little more retired, as if he did not want anyone still within the church, perhaps the sacristan, to observe this meeting as he left, for he drew his companion deep into the third carrel, and there sat down with him. Richard could easily have slid round the corner and out of the cloister now that the way was free, but he did not do so. Pure human curiosity kept him mute and still where he was, almost holding his breath, a little pitcher with very long ears.

'This malefactor of whom you spoke,' began Jerome, 'he who assaulted your steward and has run from you – how did you say he was called?'

'His name is Brand. Why, have you any word of him?'

'No, certainly none by that name. I do firmly believe,' said Jerome virtuously, 'that it is every man's duty to help you to reclaim your villein if he can. Even more it is the duty of the church, which should always uphold justice and law, and condemn the criminal and law-breaker. You did tell us this fellow is young, about twenty years? Beardless, reddish dark as to his hair?'

'All that, yes. You know of such a one?' demanded Drogo sharply.

'It *may* not be the same man, but there is one young man who would answer to such a description, only one to my knowledge who is lately come into these parts. It would be worth asking. He came here with a pilgrim, a holy man who has settled down in a hermitage only a few miles from us, on the manor of Eaton. He serves the hermit. If he is indeed your rogue, he must have imposed on that good soul, who in the kindness of his heart has given him work and shelter. If it is so, then it is only right that his eyes should be opened to the kind of servitor he is harbouring. And if he proves not to be the man, there is no harm done. But indeed I did have my doubts about him, the one time he came here with a message. He has a sort of civil insolence about him that sorts ill with a saint's service.'

Richard crouched motionless, hugging his knees, his ears stretched to catch every word that passed.

'Where is this hermitage to be found?' demanded Drogo, with the hunger of the manhunt in his voice. 'And what is the fellow calling himself?'

'He goes by the name of Hyacinth. The hermit's name is Cuthred, anyone in Wroxeter or Eaton can show you where he dwells.' And Jerome launched willingly into exact instructions as to the road, which occupied him so happily that even if there had been any small sounds from the neighbouring carrel he probably would not have heard them. But Richard's small bare feet made no sound on the flags as he slid hastily round into the archway, and fled down the court to the stables, still carrying his shoes. His hard little soles patterned like pebbles on the cobbles of the stableyard, careless of being overheard now that he was safely out of that narrow, darkening carrel, echoing hollowly to the sound of one self-righteous voice and one wolfish one plotting the capture and ruin of Hyacinth, who was young and lively and ranked as a friend. But they should not have him, not if Richard could prevent. No matter how detailed Brother Jerome's directions, that man who wanted his villein back, and certainly meant him no good if ever he got him, would still have to find his way and sort out the woodland paths as he came to them, but Richard knew every track, and could ride by the shortest way, and fast, if only he could get his pony saddled and smuggled quietly out at the gatehouse before the enemy sent a groom to saddle his own tall horse. For he was hardly likely to do it for himself if he had a servant to do it for him. The thought of the twilit woods did not daunt Richard, his heart rose excitedly to the adventure.

Luck or heaven favoured him, for it was the hour when everyone was at supper, and even the porter at the gatehouse was taking his meal within, and left the gate unwatched while he ate. If he did hear hooves, and come out to see who the rider might be, he came too late to see Richard scramble into the saddle and set off at a round trot along the Foregate towards Saint Giles. He had even forgotten that he was hungry, and felt no pang at going supperless. Besides, he was a favourite with Brother Petrus, the abbot's cook, and might be able to wheedle something out of him later. As for what was to happen when his absence was discovered, as it surely must be at bedtime even if it passed unremarked at supper, there was no point in giving any thought to that. What mattered was to find Hyacinth, and warn him, if he was indeed this Brand, that he had better get away into hiding as fast as he could, for the hunt was out after him, and close on his heels. After that, let what was bound to happen, happen!

He turned into the forest beyond Wroxeter, on a broad ride which Eilmund had cleared for the passage of his coppice wood and trimmed poles. It led directly to the forester's cottage, but also provided the quickest way to a side-path which continued to the hermitage, the obvious place to look first for Cuthred's servant. The forest here was chiefly oak, and old, the ground cover light and low, and the deep layers of the leaves of many autumns made riding silent. Richard had slackened speed among the old trees, and the pony stepped with delicate pleasure in the cushioned mould. But for the hush, the boy would never have heard the voices, for they were low and intent, and manifestly the one was a man's, the other a girl's, though their words were too soft to be distinguished, meant only for each other. Then he saw them, aside from the path, very still and very close beside the broad bole of an oak tree. They were not touching, though they had eyes only for each other, and whatever they had to say was earnest and of high importance. The shout Richard launched at sight of them startled them apart like fluttered birds.

'Hyacinth! Hyacinth!'

He rolled and fell from his pony, rather than dismounted, and flew to meet them as they started towards him.

'Hyacinth, you must hide – you must get away quickly! They're after you, if you're Brand – *are* you

75

Brand? There's a man has come looking for you, he says he's hunting a runaway villein named Brand ...'

Hyacinth, alert and quivering, held him by the shoulders, and dropped to his knees to have him eye to eye. 'What like of man? A servant? Or the man himself? And when was this?'

'After Vespers. I heard them talking – Brother Jerome told him there was a young man newly come into this country, who might be the one he's looking for. He told him where to find you, and he's coming to look for you at the hermitage now, this very night. An awful man, big and loud-mouthed. I ran to get my pony while they were still talking, I got away before him. But you mustn't go back to Cuthred, you must get away quickly and hide.'

Hyacinth caught the boy in his arms in a brief, boisterous embrace. 'You're a true and gallant friend as any man could have, and never fear for me, now I'm warned what can harm me? That's the man himself, no question! Drogo Bosiet thinks highly enough of me to waste time and men and money on hunting me down, and in the end he'll get nothing for his pains.'

'Then you *are* Brand? You *were* his villein?'

'I love you all the more,' said Hyacinth, 'for viewing my villeinage as past. Yes, the name they gave me long ago was Brand, I chose Hyacinth for myself. You and I will keep to that name. And now you and I, my friend, must part, for what you must do now is ride back to the abbey quickly, before the light's gone, and before you're missed. Come, I'll see you safe to the edge of the wood.'

'No!' said Richard, outraged. 'I'll go alone, I'm not afraid. You must vanish – now, at once!'

The girl had laid her hand on Hyacinth's shoulder. Richard saw her eyes wide and bright with resolution rather than alarm in the encroaching twilight. 'He shall, Richard! I know a place where he'll be safe.'

'You ought to try to get into Wales,' said Richard anxiously, even somewhat jealously, for this was his friend, and he was the rescuer, and almost he resented it that Hyacinth should owe any part of his salvation to someone else, and a woman, at that.

Hyacinth and Annet looked briefly at each other, and smiled, and the quality of their smiles lit up the woodland. 'No, not that,' said Hyacinth gently. 'If run I must, I'll not run far. But you need not fear for me, I shall be safe enough. Now mount, my lord, and be off with you, back where *you'll* be safe, or I won't stir a step.'

That set him in motion briskly enough. Once he looked back to wave, and saw them standing as he had left them, gazing after him. A second time he looked back, before the spot where they stood was quite hidden from him among the trees, but they were gone, vanished, and the forest was silent and still. Richard remembered his own problems ahead, and took the road homeward at an anxious trot.

Drogo Bosiet rode through the early twilight by the ways Brother Jerome had indicated to him, asking peremptorily of the villagers in Wroxeter for confirmation that he was on the best road to the cell of the hermit Cuthred. It seemed that the holy man was held in the kind of unofficial reverence common to the old Celtic eremites, for more than one of those questioned spoke of him as Saint Cuthred.

Drogo entered the forest close to where Eaton land, as the shepherd in the field informed him, bordered Eyton land, and a narrow ride brought him after almost a mile of forest to a small, level clearing ringed round with thick woodland. The stone hut in the centre was stoutly built but small and low-roofed, and showed signs of recent repair after being neglected for years. There was a little square garden enclosure round it, fenced in with a low pale, and part of the ground within had been cleared and planted. Drogo dismounted at the edge of the clearing and advanced to the fence, leading his horse by the bridle.

The evening silence was profound, there might have been no living being within a mile of the place.

But the door of the hut stood open, and from deep within a steady gleam of light showed. Drogo tethered his horse, and strode in through the garden and up to the door, and still hearing no sound, went in. The room into which he stepped was small and dim, and contained little but a pallet bed against the wall, a small table and a bench. The light burned within, in a second room, and through the open doorway, for there was no door between, he saw that this was a chapel. The lamp burned upon a stone altar, before a small silver cross set up on a carved wooden casket reliquary, and on the altar before the cross lay a slender and elegant breviary in a gilded binding. Two silver candlesticks, surely the gifts of the hermit's patroness, flanked the cross, one on either side.

Before this altar a man was kneeling motionless, a tall man in a rough black habit, with the cowl raised to cover his head. Against the small, steady light the dark figure was impressive, the long, erect back straight as a lance, the head not bowed but raised, the very image of sanctity. Even Drogo held his tongue for a moment, but no longer. His own needs and desires were paramount, a hermit's prayers could and must yield to them. Evening was rapidly deepening into night, and he had no time to waste.

'You are Cuthred?' he demanded firmly. 'They told me at the abbey how to find you.'

The dignified figure did not move, unless he unfolded his unseen hands. But he said in a measured and unstartled voice: 'Yes, I am Cuthred. What do you need from me? Come in and speak freely.'

'You have a boy who runs your errands. Where is he? I want to see him. You may well have been cozened into keeping a rogue about you unawares.'

And at that the habited figure did turn, the cowled head reared to face the stranger, and the sidelong light

78

from the altar lamp showed a lean, deep-eyed, bearded face, a long, straight, aristocratic nose, a fell of dark hair within the hood, as Drogo Bosiet and the hermit of Eyton forest looked long and steadily at each other.

Brother Cadfael was sitting by Eilmund's couch, supping on bread and cheese and apples, since like Richard he had missed his usual supper, and well content with a very discontented patient, when Annet came back from feeding the hens and shutting them in, and milking the one cow she kept for their own use. She had been an unconscionable time about it, and so her disgruntled father told her. All trace of fever had left him, his colour was good, and he was in no great discomfort, but he was in a glum fury with his own helplessness, and impatient to be out and about his business again, distrusting the abbot's willing but untutored substitutes to take proper care of his forest. The very shortness of his temper was testimony to his sound health. And the offending leg was straight and gave no great pain. Cadfael was well satisfied.

Annet came in demurely, and laughed at her father's grumbling, no way in awe of him. 'I left you in the best of company, and I knew you'd be the better for an hour or so without me, and so would I for an hour without you, such an old bear as you're become! Why should I hurry back, on such a fine evening? You know Brother Cadfael has taken good care of you, don't grudge me a breath of air.'

But by the look of her she had enjoyed something more potent than a mere breath of air. There was a brightness and a quivering aliveness about her, as if after strong wine. Her brown hair, always so smoothly banded, had shaken loose a few strands on her shoulders, Cadfael noted, as though she had wound her way through low branches that caught at the braids, and the colour in her cheeks was rosy and roused, to match the brilliance of her eyes. She had brought in a few of the month's lost leaves on her shoes. True, the byre lay just within the trees at the edge of the clearing, but there were no well-grown oaks there.

'Well, now that you're back, and I shan't be leaving him to complain without a listener,' said Cadfael, 'I'd best be getting back before it's full dark. Keep him off his feet for a few days yet, lass, and I'll let him up on crutches soon if he behaves himself. At least he's taken no harm from lying fast in the water, that's a mercy.'

'Thanks to Cuthred's boy Hyacinth,' Annet reminded them.

She flicked a swift glance at her father, and was pleased when he responded heartily: 'And that's truth if ever there was! He was as good as a son to me that day, and I don't forget it.'

And was it fancy, or did Annet's cheeks warm into a deeper rose? As good as a son to a man who had no son to be his right hand, but only this bright, confident, discreet and loving daughter?

'Possess your soul in patience,' advised Cadfael, rising, 'and we'll have you as sound as before. It's worth waiting for. And don't fret about the coppice, for Annet here will tell you they've made a good job of clearing the brook and shaved off the overhang of the bank. It will hold.' He made fast his scrip to his girdle, and turned to the door.

'I'll see you to the gate,' said Annet, and came out with him into the deep twilight of the clearing, where his horse was placidly pulling at the turf.

'Girl,' said Cadfael with his foot in the stirrup, 'you blossom like a rose tonight.'

She was just taking up the loose tresses in her hands, and smoothing them back into neatness with the rest. She turned and smiled at him. 'But I seem to have been through a thorn bush,' she said.

Cadfael leaned from the saddle and delicately picked a sear oak leaf out of her hair. She looked up to see him twirling it gently between his fingers by the stem, and wonderfully she smiled. That was how he left her, roused and braced, and surely having made up her mind to go, undaunted, through all the thorny thickets that might be in the path between her and what she wanted. She was not ready yet to confide even in her father, but it troubled her not at all that Cadfael should guess at what was in the wind, nor had she any fear of a twisted ending. Which did not preclude the possibility that others might have good reason to fear on her account.

Cadfael rode without haste through the darkening wood. The moon was already up, and bright where it could penetrate the thickness of the trees. Compline must be long over by now, and the brothers making ready for sleep. The boys would be in their beds long ago. It was cool and fresh in the green-scented forest, pleasant to ride alone and at leisure, and have time to think of timeless things that could not be accommodated in the bustle of the day, sometimes not even during the holy office or the quiet times of prayer, where by rights they belonged. There was more room for them here under this night sky still faintly luminous round the rims of vision. Cadfael rode in a deep content of mind through the thickest part of the woodland growth, with a glimmer of light from the open fields ahead before him.

It was the rustling movement on his left, among the trees, that startled him out of his muse. Something vaguely pale in the gloom moved alongside him, and he heard the slight jingling of a horse's bit and bridle. A riderless horse, wandering astray but saddled and bridled, for the small metallic sounds rang clear. He had not been riderless when he set out from his stable. In glimpses of moonlight between the branches the pale shape shone elusively, drawing nearer to the path. Cadfael had seen that light roan hide before, that same afternoon in the great court of the abbey.

He dismounted in haste, and called, advancing to take

81

Chapter Six

AT SO late an hour there was small chance of reaching immediate help at either abbey or castle, and none of deriving any knowledge from the darkening scene here in the forest. All Cadfael could do, thus alone, was to kneel beside the mute body and feel for a heartbeat or pulse, and listen for any faint sign of breathing. But though Drogo's flesh was warm, and yielded pliably to handling, there was no breath in him, and the heart in his great chest, almost certainly pierced by the thrust from behind, was stonily still. He could not have been dead very long, but the gush of blood that had sprung out with the blade had ceased to flow, and was beginning to dry at its edges into a dark crust. More than an hour ago, Cadfael thought, judging by what signs he had, perhaps as much as two hours. And his saddle-roll cut loose and taken. Here, in our woods! When did any man ever hear of footpads so close? Or has some cutthroat from the town heard of Eilmund being laid up at home, and ventured to try his luck here for a chance traveller riding alone?

Delay could not harm Drogo now, and daylight might show at least some trace to lead to his murderer. Best leave him so, and take word to the castle, where there was always a guard waking, and leave a message for Hugh, to be delivered as soon as there was light. At midnight the brothers would rise for Matins, and the same grim news could and should be delivered then to Abbot Radulfus. The dead man was the abbey's guest, and his son expected within a few days, and to the abbey he must be taken for proper and reverent care.

No, there was nothing more to be done for Drogo Bosiet, but at least he could get the horse back to his stable. Cadfael mounted, and gathered the loose bridle in his left hand, and the horse came with him docilely. There was no haste. He had until midnight. No need to save time, since even if he reached his bed before Matins, sleep would be impossible. Better take care of the horses and then wait for the bell.

Abbot Radulfus came early to the church for Matins, to find Cadfael waiting for him in the south porch as he crossed from his lodging. The bell in the dortoir was only just sounding. It takes but a few moments to say bluntly that a man is dead, and by an act of man, not of God.

Radulfus was never known to waste words in exclamation, and did not do so now at the news that a guest of his house had come to an unlawful end in the abbey's own forest. The gross affront and grosser wrong he accepted in sombre silence, and the right and duty of retribution, as incumbent now upon the church as on the secular authority, he took up with a deep assenting nod of his head, and a grim tightening of his long, firm lips. In the hush while he thought, they heard the soft, sandalled steps of the brothers descending the night stairs.

'And you have left word for Hugh Beringar?' asked the abbot.

'At his house and at the castle.'

'No man can do more, then, until first light. He must be brought here, for here his son will come. But you – you will be needed, you can lead straight to where he lies. Go now, I excuse you from the office, go and take some

84

rest, and at dawn ride to join the sheriff. Say to him that I will send a party after, to bring the body home.'

In the first hesitant light of a chill morning they stood over Drogo Bosiet's body, Hugh Beringar and Cadfael, a sergeant of Hugh's garrison and two men-at-arms, all silent, all with eyes fixed on the great patch of encrusted blood that soaked the back of the rich riding coat. The grass hung as heavy and flattened with dew as if after rain, and the moisture had gathered in great pearls in the woollen pile of the dead man's clothing, and starred the bushes in a treasury of cobwebs.

'Since he plucked out the dagger from the wound,' said Hugh, 'most likely he took it away with him. But we'll look about for it, in case he discarded it. And you say the straps of the saddle-roll were sliced through? After the slaying - he needed the knife for that. Quicker and easier in the dark to cut it loose than unbuckle it, and whoever he was, he wouldn't want to linger. Strange, though, that a mounted man should fall victim to such an attack. At the least sound he had only to spur and draw clear, surely.'

'But I think,' said Cadfael, studying how the body lay, 'that he was on foot here, and leading the horse. He was a stranger, and the path here is very narrow and the trees crowd close, and it was dark or getting dark. See the leaves that have clung to his boot soles. He never had time to turn, the one stroke was enough. Where he had been I don't know, but he was on his way back to his lodging in our guest hall when he was struck down. With no struggle and little noise. The horse had taken no great alarm, he strayed only a few yards.'

'Which argues an expert footpad and thief,' said Hugh. 'But do you believe in that? In my writ and so close to the town?'

'No. But some secret rogue, perhaps even a sneak thief out of the town, might risk one exploit, knowing

Eilmund is laid up at home. But this is guessing,' said Cadfael, shaking his head. 'Now and then even a poacher might be tempted to try murder, if he came on a man of substance, alone and at night. But guessing is small use.'

The party sent by Abbot Radulfus to carry Drogo back to the abbey were already winding their way along the path with their litter. Cadfael knelt in the grass, soaking his habit at the knees in the plenteous dew, and carefully turned the stiffening body face upward. The heavy muscling of the cheeks had fallen slack, the eyes, so disproportionately small for the massive countenance, were half open. He looked older and less arrogantly brutal in death, a mortal man like other men, almost piteous. The hand that had lain hidden under his body wore a heavy silver ring.

'Something the thief missed,' said Hugh, looking down with something of startled regret in his face for so much power now powerless.

'Another sign of haste. Or he would have ransacked every garment. And proof enough that the body was not moved. He lies as he fell, facing towards Shrewsbury. It's as I said, he was on his way home.'

'There's a son expected, you said? Come,' said Hugh, 'we can leave him to your men now, and my fellows will comb the woods all round in case there's sign or trace to be found, though I doubt it. You and I will be off back to the abbey, and see what the abbot has brought to light at chapter. For someone must surely have put some notion into his mind, to send him out again so late.'

The sun was above the rim of the world, but veiled and pale, as they mounted and turned back along the narrow ride. The spider-draped bushes caught the first gleams that pierced the mist, and flashed in coruscations of diamonds. When they emerged into the open, low-lying fields the horses waded through a shallow lilac-tinted sea of vapour.

'What do you know of this man Bosiet,' asked Hugh, 'more than he has told me, or I have gleaned without his telling?'

'Little enough, I expect. He's lord of several manors in Northamptonshire, and some little while since a villein of his, as like as not for a very good reason, laid his steward flat and put him to bed for some days, and then very wisely took to his heels before they could lay hands on him. Bosiet and his men have been hunting for the fellow ever since. They must have wasted a good while searching the rest of the shire, I fancy, before they got word from someone that he'd made for Northampton and seemed to be heading north and west. And between them they've followed this far, making drives in both directions from every halt. He must have cost them far above his value, valuable though they say he is, but it's his blood they're after first and foremost, and seemingly they set a higher price on that than on his craft, whatever that may be. There was a very vigorous hate there,' said Cadfael feelingly. 'He brought it to chapter with him. Father Abbot was not greatly taken with the notion of helping him to the sort of revenge he'd be likely to take.'

'And shrugged him off on to me,' said Hugh, briefly grinning. 'Well, small blame to him. I took your word for it, and stayed out of his way as long as I could. In any case I could give him no help. What else do you know of him?'

'That he has a groom named Warin, the one that rode with him, though not, it seems, on his last ride. Maybe he'd sent his man on some other errand, and couldn't wait once he got the word, but set off alone. He's – he *was* – a man who liked to use his fists freely on his servants, for any offence or none. At least he'd laid Warin's face open for him, and according to the groom that was no rarity. As for the son, according to Warin he's much like his father, and just as surely to be avoided. And he'll be coming from Stafford any day now.'

87

'To find he has to coffin his father's body and take it home for burial,' said Hugh ruefully.

'To find he's now lord of Bosiet,' said Cadfael. 'That's the reverse of the coin. Who knows which side up it will look to him?'

'You're grown very cynical, old friend,' remarked Hugh, wryly smiling.

'I'm thinking,' Cadfael owned, 'of reasons why men do murder. Greed is one, and might be spawned in a son, waiting impatiently for his inheritance. Hate is another, and a misused servant might entertain it willingly if chance offered. But there are other and stranger reasons, no doubt, like a simple taste for thieving, and a disposition to make sure the victim never blabs. A pity, Hugh, a great pity there should be so much hurrying on of death, when it's bound to reach every man in its own good time.'

By the time they emerged on to the highroad at Wroxeter the sun was well up, and the mist clearing from its face, though the fields still swam in pearly vapour. They made good speed from there along the road to Shrewsbury, and rode in at the gatehouse after the end of High Mass, when the brothers were dispersing to their work until the hour of the midday meal.

'The lord abbot's been asking after you,' said the porter, coming out from his lodge at sight of them. 'He's in his parlour, and the prior with him, and asks that you'll join him there.'

They left their horses to the grooms, and went at once to the abbot's lodging. In the panelled parlour Radulfus looked up from his desk, and Prior Robert, very erect and austere on a bench beside the window, looked down his nose with a marked suggestion of disapproval and withdrawal. The complexities of law and murder and manhunt had no business to intrude into the monastic domain, and he deplored the necessity to recognise their existence, and the very processes of dealing with them

88

when they did force a breach in the wall. Close to his elbow, unobtrusive in his shadow, stood Brother Jerome, his narrow shoulders hunched, thin lips drawn tight, pale hands folded in his sleeves, the image of virtue assailed and bearing the cross with humility. There was always a strong element of complacency in Jerome's humility, but this time there was also a faintly defensive quality, as though his rightness had somehow, if only by implication, been questioned.

'Ah, you are back!' said Radulfus. 'You have not brought back the body of our guest so quickly?'

'No, Father, not yet, they will be following us, but on foot it will take some time. It is just as Brother Cadfael reported it to you in the night. The man was stabbed in the back, probably as he was leading his horse, the path there being narrow and overgrown. You will know already that his saddle-roll was cut loose and stolen. By what Brother Cadfael observed of the body when he found it, the thing must have been done about the time of Compline, perhaps a little before. There's nothing to show by whom. By the hour, he must have been on his way back here to your guest hall. By the way he faced as he fell, also, for the body was not moved, or his ring would have been taken, and he still wears it. But as to where he had been in those parts, there's no knowing.'

'I think,' said the abbot, 'we have something to show on that head. Brother Jerome here will tell you what he has now told to Prior Robert and me.'

Jerome was usually only too ready to hear his own voice, whether in sermon, homily or reproof, but it was noticeable that this time he was assembling his words with more than normal care.

'The man was a guest and an upright citizen,' he said, 'and had told us at chapter that he was pursuing an offender against the law, one who had committed assault against the person of his steward and done him grievous harm, and then absconded from his master. I took

89

thought afterwards that there was indeed one newcomer in these parts who might well be the man he sought, and I considered it the duty of every one of us to help the cause of justice and law. So I spoke to the lord of Bosiet. I told him that the young man who serves the hermit Cuthred, and who came here with him only a few weeks ago, does answer to the description he gave of his runaway villein Brand, though he calls himself Hyacinth. He is of the right age, his colouring as his master described it. And no one here knows anything about him. I thought it only right to tell him the truth. If the young man proved not to be Brand, there was no harm to him.'

'And you told him, I believe,' said the abbot neutrally, 'how to get to the hermit's cell, where he could find this young man?'

'I did, Father, as was my duty.'

'And he at once set off to ride to that place.'

'Yes, Father. He had sent his groom on an errand into the town, he was obliged to saddle up for himself, but he did not wish to wait, since most of the day was gone.'

'I have spoken to the groom Warin, since we learned of his master's death,' said the abbot, looking up at Hugh. 'He was sent to enquire after any craftsman in fine leather-work in Shrewsbury, for it seems that was the young man's craft also, and Bosiet thought he might have tried to get work within the borough among those who could use his skills. There is no blame can attach to the servant, by the time he returned his master was long gone. His errand could not wait, it seems, until morning.' His voice was measured and considered, with no inflection of approval or disapproval. 'That solves, I think, the problem of where he had been.'

'And where I must follow him,' said Hugh, enlightened. 'I'm obliged to you, Father, for pointing me the next step of the road. If he did indeed talk to Cuthred, at least we may learn what passed, and whether he got the answer he wanted – though plainly he was returning alone. Had he been bringing a captive villein with him, he would hardly have left him with free hands and a dagger about him. With your permission, Father, I'll keep Brother Cadfael with me as witness, rather than take men-at-arms to a hermitage.'

'Do so,' said the abbot willingly. 'This unfortunate man was a guest of our house, and we owe him every effort which may lead to the capture of his murderer. And every proper rite and service that can still be paid to his corpse. Robert, will you see to it that the body is reverently received when it comes? And Brother Jerome, you may assist. Your zeal to be of help to him should not be frustrated. You shall keep a night vigil with him in prayers for his soul.'

So there would be two lying side by side in the mortuary chapel tonight, Cadfael thought as they went out together from the parlour: the old man who had closed a long life as gently as a spent flower sheds it petals, and the lord of lands taken abruptly in his malice and hatred, with no warning, and no time to make his peace with man or God. Drogo Bosiet's soul would be in need of all the prayers it could get.

'And has it yet entered your mind,' asked Hugh abruptly, as they rode out along the Foregate for the second time, 'that Brother Jerome in his zeal for justice may have helped Bosiet to his death?'

If it had, Cadfael was not yet minded to entertain the thought. 'He was on his way back,' he said cautiously, 'and empty-handed. It argues that he was disappointed. The boy is not his lost villein.'

'It could as well argue that he is, and saw his doom bearing down on him in time to vanish. How then? He's been in the woods there now long enough to know his way about. How if he was the hand that held the dagger?'

No denying that it was a possibility. Who could have better reason for slipping a knife into Drogo Bosiet's

91

back than the lad he meant to drag back to his own manor court, flay first, and exploit afterwards lifelong? 'It's what will be said,' agreed Cadfael sombrely. 'Unless we find Cuthred and his boy sitting peacefully at home minding their own business and meddling with no one else's. Small use guessing until we hear what happened there.'

They approached the projecting tongue of Eaton land by the same path Drogo had used, and saw the small clearing in thick woodland open before them almost suddenly, as he had seen it, but in full daylight, while he had come in early dusk. Muted sunlight filtering through the branches turned the sombre grey of the stone hut to dull gold. The low pales of the fence that marked out the garden were set far apart, a mere sketched boundary, no bar to beast or man, and the door of the hut stood wide open, so that they saw through into the inner room where the constant lamp on the stone altar showed tiny and dim as a single spark, almost quenched by the light falling from the tiny shutterless window above. Saint Cuthred's cell, it seemed, stood wide open to all who came.

A part of the enclosed garden was still wild, though the grass and herbage had been cut, and there the hermit himself was at work with mattock and spade, heaving up the matted clods and turning the soil below as he cleared it. They watched him at it as they approached, inexpert but dogged and patient, plainly unused to handling such tools or stooping to such labours as should have fallen to Hyacinth. Who, by the same token, was nowhere to be seen.

A tall man, the hermit, long-legged, long-bodied, lean and straight, his coarse dark habit kilted to his knees, and the cowl flung back on his shoulders. He saw them coming and straightened up from his labours with the mattock still in his hands, and showed them a strong, fleshless face, olive-skinned and deep-eyed, framed in a thick bush

Chapter Seven

I T HAD always been brother Jerome's contention, frequently and vociferously expressed, that Brother Paul exercised far too slack an authority over his young charges, both the novices and the children. It was Paul's way to make his supervision of their days as unobtrusive as possible except when actually teaching, though he was prompt to appear if any of them needed or wanted him. But such routine matters as their ablutions, their orderly behaviour at meals, and their retiring at night and rising in the morning were left to their good consciences and to the sound habits of cleanliness and punctuality they had been taught. Brother Jerome was convinced that no boy under sixteen could be trusted to keep any rule, and that even those who had reached that mature age still had more of the devil in them than of the angels. He would have watched and hounded and corrected their every movement, had he been master of the boys, and made a great deal more use of punishments than ever Paul could be brought to contemplate. It was pleasure to him to be able to say, with truth, that he had always prophesied disaster from such lax stewardship.

Three schoolboys and nine novices, in a range of ages from nine years up to seventeen, are quite enough active youngsters to satisfy the casual eye at breakfast, unless

97

someone has reason to count them, and discover that they fall one short of the right tally. Probably Jerome would have counted them on every occasion, certain that sooner or later there would be defaulters. Brother Paul did not count. And as he was needed at chapter and afterwards that day on specific business concerning his office, he had confided the morning's schooling to the most responsible of the novices, another policy which Jerome deplored as ruinous to discipline. In church the small fry occupied such insignificant places that one more or less would never be noticed. So it was only late in the afternoon, when Paul mustered his flock again into the schoolroom, and separated the class of novices from the younger boys, that the absence of Richard was at last manifest.

Even then Paul was not at first alarmed or disturbed. The child was simply loitering somewhere, forgetful of time, and would appear at a run at any moment. But time slid by and Richard did not come. Questioned, the three boys remaining shuffled their feet uneasily, shifted a little closer together to have the reassurance of shoulder against shoulder, shook their heads wordlessly, and evaded looking Brother Paul in the eye. The youngest in particular looked less than happy, but they volunteered nothing, which merely convinced Paul that Richard was deliberately playing truant, that they were well aware of it and disapproved but would not let out one word to betray him. That he refrained from threatening them with dire penalties for such refractory silence would only have confirmed Jerome in his black disapproval of such an attitude.

Jerome encouraged tale-bearers. Paul had a sneaking sympathy with the sinful solidarity that would invite penalties to fall on its own head rather than betray a companion. He merely stated firmly that Richard should be called to account for his behaviour later and pay the penalty of his foolishness, and proceeded with the lesson. But he was increasingly aware of his pupils' inattention and uneasiness, and the guilty glances they slid sidelong at one another over their letters. By the time they were dismissed he felt that the youngest, at any rate, was on the verge of blurting out whatever he knew, and his very distress argued that there was more behind this defection than the mere capricious cutting of a class.

Paul called the child back as they were leaving, half-gratefully, half-fearfully. 'Edwin, come here to me!'

Understandably, the other two fled, certain now that the sky was about to fall on them, and in haste to avoid the first shock, whatever followed later. Edwin halted, turned, and slowly trailed his way back across the room, his eyes lowered to the small feet he was dragging reluctantly along the boards of the floor. He stood before Brother Paul, and trembled. One knee was still band-aged, and the linen had slipped awry. Without thinking, Paul unwound it and made it neat again.

'Edwin, what is it you know about Richard? Where is he?'

The child gulped out with utter conviction: 'I don't *know*!' and burst into tears. Paul drew him close and let him bury his nose in a long-suffering shoulder.

'Tell me! When did you last see him? When did he go?'

Edwin sobbed inarticulately into the rough woollen folds, until Paul held him off and peered into the smudged and woeful face. 'Come! Tell me everything you know.'

And it came out in a flood, between hectic sniffs and sobs. 'It was yesterday, after Vespers. I saw him, he took his pony and rode out along the Foregate. I thought he'd come back, but he didn't, and we were frightened — We didn't want him to be caught, he'd be in such terrible trouble — We didn't want to tell, we thought he'd come back and no one need know . . .'

'Do you tell me,' demanded Paul, appalled and for once sounding formidable, 'that he did not sleep here in his bed last night? That he's been gone since yesterday and not a word said?'

99

A fresh burst of despairing tears distorted Edwin's round flushed face, and his violently nodding head admitted the impeachment.

'And all of you knew this? You three? Did you never think that he might be hurt somewhere, or in danger? Would he stay out all night willingly? Oh, child, why did you not tell me? All this time we've lost!' But the boy was frightened enough already, there was nothing to be done with him but hush and reassure and comfort him, where reassurance and comfort were very hard to find. 'Now, tell me – you saw him go, mounted. After Vespers? Did he not say what he intended?'

Edwin, very drearily, gathered what sense he had left and fumbled out the rest of it. 'He came too late for Vespers. We were down on the Gaye, by the river, he didn't want to come in, and when he did run after us it was too late. I think he waited to try and slip in with us when we came out of church, but Brother Jerome was standing talking to – to that man, the one who ...'

He began to whimper again, recalling what he should not have seen, but of course had, the bearers of the litter coming in at the gatehouse, the bulky body motionless, the powerful face covered. 'I waited at the school door,' whispered the tearful voice, 'and I saw Richard come running out and down to the stables, and then he came back with his pony, and led it out at the gate in a great hurry, and rode away. And that's all I know. I thought he would soon come back,' he wailed hopelessly. 'We didn't want to get him into trouble . . .'

If they had recoiled from doing that, they had certainly given him ample time and scope to get himself into trouble, deeper than any disloyalty of theirs might have plunged him. Brother Paul resignedly shook and patted his penitent into relative calm.

'You have been very wrong and foolish, and if you're in disgrace it's no more than you deserve. But answer everything truthfully now, and we'll find Richard safe

100

and sound. Go now, at once, and find the other two, and the three of you wait here until you are sent for.'

And Paul was off at a shaken run to take the bad news first to Prior Robert and then to the abbot, and then to confirm that the pony Dame Dionisia had sent as bait to her grandson was indeed gone from his stall. And there was great clamour and running about and turning grange court and barns and guest halls inside out, in case the culprit had not, after all deserted the enclave, or for sounder reasons had returned to it furtively, to try and conceal the fact that he had ever left it. The wretched schoolboys, tongue-lashed by Prior Robert and threatened with worse when anyone had time to perform it, cowered shivering and reduced to tears by the enormity of what had seemed to them good intentions, and having survived the first storm of recriminations, settled down stoically to endure the rest supperless and outcast. Not even Brother Paul had time to offer them any further reassuring words, he was too busy searching through the complex recesses of the mill and nearer alleys of the Foregate.

Into this frenzy of alarm and activity Cadfael came riding in the early evening, after parting from Hugh at the gate. This very night there would be sergeants out dragging the woods from Eyton westward for the fugitive who might or might not be Brand, but must at all costs be captured. Hugh was no fonder of manhunts than was Cadfael, and many a misused serf had been driven at last to flight and outlawry, but murder was murder, and the law could not stomach it. Guilty or innocent, the youth Hyacinth would have to be found. Cadfael dismounted at the gatehouse with his mind full of one vanished youngster, to be met by the spectacle of agitated brothers running hither and thither among all the monastic buildings in search of a second one. While he was gaping in amazement at the sight, Brother Paul came bearing down upon him breathless and hopeful.

101

'Cadfael, you've been in the forest. You haven't seen hide or hair of young Richard, have you? I'm beginning to think he must have run home ...'

'The last place he'd be likely to go,' said Cadfael reasonably, 'while he's wary of his grandmother's intentions. Why? Do you tell me you've mislaid the imp?'

'He's gone – gone since last night, and we never knew it until an hour ago.' Paul poured out the dismal story in a cascade of guilt and remorse and anxiety. 'I am to blame! I have failed in my duty, been too complacent, trusted them too far ... But why should he run away? He was happy enough. He never showed signs ...'

'Doubtless he had his reasons,' said Cadfael, scrubbing thoughtfully at his blunt brown nose. 'But back to the lady? I doubt it! No, if he went off in such haste it was something new and urgent that sent him running. Last night after Vespers, you said?'

'Edwin tells me Richard dawdled too long by the river, and came too late for Vespers, and must have been lurking in the cloister to slip in among the rest of the boys when they came out. But he could not do it because Jerome stood there in the archway, waiting to speak to Bosiet, who had attended among the guests. But when Edwin looked back he saw Richard come running out down to the stables, and then out at the gate in a hurry.'

'Did he so!' said Cadfael, enlightened. 'And where was Jerome, then, and Bosiet, that the boy was able to make off undetected?' But he did not wait for an answer. 'No, never trouble to guess. We already know what they had to talk about, between the two of them – a small matter, and private. Jerome wanted no other audience, but it seems he had one of whom he knew nothing. Paul, I must leave you to your hunt a little while longer, and ride after Hugh Beringar. He's already committed to a search for one vanished lad, he may as well make it for two, and drag the coverts but once.'

*   *   *

Hugh, overtaken under the arch of the town gate, reined in abruptly at the news, and turned to stare meditatively at Cadfael. 'So you think that's the way of it!' he said and whistled. 'Why should he care about a young fellow he's barely seen and never spoken to? Or have you reason to think the two of them have had their heads together?'

'No, none that I know of. Nothing but the timing of it, but that links the pair closely enough. Not much doubt what Richard overheard, and none that it sent him hotfoot on some urgent errand. And before Bosiet can get to the hermitage, Hyacinth vanishes.'

'And so does Richard!' Hugh's black brows drew together, frowning over the implications. 'Do you tell me if I find the one I shall have found both?'

'No, that I gravely doubt. The boy surely meant to be back in the fold before bedtime, and all innocence. He's no fool, and he has no reason to want to leave us. But all the more reason we should be anxious about him now. He would be back with us, surely, if something had not prevented. Whether his pony's thrown him somewhere, and he's hurt, or lost – or whether . . . They're wondering if he's run home to Eaton, but that's rankly impossible. He never would.'

Hugh had grasped the unspoken suggestion which Cadfael himself had hardly had time to contemplate. 'No, but he might be taken there! And by God, so he might! If some of Dionisia's people happened on him alone in the woods, they'd know how to please their lady. Oh, I know the household there are Richard's people, not hers, but there must be one or two among them would take the chance of present favours if it offered. Cadfael, old friend,' said Hugh heartily, 'you go back to your workshop and leave Eaton to me. As soon as I've set my men on the hunt, yes, for both, I'll go myself to Eaton and see what the lady has to say for herself. If she baulks at letting me turn her manor inside out for the one lad, I shall know she has the other hidden away somewhere about the place, and I can force her hand. If Richard's there, I'll have him out for you by tomorrow, and back in Brother Paul's arms,' promised Hugh buoyantly. 'Even if it costs the poor imp a whipping,' he reflected with a sympathetic grin, 'he may find that preferable to being married off on his grandmother's terms. At least the sting doesn't last so long.'

Which was a very perverse blasphemy against marriage, Cadfael thought and said, coming from one who had such excellent reason to consider himself blessed in his wife and proud of his son. Hugh had wheeled his horse towards the steep slope of the Wyle, but he slanted a smiling glance back over his shoulder.

'Come up to the house with me now, and complain of me to Aline. Keep her company while I'm off to the castle to start the hunt.'

And the prospect of sitting for an hour or so in Aline's company, and playing with his godson Giles, now approaching three years old, was tempting, but Cadfael shook his head, reluctantly but resignedly. 'No, I'd best be going back. We'll all be busy hunting our own coverts and asking along the Foregate until dark. There's no certainty where he'll be, we dare miss no corner. But God speed your search, Hugh, for it's more likely than ours.'

He walked his horse back over the bridge towards the abbey with a slack rein, suddenly aware he had ridden far enough for one day, and looked forward with positive need to the stillness and soul's quiet of the holy office, and the vast enclosing sanctuary of the church. The thorough search of the forest must be left to Hugh and his officers. No point even in spending time and grief now wondering where the boy would spend the coming night, though an extra prayer for him would not come amiss. And tomorrow, thought Cadfael, I'll go and visit Eilmund, and take him his crutches, and keep my eyes open on the way. Two missing lads to search for. Find one, find both? No, that was too much to hope for. But if he found one, he might also be a long step forward towards finding the other.

There was a newly-arrived guest standing at the foot of the steps that led up to the door of the guest hall, watching with contained interest the continuing bustle of a search which had now lost its frenetic aspect and settled down grimly into the thorough inspection of every corner of the enclave, besides the parties that were out enquiring along the Foregate. The obsessed activity around him only made his composed stillness the more striking, though his appearance otherwise was ordinary enough. His figure was compact and trim, his bearing modest, and his elderly but well-cared-for boots, dark chausses and good plain cotte cut short below the knee, were the common riding gear of all but the highest and the lowest who travelled the roads. He could as well have been a baron's sub-tenant on his lord's business as a prosperous merchant or a minor nobleman on his own. Cadfael noticed him as soon as he dismounted at the gate. The porter came out from his lodge to plump himself down on the stone bench outside with a gusty sigh, blowing out his russet cheeks in mild exasperation.

'No sign of the boy, then?' said Cadfael, though plainly expecting none.

'No, nor likely to be, not within here, seeing he went off pony and all. But make sure first here at home, they say. They're even talking of dragging the mill-pond. Folly! What would he be doing by the pool, when he went off at a trot along the Foregate – that we do know. Besides, he'll never drown, he swims like a fish. No, he's well away out of our reach, whatever trouble he's got himself into. But they must needs turn out all the straw in the lofts and prod through the stable litter. You'd best hurry and keep a sharp eye on your workshop, or they'll be turning that inside out.'

Cadfael was watching the quiet dark figure by the guest hall. 'Who's the newcomer?'

'One Rafe of Coventry. A falconer to the earl of Warwick. He has dealings with Gwynedd for young birds to train, so Brother Denis tells me. He came not a quarter of an hour since.'

'I took him at first to be Bosiet's son,' said Cadfael, 'but I see he's too old – more the father's own generation.'

'So did I take him for the son. I've been keeping a sharp watch for him, for someone has to tell him what's waiting for him here, and I'd rather it was Prior Robert than take it on myself.'

'I like to see a man,' said Cadfael appreciatively, his eyes still on the stranger, 'who can stand stock still in the middle of other people's turmoil, and ask no questions. Ah, well, I'd better get this fellow unsaddled and into his stall, he's had a good day's exercise with all this coming and going. And so have I.'

And tomorrow, he thought, leading the horse at a leisurely walk down the length of the great court towards the stable yard, I must be off again. I may be astray, but at least let's put it to the test.

He passed close to where Rafe of Coventry stood, passively interested in the bustle for which he asked no explanation, and thinking his own thoughts. At the sound of hooves pacing slowly on the cobbles he turned his head, and meeting Cadfael's eyes by chance, gave him the brief thaw of a smile and a nod by way of greeting. A strong but uncommunicative face he showed, broad across brow and cheekbones, with a close-trimmed brown beard and wide-set, steady brown eyes, wrinkled at the corners as if he lived chiefly in the open, and was accustomed to peering across distances.

'You're bound for the stables, Brother? Be my guide there. No reflection on your grooms, but I like to see my own beast cared for.'

'So do I,' said Cadfael warmly, checking to let the

stranger fall into step beside him. 'It's a lifetime's habit. If you learn it young you never lose it.' They matched strides neatly, being of the same modest stature. In the stable yard an abbey groom was rubbing down a tall chestnut horse with a white blaze down his forehead, and hissing gently and contentedly to him as he worked.

'Yours?' said Cadfael, eyeing the beast appreciatively.

'Mine,' said Rafe of Coventry briefly, and himself took the cloth from the groom's hand. 'My thanks, friend! I'll take him myself now. Where may I stable him?' And he inspected the stall the groom indicated, with a long, comprehensive glance round and a nod of satisfaction. 'You keep a good stable here, Brother, I see. No offence that I prefer to do my own grooming. Travellers are not always so well provided, and as you said, it's habit.'

'You travel alone?' said Cadfael, busy unsaddling but with a sharp eye on his companion all the same. The belt that circled Rafe's hips was made to carry sword and dagger. No doubt he had shed both in the guest hall with his cloak and gear. A falconer is not easily fitted into a category where travel is concerned. A merchant would have had at least one able-bodied servant with him for protection, probably more. A soldier would be self-sufficient, as this man chose to be, and carry the means of protecting himself.

'I travel fast,' said Rafe simply. 'Numbers drag. If a man depends only on himself, there's no one can let him fall.'

'You've ridden far?'

'From Warwick.' A man of few words and no curiosity, this falconer of the earl's. Or did that quite hold good? Concerning the search for the lost boy he showed no disposition to ask questions, but he was taking a measured interest in the stables and the horses they held. Even after he had satisfied himself of his own beast's welfare, he still stood looking round him at the rest with a keen professional eye. The mules and the working horses he passed by, but halted at the pale roan that had belonged to Drogo Bosiet. That was understandable enough in a lover of good horseflesh, for the roan was a handsome animal and clearly from stock of excellent quality.

'Can your house afford such bloodstock?' He passed a hand approvingly over the glossy shoulder and stroked between the pricked ears. 'Or does this fellow belong to a guest?'

'He did,' said Cadfael, himself sparing of words.

'He *did*? How is that?' Rafe had turned alertly to stare, and in the unrevealing face the eyes were sharp and intent.

'The man who owned him is dead. He's lying in our mortuary chapel this moment.' The old brother had gone to his rest in the cemetery that same morning, Drogo had the chapel to himself now.

'What kind of man was that? And how did he die?' On this head he had questions enough to ask, startled out of his detachment and indifference.

'We found him dead in the forest, a few miles from here, with a knife wound in his back. And robbed.' Cadfael was never quite sure why he himself had become so reticent at this point, and why, for instance, he did not simply name the dead man. And had his companion persisted, as would surely have been natural enough, he would have answered freely. But there the questioning stopped. Rafe shrugged off the implied perils of riding alone in the forests of the border shires, and closed the low door of the stall on his contented horse.

'I'll bear it in mind. Go well armed, I say, or keep to the highroads.'

He dusted his hands and turned towards the gateway of the yard. 'Well, I'll go and make ready for supper.' And he was off at a purposeful walk, but not immediately towards the guest hall. Instead, he crossed to the archway of the cloister, and entered there. Cadfael found something so significant in that arrow-straight progress towards the church that he followed, candidly curious and officiously helpful, and finding Rafe of Coventry standing hesitant by the parish altar, looking round him at the multiplicity of chapels contained in transepts and chevet, directed him with blunt simplicity to the one he was looking for.

'Through here. The arch is low, but you're my build, no need to stoop your head.'

Rafe made no effort to disguise or disclaim his purpose, or to reject Cadfael's company. He gave him one calm, considering look, nodded his acknowledgements, and followed. And in the stony chill and dimming light of the chapel he crossed at once to the bier where Drogo Bosiet's body lay reverently covered, with candles burning at head and feet, and lifted the cloth from the dead face.

Very briefly he studied the fixed and pallid features, and again covered them, and the movements of his hands as they replaced the cloth had lost their urgency and tension. He had time even for simple human awe at the presence of death.

'You don't, by any chance, know him?' asked Cadfael.

'No, I never saw him before. God rest his soul!' And Rafe straightened up from stooping over the bier, and drew a liberating breath. Whatever his interest in the body had been, it was over.

'A man of property, by the name of Drogo Bosiet, from Northamptonshire. His son is expected here any day now.'

'Do you tell me so? A bleak coming that will be for him.' But the words he used now were coming from the surface of his mind only, and answers concerned him scarcely at all. 'Have you many guests at this season? Of my own years and condition, perhaps? I should enjoy a game of chess in the evening, if I can find a partner.'

If he had lost interest in Drogo Bosiet, it seemed he was still concerned to know of any others who might have come here as travellers. Any of his own years and condition!

'Brother Denis could give you a match,' said Cadfael, deliberately obtuse. 'No, it's a quiet time with us. You'll find the hall half-empty.' They were approaching the steps of the guest hall, side by side and easy together, and the late afternoon light, overcast and still, was beginning to dim into the dove grey of evening.

'This man who was struck down in the forest,' said Rafe of Coventry. 'Your sheriff will surely have the hounds out after an outlaw so near the town. Is there suspicion of any man for the deed?'

'There is,' said Cadfael, 'though there's no certainty. A newcomer in these parts, who's missing from his master's service since the attack.' And he added, innocently probing without seeming to probe: 'A young fellow he is, maybe twenty years old ...'

Not of Rafe's years or condition, no! And of no interest to him, for he merely nodded his acceptance of the information, and by the indifference of his face as promptly discarded it. 'Well, God speed their hunting!' he said, dismissing Hyacinth's guilt or innocence as irrelevant to whatever he had on that closed and armoured mind of his.

At the foot of the guest hall steps he turned in, surely to examine, thought Cadfael, every man of middle years who would come to supper in hall. Looking for one in particular? Whose name, since he did not ask for names, would be unhelpful, because false? One, at any rate, who was not Drogo Bosiet of Northamptonshire!

Chapter Eight

HUGH came to the manor of Eaton early in the morning, with six mounted men at his back, and a dozen more deployed behind him between the river and the highroad, to sweep the whole expanse of field and forest from Wroxeter to Eyton and beyond. For a fugitive murderer they might have to turn the hunt westward, but Richard must surely be somewhere here in this region, if he had indeed set out to warn Hyacinth of the vengeance bearing down on him. Hugh's party had followed the direct road from the Abbey Foregate to Wroxeter, an open, fast track, and thence by the most direct path into the forest, to Cuthred's cell, where Richard would have expected to find Hyacinth. By young Edwin's account he had been only a few minutes ahead of Bosiet, he would have made all haste and taken the shortest and fastest way. But he had never reached the hermitage.

'The boy Richard?' said the hermit, astonished. 'You did not ask me of him yesterday, only of the man. No, Richard did not come. I remember the young lord well, God grant no harm has come to him! I did not know he was lost.'

'And you've seen nothing of him since? It's two nights now he's been gone.'

'No, I have not seen him. My doors are always open,

111

even by night,' said Cuthred, 'and I am always here if any man needs me. Had the child been in any peril or distress within reach of me, he would surely have come running here. But I have not seen him.'

It was simple truth that both doors stood wide, and the sparse furnishings of both living room and chapel were clear to view.

'If you should get any word of him,' said Hugh, 'send to me, or to the abbey, or if you should see my men drawing these coverts round you – as you will – give them the message.'

'I will do so,' said Cuthred gravely, and stood at the open gateway of his little garden to watch them ride away towards Eaton.

John of Longwood came striding out from one of the long barns lining the stockade, as soon as he heard the dull drumming of many hooves on the beaten earth of the yard. His bare arms and balding crown were the glossy brown of oak timber, for he spent most of his time out and active in all weathers, and there was no task about the holding to which he could not turn his hand. He stared at sight of Hugh's men riding in purposefully at the gate, but in wonder and curiosity rather than consternation, and came readily to meet them.

'Well, my lord, what's afoot with you so early?' He had already taken in the significance of their array. No hounds, no hawks, but steel by their sides, and two of them archers shouldering bows. This was another kind of hunt. 'We've had no trouble hereabouts. What's the word from Shrewsbury?'

'We're looking for two defaulters,' said Hugh briskly. 'Don't tell me you haven't heard we have a man murdered between here and the town, two nights ago. And the hermit's boy is fled, and suspect of being the man's runaway villein, with good reason to make away with him and run for the second time. That's the one quarry we're after.'

112

'Oh, ay, we'd heard about him,' said John readily, 'but I doubt he's a good few miles from here by this time. We've not seen hide or hair of him since late that afternoon, when he was here to fetch some honey cakes our dame had for Cuthred. She was not best pleased with him, neither, I heard her scolding. And for sure he was an impudent rogue. But the start he's had, I fancy you won't see him again. I never saw him carry steel, though,' said John by way of a fair-minded afterthought, and frowned over the resultant doubt. 'There's a chance at least that some other put an end to his master. The threat to haul him back to villeinage would be enough to make the lad take to his heels, the faster the better. In unknown country his lord would be hard put to it to track him down. No need, surely, to kill him. Small inducement to stay and take the risk.'

'The fellow's neither convicted nor charged yet,' said Hugh, 'nor can be until he's taken. But neither can he be cleared until then. And either way I want him. But we're after another runaway, too, John. Your lady's grandson, Richard, rode out of the abbey precinct that same evening, and hasn't come back.'

'The young lord!' echoed John, stricken open-mouthed with astonishment and consternation. 'Two nights gone, and only now we get to hear of it? God help us, she'll run mad! What happened? Who fetched the lad away?'

'No one fetched him. He up and saddled his pony and off he went, alone, of his own will. And what's befallen him since nobody knows. And since one of the pair I'm seeking may be a murderer, I'm leaving no barn un-ransacked and no house unvisited, and with orders to every man to keep a sharp lookout for Richard, too. Granted you're a good steward, John, not even you can know what mouse has crept into every byre and sheep fold and storehouse on the manor of Eaton. And that's what I mean to know, here and everywhere between here

113

and Shrewsbury. Go in and tell Dame Dionisia I'm asking to speak with her.'

John shook his head helplessly, and went. Hugh dismounted, and advanced to the foot of the stairs that led up to the hall door, above the low undercroft, waiting to see how Dionisia would bear herself when she emerged from the broad doorway above. If she really had not heard of the boy's disappearance until this moment, when her steward would certainly tell her, he could expect a fury, fuelled all the more by genuine dismay and grief. If she had, then she had had time to prepare herself to present a fury, but even so she might let slip something that would betray her. As for John, his honesty was patent. If she had the boy hidden away, John had had no part in it. He was not an instrument she would have used for such a purpose, for he was stubbornly determined to be Richard's steward rather than hers.

She came surging out from the shadow of the doorway, blue skirts billowing, imperious eyes smouldering. 'What's this I hear, my lord? It surely cannot be true! Richard missing?'

'It is true, madam,' said Hugh watching her intently, and undisturbed by the fact of having to look up to do it, as indeed he would have had to do even if she had come darting down the steps to his level, for she was taller than he. 'Since the night before last he's been gone from the abbey school.'

She flung up her clenched hands with an indignant cry. 'And only now am I told of it! Two nights gone! Is that the care they take of their children? And these are the people who deny me the charge of my own flesh and blood! I hold the abbot responsible for whatever distress or harm has come to my grandson. The guilt is on his head. And what are you doing, my lord, to recover the child? Two days you tell me he's been lost, and late and laggard you come to let me know of it ...'

The momentary hush fell only because she had to stop

114

to draw breath, standing with flashing eyes at the head of the steps, tall and greying fair and formidable, her long patrician face suffused with angry blood. Hugh took ruthless advantage of the lull, while it lasted, for it would not last long.

'Has Richard been here?' he demanded bluntly, challenging her show of furious deprivation and loss.

She caught her breath, standing open-mouthed. '*Here?* No, he did not come here. Should I be thus distraught if he had?'

'You would have sent word to the abbot, no doubt,' said Hugh guilelessly, 'if he had come running home? They are no less anxious about him at the abbey. And he rode away alone, of his own will. Where should we first look for him but here? But you tell me he is not here, has not been here. And his pony has not come wandering home to his old stable?'

'He has not, or I should have been told at once. If he'd come home riderless,' she said, her nostrils flaring, 'I would have had every man who is mine scouring the woods for Richard.'

'My men are busy this minute doing that very thing,' said Hugh. 'But by all means turn out Richard's people to add to the number, and welcome. The more the better. Since it seems we've drawn blank,' he said, still thoughtfully studying her face, 'and after all, he is not here.'

'No,' she blazed, 'he is not here! No, he has not been here! Though if he left of his own will, as you claim, perhaps he meant to come home to me. And for whatever has befallen him on the way I hold Radulfus to blame. He is not fit to have charge of a noble child, if he cannot take better care of him.'

'I will tell him so,' said Hugh obligingly, and went on with aggravating mildness: 'My present duty is to continue the search, then, both for Richard and for the thief who killed an abbey guest in Eyton forest. You need not fear, madam, that my search will not be thorough.

115

Since I cannot expect you to make daily rounds of every corner of your grandson's manor, no doubt you'll be glad to allow me free access everywhere, to do that service for you. You'll wish to set the example to your tenants and neighbours.'

She gave him a long, long, hostile look, and as suddenly whirled on John of Longwood, who stood impassive and neutral at her elbow. In the gale of her movements her long skirt lashed like the tail of an angry cat.

'Open my doors to these officers. All my doors! Let them satisfy themselves I'm neither harbouring a murderer nor hiding my own flesh and blood here. Let all our tenants know it's my will they should submit to search as freely as I do. My lord sheriff,' she said, looking down with immense dignity upon Hugh, 'enter and search wherever you wish.'

He thanked her with unabashed civility, and if she saw the glint in his eye, that just fell short of becoming an open smile, she scorned to acknowledge it, but turned her straight back and withdrew with a rapid and angry gait into the hall, leaving him to a search he already felt must prove fruitless. But there was no certainty, and if she had calculated that such a rash and sweeping invitation would be taken as proof, and send them away satisfied, even shamefaced, she was much deceived. Hugh set to work to probe every corner of Dionisia's hall and solar, kitchens and stores, examined every cask and handcart and barrel in the undercroft, every byre and barn and stable that lined the stockade, the smith's workshop, every loft and larder, and moved outward into the fields and sheep folds, and thence to the huts of every tenant and cotter and villein on Richard's land. But they did not find Richard.

Brother Cadfael rode for Eilmund's assart in the middle of the afternoon, with the new crutches Brother Simon had cut to the forester's measure slung alongside, good, sturdy props to bear a solid weight. The fracture appeared to be knitting well, the leg was straight and not shortened. Eilmund was not accustomed to lying by inactive, and was jealous of any other hands tending his woodlands. Once he got hold of these aids Annet would have trouble keeping him in. It was in Cadfael's mind that her father's helplessness had afforded her an unusual measure of freedom to pursue her own feminine ploys, no doubt innocent enough, but what Eilmund would make of them when he found out was another matter.

Approaching the village of Wroxeter, Cadfael met with Hugh riding back towards the town, after a long day in the saddle. Beyond, in fields and woodlands, his officers were still methodically combing every grove and every headland, but Hugh was bound back to the castle alone, to collect together whatever reports had been brought in, and consider how best to cover the remaining ground, and how far the search must be extended if it had not yet borne fruit.

'No,' said Hugh, answering the unasked question almost as soon as they were within hail of each other, 'she has not got him. By all the signs she did not even know you'd lost him until I brought the word, though it's no great trick, I know, for any woman to put on such an exclaiming show. But we've parted every stalk of straw in her barns, and what we've missed must be too small ever to be found. No black pony in the stables. Not a soul but tells the same story, from John of Longwood down to the smith's boy. Richard is not there. Not in any cottage or byre in this village. The priest turned out his house for us, and went with us round the manor, and he's an honest man.'

Cadfael nodded sombre confirmation of his own doubts. 'I had a feeling there might be more to it than that. It would be worth trying yonder at Wroxeter, I suppose. Not that I see Fulke Astley as a likely villain – he's too fat and too cautious.'

'I'm just come from there,' said Hugh. 'Three of my men are still prodding into the last corners, but I'm satisfied he's not there, either. We'll miss no one – manor, cottage, assart, all. Of what falls alike on them all none of them can well complain. Though Astley did bristle at letting us in. A matter of his seigneurial dignity, for there was nothing there to find.'

'The pony,' said Cadfael, gnawing a considering lip, 'must be shut away somewhere.'

'Unless,' said Hugh sombrely, 'the other fugitive has ridden him hard out of the shire, and left the boy in such case that he cannot bear witness – even when we find him.'

They stared steadily upon each other, mutely admitting that it was a black and bitter possibility, but one that could not be altogether banished.

'The child ran off to him, if that is indeed what he did,' Hugh pursued doggedly, 'without saying a word to any other. How if it was indeed to a rogue and murderer he went, in all innocence? The cob is a sturdy little beast, big for Richard, the hermit's boy a light weight, and Richard the only witness. I don't say it is so. I do say such things have happened, and could happen again.'

'True, I would not dispute it,' admitted Cadfael.

There was that in his tone that caused Hugh to say with certainty: 'But you do not believe it.' It was something of which Cadfael himself had been less certain until that moment. 'Do you feel your thumbs pricking? I know better than to ignore the omen if you do,' said Hugh with a half-reluctant smile.

'No, Hugh.' Cadfael shook his head. 'I know nothing that isn't known to you, I am nobody's advocate in this matter – except Richard's – I've barely exchanged a word with this boy Hyacinth, never seen him but twice, when he brought Cuthred's message to chapter and when he

118

came to fetch me to the forester. All I can do is keep my eyes open between here and Eilmund's house, and that you may be sure I shall do – perhaps even do a little beating of the bushes myself along the way. If I have anything to tell, be sure you'll hear it before any other. Be it good or ill, but God and Saint Winifred grant us good news!'

On that promise they parted, Hugh riding on to the castle to receive whatever news the watch might have for him thus late in the afternoon, Cadfael moving on through the village towards the edge of the woodland. He was in no hurry. He had much to think about. Strange how the very act of admitting that the worst was possible had so instantly strengthened his conviction that it had not happened and would not happen. Stranger still that as soon as he had stated truthfully that he knew nothing of Hyacinth, and had barely spoken a word to him, he should find himself so strongly persuaded that very soon that lack might be supplied, and he would learn, if not everything, all that he needed to know.

Eilmund had regained his healthy colour, welcomed company eagerly, and could not be restrained from trying out his crutches at once. Four or five days cooped up indoors was a sore test of his temper, but the relief of being able to hurple vigorously out into the garden, and finding himself a fast learner in the art of using his new legs, brought immediate sunny weather with him. When he had satisfied himself of his competence, he sat down willingly, at Annet's orders, to share a supper with Cadfael.

'Though by rights I ought to be getting back,' said Cadfael, 'now I know how well you're doing. The bone seems to be knitting straight and true as a lance, and you'll not need me here harrying you every day. And speaking of inconvenient visitors, have you had Hugh Beringar or his men here today searching the woods around? You'll have heard before now they're hunting Cuthred's boy Hyacinth for suspicion of killing his master? And there's young Richard missing, too.'

'We heard of the both only last night,' said Eilmund. 'Yes, they were here this morning, a long line of the garrison men working their way along every yard of the forest between road and river. They even looked in my byre and henhouse. Will Warden grumbled himself it was needless folly, but he had his orders. Why waste time, he says, aggravating a good fellow we all know to be honest, but it's as much as my skin's worth to leave out a single hut or let my beaters pass by a solitary bush, with his lordship's sharp eye on us all. Do you know, have they found the child?'

'No, not yet. He's not at Eaton, that's certain. If it's any comfort, Eilmund, Dame Dionisia had to open her doors to the search, too. Noble and simple, they'll all fare alike.'

Annet waited upon them in silence, bringing cheese and bread to the table. Her step was as light as always, her face as calm, only at the mention of Richard did her face cloud over in anxious sympathy. There was no knowing what went on behind her composed face, but Cadfael hazarded his own guesses. He took his leave in good time, against Eilmund's hospitable urgings.

'I've been missing too many services, these last days, I'd best get back to my duty, and at least put in an appearance for Compline tonight. I'll come in and see you the day after tomorrow. You take care how you go. And, Annet, don't let him stay on his feet too long. If he gives you trouble, take his props away from him.'

She laughed and said that she would, but her mind, Cadfael thought, was only half on what she said, and she had not made any move to second her father's protest at such an early departure. Nor did she come out to the gate with him this time, but only as far as the door, and there stood to watch him mount, and waved when he looked back before beginning to thread the narrow path between the trees. Only when he had vanished did she turn and go back into the cottage.

Cadfael did not go far. A few hundred yards into the woods there was a hollow of green surrounded by a deep thicket, and there he dismounted and tethered his horse, and made his way back very quietly and circumspectly to a place from which he could see the house door without himself being seen. The light was dimming gently into the soft green of dusk, and the hush was profound, only the last birdsong broke the forest silence.

In a few minutes Annet came out to the door again, and stood for a little while braced and still, her head alertly reared, looking all round the clearing and listening intently. Then, satisfied, she set off briskly out of the fenced garden and round to the rear of the cottage. Cadfael circled with her in the cover of the trees. Her hens were already securely shut in for the night, the cow was in the byre; from these customary evening tasks Annet had come back a good hour ago, while her father was trying out his crutches in the grassy levels of the clearing. It seemed there was one more errand she had to do before the full night came down and the door was closed and barred. And she went to it at a light and joyous run, her hands spread to part the bushes on either side as she reached the edge of the clearing, her light brown hair shaking loose from its coil and dancing on her shoulders, her head tilted back as though she looked up into the trees, darkening now over her head and dropping, silently and moistly, the occasional withered leaf, the tears of the aging year.

She was not going far. No more than a hundred paces into the woods she halted, poised still in the same joyous attitude of flight, under the branches of the first of the ancient oaks, still in full but tarnished leafage. Cadfael, not far behind her in the shelter of the trees, saw her throw back her head and send a high, melodious whistle

121

up into the crown of the tree. From somewhere high above a soft shimmering of leaves answered, dropping through the branches as an acorn might fall, and in a moment the descending shiver of movement reached the ground in the shape of a young man sudden and silent as a cat, who swung by his hands from the lowest bough and dropped lightly on his feet at Annet's side. As soon as he touched ground they were in each other's arms.

So he had not been mistaken. The two of them had barely set eyes on each other when they fell to liking, blessed as they were with the good ground of his services to her father. With Eilmund laid up helpless in the house she could go freely about her own secret business of hiding and feeding a fugitive, but what would they do now that the forester was likely to be up and about, however limited his range must remain? Was it fair to present her father with such a problem in loyalties, and he an official involved with law, if only forest law? But there they stood linked, as candidly as children, with such a suggestion of permanence about their embrace that it surely would take more than father or lord or law or king to disentangle them. With her long mane of hair loosed, and her feet bare, and Hyacinth's classic elegance of shape and movement, and fierce, disquieting beauty, they might have been two creatures bred out of the ancient forest, faun and nymph out of a profane but lovely fable. Not even the gathering twilight could dim their brightness.

Well, thought Cadfael, surrendering to the vision, if this is what we have to deal with, from this we must go on, for there's no going back. And he stepped rustling out of the bushes, and walked towards them without conceal.

They heard him and sprang round instantly with heads reared, cheek to cheek, like deer scenting danger. They saw him, and Annet flung out her arms and shut Hyacinth behind her against the bole of the tree, her face

122

blanched and sharp as a sword, and as decisively Hyacinth laughed, lifted her bodily aside, and stepped before her.

'As if I needed the proof!' said Cadfael, to afford them whatever reassurance his voice might convey, and he halted without coming too close, though they knew already there was no point in running. 'I'm not the law. If you've done no wrong you've nothing to fear from me.'

'It takes a bolder man than I am,' said Hyacinth's clear voice softly, 'to claim he's done no wrong.' Even in the dimming light his sudden, unnerving smile shone perceptibly for a moment. 'But I've done no murder, if that's what you mean. Brother Cadfael, is it?'

'It is.' He looked from one roused and wary face to the other, and saw that they were breathing a little more easily and every moment less tensed for flight or attack. 'Lucky for you they brought no hounds with them this morning. Hugh never likes to hunt a man with hounds. I'm sorry, lad, if my visit tonight kept you fretting longer than you need have done in your nest up there. I hope you spend your nights in better comfort.'

At that they both smiled, still somewhat cautiously and with eyes alert and wild, but they said nothing.

'And where did you hide through the sergeant's search, that they never got wind of you at all?'

Annet made up her mind, with the same thorough practical resolution with which she did everything. She stirred and shook herself, the glossy cloak of her hair billowing into a pale cloud about her head. She drew breath deeply, and laughed.

'If you must know, he was under the brychans of Father's bed, while Will Warden sat on the bench opposite drinking ale with us, and his men peered in among my hens and forked through the hay in the loft, outside. You thought, I believe,' she said, coming close to Cadfael and drawing Hyacinth after her by the hand, 'that Father was in ignorance of what I was doing. Did

123

you hold that against me, even a little? No need, he knows all, has known it from the beginning, or at least from the moment this manhunt began. And now that you've found us out, had we not better all go into the house, and see what our four heads can come up with for the future, to get us all out of this tangle?'

'They'll not come here again,' said Eilmund comfortably, presiding over this meeting in his house from the throne of his bed, the same bed under which Hyacinth had couched secure in the presence of the hunters. 'But if they do, we'll know of it in time. Never twice the same hiding place.'

'And never once any qualms that you might be hiding a murderer?' asked Cadfael, hopeful of being convinced.

'No need for any! From the start of it I knew I was not. And you shall know it, too. I'm talking of proof positive, Cadfael, not a mere matter of faith, though faith's no mere matter, come to that. You were here last night, it was on your way back you found the man dead, and dead no more than an hour when you found him. Do you say aye to that?'

'More than willingly, if it helps your proof along.'

'And you left me when Annet here came back from doing the work that keeps her busy in the evening. You'll call to mind I said she'd been long enough about it, and so she had, well above an hour. For good reason, she'd been meeting with this youngster here, and whatever they were about, they were in no hurry about it, which won't surprise you greatly, I daresay. In short, these two were together in the woods a mile or so from here from the time she left you and me together, until she came back nigh on two hours later. And there young Richard found them, and this lad she brought back with her here, and ten minutes after you were gone she brought him in to me. No murderer, for all that while he was with her, or me, or the both of us, and in this house he slept that night. He never was near the man who was killed, and we can swear to it.'

'Then why have you not …' Cadfael began, and as hastily caught himself back from the needless question, and held up a hand to ward off the obvious answer. 'No, say no word! I see very well why. My wits are grown dull tonight. If you came forward to tell Hugh Beringar he's after a man proven innocent, true enough you could put that danger away from him. But if one Bosiet is dead, there's another expected at the abbey any day now – he may be there this minute, for all I know. As bad as his sire, so says the groom, and he has good reason to know, he bears the marks of it. No, I see how you're bound.'

Hyacinth sat in the rushes on the floor at Annet's feet, hugging his drawn up knees. He said without passion or emphasis, but with the calm finality of absolute resolution: 'I am not going back there.'

'No, no more you shall!' said Eilmund heartily. 'You'll understand, Cadfael, that when I took the lad in, there was no question of murder at all. It was a runaway villein I chose to shelter, one with good reason to run, and one that had done me the best of turns any man could do for another. I liked him well, I would not for any cause have sent him back to be misused. And then, when the cry of murder did arise, I had no call to feel any differently, for I knew he had no part in it. It went against the grain not to be able to go out and say so to sheriff and abbot and all, but you see it was impossible. And the upshot of it is, here we are with the lad on our hands, and how are we best to make sure of his safety?'

Chapter Nine

IT WAS already taken for granted by all of them, it seemed, that Cadfael was on their side, and wholeheartedly a party to their conspiracy. How could it be otherwise? Here was absolute proof that the boy was no murderer, proof that could be laid in Hugh Beringar's hands with confidence in his justice, no question of that. But it could not be done without exposing Hyacinth to the very danger from which he had escaped once, and could hardly hope to escape a second time. Hugh was bound by law as fast as any man, even his gift for turning a blind eye and a deaf ear would not help Hyacinth if once Bosiet got wind of where he was and who was sheltering him.

'Between us,' said Cadfael, though somewhat dubiously, 'we might be able to get you away out of the county and into Wales, clean away from pursuit ...'

'No,' said Hyacinth firmly, 'I won't run. I'll hide for as long as I must, but I won't run any further. It's what I meant to do, when I set off this way, but I've changed my mind.'

'Why?' demanded Cadfael simply.

'For two good reasons. One, because Richard's lost, and Richard saved my skin for me by bringing warning, and I'm his debtor until I know he's safe, and back where he should be. And two, because I want my freedom here

126

in England, here in Shrewsbury, and I mean to get work in the town when I can with safety, and earn my living, and take a wife.' He looked up with a bright, challenging flash of his amber eyes at Eilmund, and smiled. 'If Annet will have me!'

'You'd best ask my leave about that,' said Eilmund, but with such good humour that it was plain the idea was not entirely new to him, nor necessarily unwelcome.

'So I will, when the time comes, but I would not offer you or her what I am and have now. So let that wait, but don't forget it,' warned the faun, gleaming. 'But Richard I must find, I will find! That's first!'

'What can you do,' said Eilmund practically, 'more than Hugh Beringar and all his men are doing? And you a hunted man yourself, with the hounds close on your tail! You stay quiet like a sensible lad, and hide your head until Bosiet's hunt for you starts costing him more even than his hatred's worth. As it will, in the end. He has manors at home now to think about.'

But whether Hyacinth was, by ordinary standards, a sensible lad was a matter for conjecture. He sat very still, in that taut, suggestive way he had, that promised imminent action, the soft glow of Annet's fire glowing in the subtle planes of his cheeks and brow, turning his bronze to gold. And Annet, beside him on the cushioned bench by the wall, had something of the same quality. Her face was still, but her eyes were sapphire bright. She let them talk about her in her presence, and felt no need to add a word on her own account, nor did she so much as touch Hyacinth's slender shoulder to confirm her secure tenure. Whoever had doubts about Annet's claims on the future, Annet had none.

'Richard left you as soon as he'd delivered his warning?' asked Cadfael.

'He did. Hyacinth wanted to go with him to the edge of the wood,' said Annet, 'but he wouldn't have it. He wouldn't stir unless Hyacinth went into hiding at once, so we promised. And he set off back along the track. And we came back here to Father, as he's told you, and saw no one else along the way. Richard would not have gone anywhere near Eaton, or I'd have thought his grandmother might have taken him. But he was bent on getting back to his bed.'

'It was what we all thought,' owned Cadfael, 'not least Hugh Beringar. But he was there early and turned the place wrong side out, and the boy is not there. I think John of Longwood and half the household beside would have told if he'd been seen there. Dame Dionisia is a formidable lady, but Richard is the lord of Eaton, it's his bidding they'll have to do in the future, not hers. If they dared not speak out before her face, they'd have done it softly behind her back. No, he is not there.'

It was long past time for Vespers. Even if he started back now he would be too late for Compline, but still he sat stubbornly going over this whole new situation in his mind, looking for the best way forward, where there seemed to be nothing to be done but wait, and continue to evade the hunt. He was grateful that Hyacinth was no murderer, that at least was a gain. But how to keep him out of the hands of Bosiet was another matter.

'For God's sake, boy,' he said, sighing, 'what was it you did to your overlord, there in Northamptonshire, to get yourself so bitterly hated? Did you indeed assault his steward?'

'I did,' acknowledged Hyacinth with satisfaction, and a red reminiscent spark kindled in his eyes. 'It was after the last of the harvest, and there was a girl gleaning in the poor leavings in one of the demesne fields. There never was a girl safe from him if he came on her alone. It was only by chance I was near. He had a staff, and dropped her to swing at my head with it when I came at him. I got a few bruises, but I laid him flat against the stones under the headland, clean out of his wits. So there was nothing I could do but run for it. I'd nothing to leave, no land –

Drogo distrained on my father two years before, when he was in his last illness and I had all to do, our fields and Bosiet's harvest labour, and we ended in debt. He'd been after us a long while, he said I was for ever rousing his villeins against him ... Well, if I was it was for their rights. There are laws to defend life and limb even for villeins, but they meant precious little in Bosiet's manors. He'd have had me half-killed for attacking the steward – He'd have had me hanged if I hadn't been profitable to him. It was the chance he'd been waiting for.'

'How were you profitable to him?' asked Cadfael.

'I had a turn for fine leather-work – belts, harness, pouches, and the like. When he'd made me landless he offered to leave me the toft if I'd bind myself to turn over all my work to him for my keep. I'd no choice, I was still his villein. But I began to do finer tooling and gilding. He wanted to get some favour out of the earl once, and he had me make a book cover to give him as a present. And then the prior of the Augustinian canons at Huntingdon saw it, and ordered a special binding for their great codex, and the sub-prior of Cluny at Northampton wanted his best missal rebound, and so it grew. And they paid well, but I got nothing out of it. Drogo's done well out of me. That's the other reason he wanted me back alive. And so will his son Aymer want me.'

'If you have a trade the like of that at your finger-ends,' said Eilmund approvingly, 'you can make your way anywhere, once you're free of these Bosiets. Our abbot might very well put some work your way, and some town merchant would be glad to have you in his employ.'

'Where and how did you meet with Cuthred?' asked Cadfael, curiously.

'That was at the Cluniac priory in Northampton. I lay up for the night there, but I dared not go into the enclave, there were one or two there who knew me. I got food by sitting with the beggars at the gate, and when I was making off before dawn, Cuthred was for starting too, having spent the night in the guest hall.' An abrupt dark smile plucked at the corners of Hyacinth's eloquent lips. He kept his startling eyes veiled under their high-arched golden lids. 'He proposed we should travel together. Out of charity, surely. Or so that I should not have to thieve for my food, and sink into a worse condition even than before.' As abruptly he looked up, unveiling the full brilliance of wide eyes fixed full and solemnly on Eilmund's face. The smile had vanished.

'It's time you knew the worst of me, I want no lies among this company. I came this way owing the world nothing, and ripe for any mischief, and a rogue and a vagabond I could be, and a thief I have been at need. Before you shelter me another hour, you should know what cause you have to think better of it. Annet,' he said, his voice soft and assuaged on her name, 'already knows what you must know too. You have that right. I told her the truth the night Brother Cadfael was here to set your bone.'

Cadfael remembered the motionless figure sitting patiently outside the cottage, the urgent whisper: 'I must speak to you!' And Annet coming out into the dark, and closing the door after her.

'It was I,' said Hyacinth with steely deliberation, 'who dammed the brook with bushes so that your seedlings were flooded. It was I who undercut the bank and bridged the ditch so that the deer got into the coppice. It was I who shifted a pale of the Eaton fence to let out the sheep to the ash saplings. I had my orders from Dame Dionisia to be a thorn in the flesh to the abbey until they gave her her grandson back. That was why she set up Cuthred in his hermitage, to put me there as his servant. And I knew nothing then of any of you, and cared less, and I was not going to quarrel with what provided me a comfortable living and a safe refuge until I could do better. It's my doing, more's the pity, that the worse

130

thing happened, and the tree came down on you and pinned you in the brook, my doing that you're lamed and housebound here – though that slip came of itself, I didn't touch it again. So now you know,' said Hyacinth, 'and if you see fit to take the skin off my back for it, I won't lift a hand to prevent, and if you throw me out afterwards, I'll go.' He reached up a hand to Annet's hand and added flatly: 'But not far!'

There was a long pause while two of them sat staring at him, intently and silently, and Annet watched them no less warily, all of them withholding judgement. No one had exclaimed against him, no one had interrupted this half-defiant confession. Hyacinth's truth was used like a dagger, and his humility came very close to arrogance. If he was ashamed, it did not show in his face. Yet it could not have been easy to strip himself thus of the consideration and kindness father and daughter had shown him. If he had not spoken, clearly Annet would have said no word. And he had not pleaded, nor attempted any extenuation. He was ready to take what was due without complaint. Doubtful if anyone, however eloquent or terrible a confessor, would ever get this elusive creature nearer to penitence than this.

Eilmund stirred, settling his broad shoulders more easily against the wall, and blew out a great, gusty breath. 'Well, if you brought the tree down on me, you also hoisted it off me. And if you think I'd give up a runaway villein to slavery again because he'd played a few foul tricks on me, you're not well acquainted with my simple sort. I fancy the fright I gave you that day was all the thrashing you needed. And since then you've done me no more injury, for from all I hear there's been quiet in the woods from that day. I doubt if the lady's satisfied with her bargain. You show sense, and stay where you are.'

'I told him,' said Annet, confidently smiling, 'you would not pay back injury for injury. I never said a word, I knew he would out with it himself. And Brother

Cadfael knows now Hyacinth's no murderer, and has owned to the worst he knows about himself. There's not one of us here will betray him.'

No, not one! But Cadfael sat somewhat anxiously pondering what could best be done now. Betrayal was impossible, certainly, but the hunt would go on, and might well drag all these woods over again, and in the meantime Hugh, in his natural concentration on this most likely quarry, might be losing all likelihood of finding the real murderer. Even Drogo Bosiet was entitled to justice, however he infringed the rights of others. Withholding from Hugh the certainty and proof of Hyacinth's innocence might be delaying the reassessment that would set in motion the pursuit of the guilty.

'Will you trust me, and let me tell Hugh Beringar what you have told me? Give me leave,' urged Cadfael hastily, seeing their faces stiffen in consternation, 'to deal with him privately — '

'No!' Annet laid her hand possessively on Hyacinth's shoulder, burning up like a stirred fire. 'No, you can't give him up! We have trusted you, you can't fail us.'

'No, no, no, not that! I know Hugh well, he would not willingly give up a villein to mistreatment, he is for justice even before law. Let me tell him only that Hyacinth is innocent, and show him the proof. I need say nothing as to how I know or where he is, Hugh will take my word. Then he can hold off this search and leave you alone until it's safe for you to come forth and speak openly.'

'No!' cried Hyacinth, on his feet in one wild, smooth movement, his eyes two yellow flames of alarm and rejection. 'Not a word to him, never a word! If we'd thought you'd go to him we'd never have let you in to us. He's the sheriff, he must take Bosiet's part – he has manors, he has villeins of his own, do you think he'd ever side with me against my legal lord? I should be dragged back at Aymer's heels, and buried alive in his prison.'

132

Cadfael turned to Eilmund for help. 'I swear to you I can lift this suspicion from the lad by speaking with Hugh. He'll take my word and hold off from the hunt – withdraw his men, or send them elsewhere. He has still Richard to find. Eilmund, you know Hugh Beringar better than to doubt his fairness.'

But no, Eilmund did not know him, not as Cadfael knew him. The forester was shaking his head doubtfully. A sheriff is a sheriff, pledged to law, and law is rigid and weighted, all in all, against the peasant and the serf and the landless man. 'He's a decent, fair-minded man, sure enough,' said Eilmund, 'but I dare not stake this boy's life on any king's officer. No, leave us keep as we are, Cadfael. Say nothing to any man, not until Bosiet's come and gone.'

They were all linked against him. He did his best, arguing quietly what ease it would be to know that the hunt would not be pressed home against Hyacinth, that his innocence, once communicated privily to Hugh, would set free the forces of law to look elsewhere for Drogo's murderer, and also allow them to press their search for Richard more thoroughly, and with more resources, through these forests where the child had vanished. But they had their arguments, too, and there was matter in them.

'If you told the sheriff, even secretly,' urged Annet, 'and if he did believe you, he would still have Bosiet to deal with. His father's man will tell him it's as good as certain his runaway is somewhere here in hiding, murderer or no. He'll go the length of using hounds, if the sheriff draws his men off. No, say nothing to anyone, not yet. Wait until they give up and go home. Then we'll come forth. Promise! Promise us silence until then!'

There was nothing to be done about it. He promised. They had trusted him, and against their absolute prohibition he could not hold out. He sighed and promised.

It was very late when he rose at last, his word given, to

begin the night ride back to the abbey. He had given a promise also to Hugh, never thinking how hard it might be to keep. He had said that if he had anything to tell, Hugh should hear it before any other. A subtle, if guileless, arrangement of words, through which a devious mind could find several loopholes, but what he meant had been as clear to Hugh as it was to Cadfael. And now he could not make it good. Not yet, not until Aymer Bosiet should grow restive, count the costs of his vengeance, and think it better to go home and enjoy his new inheritance instead.

In the doorway he turned back to ask of Hyacinth one last question, a sudden afterthought. 'What of Cuthred? With you two living so close – did he have any part in all this mischief of yours in Eilmund's forest?'

Hyacinth stared at him gravely, in mild surprise, his amber eyes wide and candid. 'How could he?' he said simply. 'He never leaves his own pale.'

Aymer Bosiet rode into the great court of the abbey about noon of the next day, with a young groom at his back. Brother Denis the hospitaller had orders to bring him to Abbot Radulfus as soon as he arrived, for the abbot was unwilling to delegate to anyone else the task of breaking to him the news of his father's death. It was achieved with a delicacy for which, it seemed, there was little need. The bereaved son sat silently revolving the news and all its implications at length, and having apparently digested and come to terms with it, expressed his filial grief very suitably, but with his mind still engaged on side issues, a shrewdly calculating mind behind a face less powerful and brutal than his father's, but showing little evidence of sorrow. He did frown over the event, for it involved troublesome duties, such as commissioning coffin and cart and extra help for the journey home, and making the best possible use of such time as he could afford here. Radulfus had already had

Martin Bellecote, the master carpenter in the town, make a plain inner coffin for the body, which was not yet covered, since doubtless Aymer would want to look upon his father's face for a last time and take his farewells.

The bereaved son revolved the matter in his mind, and asked point-blank and with sharp intent: 'He had not found our runaway villein?'

'No,' said Radulfus, and if he was shaken he contrived to contain the shock. 'There was a suggestion that the young man was in the neighbourhood, but no certainty that the youth in question was really the one sought. And I believe now no one knows where he is gone.'

'My father's murderer is being sought?'

'Very assiduously, with all the sheriff's men.'

'My villein also, I trust. Whether or not,' said Aymer grimly, 'the two turn out to be the same. The law is bound to do all it can to recover my property for me. The rogue is a nuisance, but valuable. For no price would I be willing to let him go free.' He bit off the words with a vicious snap of large, strong teeth. He was as tall and long-boned as his father, but carried less flesh, and was leaner in the face; but he had the same shallowly-set eyes of an indeterminate, opaque colour, that seemed all surface and no depth. Thirty years old, perhaps, and pleasurably aware of his new status. Proprietorial satisfaction had begun to vibrate beneath the hard level of his voice. Already he spoke of 'my property'. That was one aspect of his bereavement which certainly had not escaped him.

'I shall want to see the sheriff concerning this fellow who calls himself Hyacinth. If he has run, does not that make it more likely he is indeed Brand? And that he had a hand in my father's death? There's a heavy score against him already. I don't intend to let such a debt go unpaid.'

'That is a matter for the secular law, not for me,' said Radulfus with chill civility. 'There is no proof of who killed the lord Drogo, the thing is quite open. But the

135

man is being sought. If you will come with me, I'll take you to the chapel where your father lies.'

Aymer stood beside the open coffin on its draped bier, and the light of the tall candles burning at Drogo's head and feet showed no great change in his son's face. He gazed down with drawn brows, but it was the frown of busy thought rather than grief or anger at such a death.

'I feel it bitterly,' said the abbot, 'that a guest in our house should come to so evil an end. We have said Masses for his soul, but other amends are out of my scope. I trust we may yet see justice done.'

'Indeed!' agreed Aymer, but so absently that it was plain his mind was on other things. 'I have no choice but to take him home for burial. But I cannot go yet. This search cannot be so soon abandoned. I must ride into the town this afternoon and see this master carpenter of yours, and have him make an outer coffin and line it with lead, and seal it. A pity, he could have lain just as properly here, but the men of our house are all buried at Bosiet. My mother would not be content else.'

He said it with a note of vexation in his musings. But for the necessity of taking home a corpse he could have lingered here for days to pursue his hunt for the escaped villein. Even as things stood he meant to make the fullest use of his time, and Radulfus could not help feeling that it was the villein he wanted most vindictively, not his father's murderer.

By chance Cadfael happened to be crossing the court when the newcomer took horse again, early in the afternoon. It was his first glimpse of Drogo's son, and he stopped and drew aside to study him with interest. His identity was never in doubt, for the likeness was there, though somewhat tempered in this younger man. The curiously shallow eyes, so meanly diminished by their lack of the shadow and form deep sockets provide, had the same flat malevolence, and his handling of horseflesh as he mounted was more considerate by far than his

136

manner towards his groom. The hand that held his stirrup was clouted aside by the butt of his whip as soon as he was in the saddle, and when Warin started back from the blow so sharply that the horse took fright and clattered backwards on the cobbles, tossing up his head and snorting, the rider swung the whip at the groom's shoulders so readily and with so little apparent anger or exasperation that it was plain this was the common currency of his dealings with his underlings. He took only the younger groom with him into the town, himself riding his father's horse, which was fresh and spoiling for exercise. No doubt Warin was only too glad to be left behind here in peace for a few hours.

Cadfael overtook the groom and fell into step beside him as he turned back towards the stables. Warin looked round to show him a bruise rapidly fading, but still yellow as old parchment, and a mouth still elongated by the healing scar at one corner.

'I've not seen you these two days,' said Cadfael, eyeing the traces of old violence and alert for new. 'Come round with me into the herb garden, and let me dress that gash again for you. He's safely away for an hour or two, I take it, you can breathe easily. And it would do with another treatment, though I see it's clean now.'

Warin hesitated only for a moment. 'They've taken the two fresh horses, and left me the others to groom. But they can wait a while.' And he went willingly at Cadfael's side, his lean person, a little withered before its time, seeming to expand in his lord's absence. In the pleasant aromatic coolness of the workshop, under the faintly stirring herbs that rustled overhead, he sat eased and content to let his injury be bathed and anointed, and was in no hurry to get back to his horses even when Cadfael had done with him.

'He's hotter even than the old one was on Brand's heels,' he said, shaking a helpless but sympathetic head over his former neighbour's fortunes. 'Torn two ways,

137

between wanting to hang him and wanting to work him to death for greed, and it isn't whether or not Brand killed the old lord that will determine which way the cat jumps, for there was no great love lost there, neither. Not much love in all that household to be gained or lost. But good haters, every one.'

'There are more of them?' Cadfael asked with interest. 'Drogo has left a widow?'

'A poor pale lady, all the juice crushed out of her,' answered Warin, 'but better born than the Bosiets, and has powerful kin, so they have to use her better than they use anyone else. And Aymer has a younger brother. Not so loud nor so violent, but sharper witted and better able to twist and turn. That's all of them, but it's enough.'

'Neither one of them married?'

'Aymer's had one wife, but she was a sickly thing and died young. There's an heiress not far from Bosiet they both fancy now – though by rights it's her lands they fancy. And if Aymer is the heir, Roger's far the better at making himself agreeable. Not that it lasts beyond when he gets his way.'

It sounded a poor outlook for the girl, whichever of the two got the better of the contest, but it also sounded one possible reason why Aymer should not loiter here too long, or he might lose his advantages at home. Cadfael felt encouraged. Absence from a newly-inherited honour might even be dangerous, if there was a clever and treacherous younger brother left behind there to make calculated use of his opportunities. Aymer would be bearing that in mind, even while he grudged giving up his vindictive pursuit of Hyacinth. Cadfael still could not think of the boy as Brand, the name he had chosen for himself fitted him so much better.

'I wonder,' said Warin, unexpectedly harking back to the same elusive person, 'where Brand really got to? Lucky for him we did give him some grace – not that my lord intended it so! – for at first they thought that a man

138

with the skill he had at his finger-ends would surely make for London, and we wasted a week or more searching all the roads south. We got beyond Thame before one of his men came riding after us, saying Brand had been seen in Northampton. If he'd started off northwards, Drogo reckoned he'd continue so, and likely to bear west as he went, and make for Wales. I wonder has he reached it. Even Aymer won't follow him over the border.'

'And you picked up no more sightings of him along the way?' asked Cadfael.

'No, never a trace. But we're far out of the country where anyone would know him, and not everybody wants to get tangled into such a business. And he'll have taken another name, for sure.' Warin rose, refreshed but reluctant, to go back to his duties. 'I hope it may stand him in good stead. No matter what the Bosiets say, he was a decent lad.'

Brother Winfrid was busy sweeping up leaves under the orchard trees, for the moist autumn had caused them to fall before they took their bright seasonal colouring, in a soft green rain that rotted gently into the turf. Cadfael found himself alone and without occupation after Warin had left him. The more reason to sit down quietly and think, and a prayer or two wouldn't come amiss, either, for the boy who had gone rushing off on his black pony, on his self-appointed, mad and generous mission, for the rash young man he had set out to save, even for the hard, malignant lordling cut off without time for penitence or absolution, and bitterly in need of grace.

The bell for Vespers called him out of his musings, and he went gladly to answer it, out through the gardens and across the court to the cloister and the south door of the church, to be early in his place. In the past few days he had missed all too many services, he was in need of the reassurance of brotherhood.

There were always a few of the people of the Foregate

at Vespers, the devout old women who inhabited some of the abbey's grace houses, elderly couples retired and happy to fill up their leisure and meet their friends at church, and often guests of the house coming back from the activities of the day. Cadfael heard them stirring beyond the parish altar, in the vast spaces of the nave. Rafe of Coventry, he noted, had come in from the cloister and chosen a place from which he could see within, past the parish altar and into the choir. Kneeling at prayer, he had still that quiet composure about him, a man secure and at peace with his own body, and wearing his inscrutable face rather as a shield than as a mask. So he had not yet moved on to contact those suppliers of his in Wales. He was the only worshipper from the guest hall. Aymer Bosiet must be still about his funereal business in the town, or else beating the coverts in field and forest somewhere after his runaway.

The brothers came in and took their places, the novices and schoolboys followed. There was a bitter reminder there, for their numbers were still one short. There was no forgetting about Richard. Until he was recovered there would be no peace of mind, no lightness of heart, for any of those children.

At the end of Vespers Cadfael lingered in his stall, letting the procession of brothers and novices file out into the cloister without him. The office had its beauty and consolation, but the solitude afterwards was also salutary in its silence, after the echoes of the music had all died away, and to be here alone in this evening hour had a special beneficence, whether because of the soft, dove-coloured light or the sense of enlargement that seemed to swell the soul to inhabit and fill the last arches of the vault, as a single drop of water becomes the ocean into which it falls. There was no better time for profound prayer, and Cadfael felt the need of it. For the boy in particular, equally solitary somewhere, perhaps afraid. It was to Saint Winifred Cadfael addressed his plea, a

Welshman invoking a Welsh saint, and one to whom he felt very close, and for whom he had an almost family affection. Herself hardly more than a child at her martyrdom, she would not let harm come to another threatened child.

Brother Rhun, whom she had healed, was carefully trimming the scented candles he made for her shrine when Cadfael approached, but he turned his fair young head towards the petitioner, gave him one glance of his aquamarine eyes, that seemed to have their own innate light, and smiled and went away. Not to linger and complete his work when the prayers ended, not to hide in the shadows and watch, but clean away out of knowledge, on swift, agile, silent feet that had once gone lamely and in pain, to leave the whole listening vault ready to receive the appeal in its folded hands, and channel it aloft.

Cadfael arose from his knees comforted, without knowing or asking why. Outside, the light was fading rapidly, and here within, the altar lamp and Saint Winifred's perfumed candles made small islands of pure radiance in a great enfolding gloom, like a warm cloak against the frost of the outside world. The grace that had just touched Cadfael had a long enough reach to find Richard, wherever he was, deliver him if he was a prisoner, console him if he was frightened, heal him if he was hurt. Cadfael went out from the choir, round the parish altar and into the nave, sensible of having done what was most needful, and content to wait patiently and passively until grace should be manifested.

It seemed that Rafe of Coventry had also had solemn and personal prayers to offer, for he was just rising from his knees in the empty and silent nave as Cadfael came through. He recognised his acquaintance of the stable yard with a shadowed but friendly smile, that came and went briefly on his lips but lingered amiably in his eyes.

'Good even, Brother!' Matched in height and pace,

they fell naturally into step together as they turned towards the south porch. 'I hope to be held excused,' said Rafe, 'for coming to church booted and spurred and dusty from riding, but I came late, and had no time to make myself seemly.'

'Most welcome, however you come,' said Cadfael. 'Not everyone who lodges with us shows his face in the church. I've had small chance to see you these two days, I've been out and about myself. Have you had successful dealing in these parts?'

'Better, at least, than one of your guests,' said Rafe, casting a side glance at the narrow door that led towards the mortuary chapel. 'But no, I would not say I've found quite what I needed. Not yet!'

'His son is here now,' said Cadfael, following the glance. 'This morning he came.'

'I have seen him,' said Rafe. 'He came back from the town just before Vespers. By the look and the sound of him he's done none too well, either, with whatever he's about. I suppose it's a man he's after?'

'It is. The young man I told you of,' said Cadfael drily, and studied his companion sidelong as they crossed the lighted parish altar.

'Yes, I remember. Then he's come back empty-handed, no poor wretch tethered to his stirrup leather.' But Rafe remained tolerantly indifferent to young men, and indeed to the Bosiet clan. His thoughts were somewhere else. At the alms box beside the altar he stopped, on impulse, and dug a hand into the pouch slung at his waist, to draw out a handful of coins. One of them slipped through his fingers, but he did not immediately stoop to pick it up, but dropped three of its fellows into the box before he turned to look for the stray. By which time Cadfael had lifted it from the tiled floor, and had it in his open palm.

If they had not been standing where the altar candles gave a clear light he would have noticed nothing strange

142

about it. A silver penny like other silver pennies, the universal coin. Yet not quite like any he had seen before in the alms boxes. It was bright and untarnished, but indifferently struck, and it felt light in the hand. Clumsily arrayed round the short cross on the reverse, the moneyer's name appeared to be Sigebert, a minter Cadfael never remembered to have heard of in the midlands. And when he turned it, the crude head was not Stephen's familiar profile, nor dead King Henry's, but unmistakably a woman's, coifed and coroneted. It hardly needed the name sprawled round the rim: 'Matilda Dom. Ang.' The empress's formal name and title. It seemed her mintage was short-weight.

He looked up to find Rafe watching him steadily, and with a small private smile that held more irony than simple amusement. There was a moment of silence while they eyed each other. Then: 'Yes,' said Rafe, 'you are right. It would have been noted after I was gone. But it has a value, even here. Your beggars will not reject it because it was struck in Oxford.'

'And no long time ago,' said Cadfael.

'No long time ago.'

'My besetting sin,' said Cadfael ruefully, 'is curiosity.' He held out the coin, and Rafe took it as gravely, and with deliberation dropped it after its fellows into the alms box. 'But I am not loose-mouthed. Nor do I hold any honest man's allegiance against him. A pity there should have to be factions, and decent men fighting one another, and all of them convinced they have the right of it. Come and go freely for me.'

'And does your curiosity not extend,' wondered Rafe softly, the wry smile perceptible in his voice, 'to wondering what such a man is doing here, so far from the battle? Come, I am sure you have guessed at what I am. Perhaps you think I felt it the wiser part to get out of Oxford before it was too late?'

'No,' said Cadfael positively, 'that never did and never

143

would enter my mind. Not of you! And why should so discreet a man as that venture north into king's country?'

'No, granted that argues very little wisdom,' agreed Rafe. 'What would you guess then?'

'I can think of one possibility,' said Cadfael gravely and quietly. 'We heard here of one man who did not take flight of his own will out of Oxford, while there was time, but was sent. On his lady's business, and with that about him well worth stealing. And that he did not get far, for his horse was found straying and blood-stained, all that he had carried gone, and the man himself vanished from the face of the earth.' Rafe was watching him attentively, his face unreadable as ever, the lingering smile sombre but untroubled. 'Such a man as you seem to me,' said Cadfael, 'might well have come so far north from Oxford looking for Renaud Bourchier's murderer.'

Their eyes held, mutually accepting, even approving, what they saw. Slowly and with absolute finality Rafe of Coventry said: 'No.'

He stirred and sighed, breaking the spell of the brief but profound silence that followed. 'I am sorry, Brother, but no, you have not read me right. I am not looking for Bourchier's murderer. It was a good thought, almost I wish it had been true. But it is not.'

And with that he moved on towards the south door, and out into the early twilight in the cloister, and Brother Cadfael followed in silence, asking and offering nothing more. He knew truth when he heard it.

Chapter Ten

IT WAS about the same hour that Cadfael and Rafe of Coventry emerged from the church after Vespers, when Hyacinth stole out from Eilmund's cottage, and made his way through the deepest cover towards the river. He had been all that day pinned close within doors, for there had again been men of the garrison sweeping through the forest, and though their passage was rapid and cursory, for the aim was to carry the search further afield, and though they knew Eilmund, and felt no compulsion to investigate his holding a second time, they were still liable to look in on him in neighbourly fashion as they passed, and ask him casually if anything of note had come to his attention. Hyacinth did not take kindly to being shut within doors, nor, indeed, to hiding. By the evening he was chafing at his confinement, but by then the hunters were on their way back, abandoning the chase until the morrow, and he was free to do a little hunting of his own.

For all the wariness and fear he felt on his own account, and admitted with his infallible and fiery honesty, he could not rest for thinking of Richard, who had come running to warn him, so gallantly and thoughtlessly. But for that the boy would never have placed himself in danger. But why should there be danger to him in his own woods, among his own people? In a troubled

145

England there were lawless men living wild, no doubt of that, but this shire had gone almost untouched by the war for more than four years now, and seemed to enjoy a degree of peace and order unmatched further south, and the town was barely seven miles distant, and the sheriff active and young, and even, so far as a sheriff can be, popular with his people. And the more Hyacinth thought about it, the more clear did it seem to him that the only threat to Richard that he had ever heard of was Dame Dionisia's threat to marry him off to the two manors she coveted. For that she had persisted in every device she could think of. Hyacinth had been her instrument once, and could not forget it. She *must* be the force behind the boy's disappearance.

True, the sheriff had descended on Eaton, searched every corner, and found no trace, and no one, in a household devoted to the boy, able to cast the least suspicion on Dionisia's indignant innocence. She had no other property where she could hide either boy or pony. And though Fulke Astley might be willing to connive, feeling that he had as good a chance of securing Eaton as she had of getting her hands on his daughter's inheritance, yet Wroxeter also had been searched thoroughly, and without success.

Today the hunt had moved on, and according to all that Annet had gathered from the returning sergeants it would continue as doggedly on the morrow, but it had not yet reached Leighton, two miles down-river. And though Astley and his household preferred to live at Wroxeter, the more remote manor of Leighton was also in his hold.

It was the only starting point Hyacinth could find, and it was worth a venture. If Richard had been caught in the woods by some of Astley's men, or those from Eaton who were willing to serve Dionisia's turn, it might well have been thought wisest to remove him as far as Leighton, rather than try to hide him nearer home. Moreover, if she still intended to force this marriage on the boy – there were ways of getting the right answers out of even the most stubborn children, more by guile than by terror – she needed a priest, and Hyacinth had been about the village of Eaton long enough to know that Father Andrew was an honest man, by no means a good tool for such a purpose. The priest at Leighton, less well acquainted with the ins and outs of the affair, might be more amenable.

At least it was one thing which could be tested. It was no use Eilmund counselling him sensibly and good-naturedly to stay where he was and not risk capture; even Eilmund understood and approved what he called folly. Annet had not tried to dissuade Hyacinth, only sensibly provided him a black, much worn coat of Eilmund's too wide for him but excellent for moving invisibly by night, and a dark capuchon to shadow his face.

Between the forest and the meanderings of the river, downstream from the mill and the fisheries and the few cottages that served them, the open water meadows extended, and there the light still hung, and a faint ground mist lay veiling the green, and twined like a silver serpent along the river. But along the northern rim the forest continued, halfway to Leighton, and beyond that point the ground rose towards the last low foothills of the Wrekin, and he would have to make use of what scattered cover remained. But here where trees and grassland met he could move fast, keeping within the edge of the woods but benefiting by the light of the open fields, and the stillness and silence and the careful stealth of his own movements would ensure that he should get due warning of any other creature stirring in the night.

He had covered more than a mile when the first small sounds reached him, and he froze, and stood with pricked ears, listening intently. A single metallic note, somewhere behind him, harness briefly shaken. Then a soft brushing of bushes as something passed, and then, unmistakable though quiet, and still some distance away, a subdued voice ventured briefly what sounded like a question, and as meekly subsided. Not one person abroad in the dusk, but two, or why speak at all? And mounted, and keeping to the rim of the woodland like himself, when it would have been simpler by far to take to the meadows. Riders by night, no more anxious to be observed than he was, and going in the same direction. Hyacinth strained his ears to pick up the muted, leaf-cushioned tread of hooves, and try to determine the line they were taking through the trees. Close to the rim, for the sake of what light remained, but more concerned with secrecy than with haste.

Cautiously Hyacinth withdrew further into the forest, and stood motionles in cover to let them pass by. There was still enough light left to make them a little more than shadowy outlines as they came and passed in single file, first a tall horse that showed as a moving pallor, probably a light grey, with a big, gross man on his back, bearded, bare-headed, the folds of his caupchon draped on his shoulders. Hyacinth knew the shape and the bearing, had seen this very man mount and ride, thus sack-like but solid in the saddle, from Richard Ludel's funeral. What was Fulke Astley doing here in the night, making his way thus furtively, not by the roads but through the forest, from one to the other of his own manors? For where else could he be bound?

And the figure that followed him, on a thickset cob, was certainly a woman, and could be nobody else but his daughter, surely, that unknown Hiltrude who seemed so old and unpleasing to young Richard.

So their errand, after all, was not so mysterious. Of course they would want the marriage achieved as soon as possible, if they had Richard in their hands. They had waited these few days until both Eaton and Wroxeter had been searched, but with the hunt being spread more widely they would wait no longer. Whatever risk they might be taking, once the match was a reality they could weather whatever storms followed. They could even afford to set Richard free to return to the abbey, for nothing and no one but the authority of the church could set him free from a wife.

And that being so, what could be done to prevent? There was no time to run back either to Eilmund's house, and have Annet carry words to castle or abbey, or direct to the town, and Hyacinth still found himself humanly reluctant to throw his own chance of liberty to the winds. But it did not arise, there was no time left at all. If he went back, by the time rescue could arrive for Richard he would be married. Perhaps there might yet be time to find where they had hidden him, and whisk him away from under their noses. These two were in no hurry, and Dame Dionisia had still to make the short journey from Eaton without detection. And the priest – where would they have found a willing priest? Nothing could be done until a priest was there.

Hyacinth forsook the thick cover, and made his way deeper into the belt of forest, no longer intent on secrecy, only on speed. At the pace the riders were making he could outrun them on a path, and in this extremity he would venture even the highroad, if need be, and risk meeting others still out on their own lawful occasions. But there was a path, too near the open road for the Astleys to favour it, and merging into the road itself once it had crossed the upland ridge. Hyacinth reached it and ran, fleet and silent on the thick carpet of leaves too moist and limp to rustle under his feet.

Once out on to the open track and plunging downhill towards the village, still almost a mile distant, he drew off again into the fields dipping to the river, and ran from one scattered covert to another, assured now that he was ahead of Astley. He waded the little stream that came down from the foot of the Wrekin to reach the Severn here, and went on along the river bank. One isolated tongue of woodland came down almost to the water, and from its shelter he could see for the first time the low stockade of the manor, and the long level of the roof within, sharp and clear against the glimmer of the water and the pallor of the sky.

It was good fortune that the trees approached so closely to the stockade on the side nearest to the river bank. From tree to tree Hyacinth darted, and reaching an oak that spread branches across the barrier, climbed nimbly up into the crotch to peer cautiously within the enclosure. He was looking at the long rear face of the house, across the roofs of barn and byre and stable lining the containing fence. The same pattern of a low undercroft, with hall and chamber and kitchen above on the living floor, and the steps to the only door must be on the opposite side. Here there was no entrance except to the undercroft, and only one small window, and that was shuttered. Under it a small wing had been built out, extending the undercroft. The shingled roof was steep, the eaves dipped fairly low. Hyacinth eyed it speculatively, and debated how securely fastened those shutters might be. To reach them would be easily possible, to find a way in by that road might be more of a problem. But this rear face of the house was the only one sheltered from observation. All this nefarious activity of Astleys and Ludels would be centred round the single great doorway into the hall, on the other side.

He swung himself down to hang by his hands within the pale, and dropped into a shadowy corner between barn and stable. At least stumbling on this nocturnal journey eased him of one fear. Richard was surely here, was alive and well and presentable as they wanted him, well fed, well cared for, probably even indulged beyond normal in the hope of cajoling him into willing consent. Indulged, in fact, with everything he could desire and they furnish, except his freedom. And that was the first profound relief. Now to get him out!

Here in the darkening yard there was no one stirring. Hyacinth slid softly out of his shelter and moved round the pale from shadow to shadow, until he slipped round the corner to the eastern end of the house. There were un-shuttered windows above him here, subdued light shining through. He refuged in the deep doorway to the under-croft, and stretched his ears for voices from above, and thought that he caught wordless murmurings, as though the aim was to keep everything of this night's activities secret. Round the next corner, where the steep stairway to the hall door ascended, there was a torch fixed, he knew it by the flickering light spilled on the beaten earth before him by fitful glimpses. There were servants moving there, too, soft-stepping and low-voiced. And the dull sound of hooves, coming at a walk into the court. The bride and her father arriving, thought Hyacinth, and wondered for a fleeting moment how the girl felt about the match, and whether she was not as wronged and slighted as Richard, and even more helpless.

He drew back in some haste, for the grooms would be leading the horses to the stables, which were in the near corner of the yard, for he had heard the beasts stirring in their stalls as he hung listening in the tree. The jutting wing of the undercroft provided cover from that corner. He rounded it and flattened himself into the dark angle of the walls behind the obstruction, and heard a single groom come leading both mounts.

He could not move until the man had gone, and time was snapping at his heels like a herdsman's dog. But the groom was brisk, and wasted no time on his charges, perhaps wanting his bed, for it must be getting late. Hyacinth heard the stable door slammed to, and the rapid footsteps scurrying away round the corner of the house. Only then, when he was able to draw off and take another look at this almost blind face of the manor, did Hyacinth observe what he had missed before. Through the join in the massive shutters on this, the only shuttered window in the house in these mild nights, a hair-line of light showed. More noticeable still, in one of the boards, close to the join, there was a small round eye of light, where a slanting knot in the wood had fallen out and left a hole. Why should this rear room be shuttered and lighted, unless it had a guest, and one who must be kept safe and secret? Hyacinth doubted if the space between the stone mullions would be large enough to let a man through, but it might be wide enough for a ten-year-old boy, and one rather small for his years. With that low roof beneath the window, they would not want him to make his escape, nor would they want any inquisitive person to see him there within.

It could at least be tried. Hyacinth leaped to get a hold of the overhanging eaves, and hauled himself up on to the shingles, to lie flat there against the stone wall, listening, though he had made little noise about it, and no one stirred to take note or investigate. He drew himself cautiously up the slope of the roof to the shuttered window. The timbers were heavy and solid, and secured somehow within the room, for when he laid a hand under the centre, where they joined, and essayed to pull them apart, they held fast as iron, and he had no tools to try and force them apart, and doubted if he could have done it even if he had had a whole armoury of implements. The hinges were strong and immovable. Neither top nor bottom of the shutters yielded to force even by a hair. There must be iron bolts that could be shot from within, and securely locked. And time was running out. Richard was strong-willed, obstinate and ingenious. If it had been possible for him to break out from his prison, he would have done it long ago.

Hyacinth laid his ear to the hair-line crack, but could hear nothing moving within. He must now make sure whether he was wasting the time which was so precious and running out so fast. At the risk of being detected, he rapped with his knuckles against the shutter, and setting his lips to the tiny eye of light, sent a shrill whistle through the hole.

152

This time there was an audible gasp somewhere in the room, then a rapid scrambling, as if someone had uncurled from being coiled defensively into a corner, set foot to floor, and taken a couple of startled steps across the room, only to halt again in doubt and alarm. Hyacinth rapped again, and called softly through the hole: 'Richard, is that you?'

Light footsteps came in a rush, a small body crowded against the inner side of the shutters. 'Who is it?' whispered Richard's voice urgently, close to the crack of light. 'Who's there?'

'Hyacinth! Richard, are you alone? I can't get in to you. Is all well with you?'

'No!' breathed the voice in indignant complaint, and proving by its spirit and anger that in fact he was in very good heart and excellent condition. 'They won't let me out, they keep hammering and hammering at me to do what they want, and agree to be married. They're bringing her tonight, they're going to *make* me ...'

'I know,' groaned Hyacinth, 'but I can't get you out. And there's no time to get word to the sheriff. Tomorrow I could, but I saw them coming here tonight.'

'They won't let me out until I do what they want,' Richard hissed grievously into the crack. 'I almost said I would. They go on and on at me, and I don't know what to do, and I'm frightened they'll only take me and hide me somewhere else if I refuse, because they know every house is being searched.' His voice was losing its bold, belligerent tone and faltering into distress. It's hard for a boy of ten to stand off for long the implacable adults who hold the upper hand. 'My grandmother promised I should have whatever I liked, whatever I wanted, if I'd say the words she wants me to say. But I *don't want* a wife ...'

'Richard .... Richard ...' Hyacinth was repeating persistently into this lament, and for a while unheard. 'Listen, Richard! They'll have to bring a priest to marry you – not Father Andrew, surely, he'd have scruples – but someone. Speak to him, tell him it's against your will, tell him – Richard, have you heard who it's to be?' A new and arresting thought had entered his mind. '*Who* is to marry you?'

'I heard them,' whispered Richard, grown calm again, 'saying they couldn't trust Father Andrew. My grandmother is bringing the hermit with her to do it.'

'Cuthred? You're sure?' Hyacinth had almost forgotten to keep his voice down in his astonishment.

'Yes, Cuthred. Yes, I'm sure, I heard her say so.'

'Richard, listen, then!' Hyacinth leaned close, his lips to the crack. 'If you refuse, they'll only visit it on you, and take you away somewhere else. Better for you to do what they want. No, trust me, do what I say, it's the only way we can foil them. Believe me, you won't have anything to fear, you won't be burdened with a wife, you're safe as in sanctuary. Just do as I say, be meek and obedient, and let them think you tamed, and they may even let you take your pony and ride back to the abbey, for they'll have what they wanted, and think it can't be undone. But it can! Oh, never fret, they won't want anything more of you, not for years yet! Trust me, and do it! Will you? Quickly, before they come! Will you do it?'

Bemused and doubtful, Richard faltered: 'Yes!' but could not help protesting the next moment: 'But how can that be? *Why* do you say it's safe?'

Hyacinth pressed close and whispered the answer. He knew by the sudden shaken spurt of laughter, exuberant and brief, that Richard had caught it and understood. And just in time, for he heard from across the room the sharp clash of a door being unbolted and flung open, and the voice of Dame Dionisia, honey and gall, half cajoling and half menacing, saying firmly and loudly: 'Your bride is come, Richard. Here is Hiltrude. And you will be gracious and courteous to her, will you not, and please us all?'

Richard must have darted away from the window at the first touch of a hand on the bolt, for his small, cautious voice said just audibly, and from some yards distant: 'Yes, grandmother!' Unwillingly dutiful, reluctantly obedient, a will only half-broken, but half would do! Her gratified but still wary: 'That's my good child!' was the last thing Hyacinth heard as he edged his way carefully down the slope of the roof and dropped to the ground.

He went on his homeward way without haste, content with his night's work. There was now no urgency, he could afford to go slowly, mindful that he himself was still hunted. For the boy was alive, well fed, well cared for, and in good spirits. No actual harm had come to him, none would come, however he chafed at being a prisoner. And in the end he would have the laugh of his captors. Hyacinth made his way blithely through the soft, chilly night scented with the rising mist of the water meadows, and the deep, dank leaf mould of the woods. The moon rose, but so veiled that it gave only a dim grey light. By midnight he would be safely back in his sanctuary in Eyton forest. And in the morning, by some means Annet would contrive for the purpose, Hugh Beringar should learn exactly where to look for Brother Paul's lost schoolboy.

When it was all over, and he had done what they wanted, however grudgingly, Richard had expected to be made much of by way of gratitude, perhaps even let out from this small room which was his prison, however comfortable it might be. He was not so foolish as to suppose that they would set him free to do as he pleased. He would have to keep up this meek front for a while, and suppress the inward glee he felt at having the laugh of them in secret, before they would dare to produce him before the world, with what manner of story to account for his loss and recovery he could not guess, but they would have it all off by heart. Certainly they would say he had consented of his own will to the ceremony just completed, and to the best of their knowledge it would then be far too late for him to say anything to the contrary, since what was done could not be undone. Only Richard knew that in fact nothing had been done to need undoing. He had absolute faith in Hyacinth. Whatever Hyacinth said was sooth.

But he had considered that they would owe him thanks and indulgence for his compliance. He had preserved his sullen but subdued face, because it would have been too betraying to let even a gleam of laughter show through, but he had repeated all the words they dictated to him, had even brought himself to take Hiltrude's hand when he was told to do so, though he had never once looked at her until the sound of her soft, dull voice, repeating the vows as resignedly as his own, had jolted him into wondering for a moment if she was being forced as he was. That possibility had never occurred to him until then, and he did lift a furtive glance to her face. She was not so very old, after all, and not very tall, and did not look like a threat so much as a victim. She might not even be really plain if only she did not look so subdued and glum. His startled impulse of sympathy for her was complicated by a grain of equally surprised resentment that she should seem as depressed at marrying him as he had good cause to be at marrying her.

But after all his compliance, not a word of thanks, rather his grandmother studied him ominously and at length, and he was afraid with some lingering suspicion in her eye, and then admonished him grimly: 'You have done well to come to your duty at last, and behave yourself fittingly towards those who know best for you. See that you keep to that mind, sir! Now say your goodnight to your wife. Tomorrow you shall get to know her better.'

And he had done as he was told, and they had all left him there, still bolted in alone, though they had sent a servant with food from the supper they were no doubt enjoying in the hall. He sat brooding on his bed, thinking over all that had happened in one late evening, and all that might follow next day. Hiltrude he forgot as soon as she was out of sight. He knew about these affairs. If you were only ten years old they didn't, for some reason, make you live with your wife, not until you were grown up. While she remained under the same roof with you, you would be expected to be civil to her, perhaps even attentive, but then she would go back with her father to her own home until you were thought to be old enough to share your bed and household with her. Now that he began to think seriously about it, it seemed to Richard that there were no privileges at all attached to being married, his grandmother would go on treating him just as before, as a child of no account, ordering him about, scolding him, cuffing him if he annoyed her, even beating him if he defied her. In short, it behoved the lord of Eaton to regain his liberty by whatever means offered, and escape out of her hold. He could not be very important to her now, he had served his purpose, what mattered was the land settlement. If she felt she had secured that, she might soon be willing to let go of the instrument.

Richard rolled himself warmly in his brychans and went to sleep. If they were discussing him in hall, and debating what to do about him, that did not trouble his dreams. He was too young and too innocently hopeful to take his problems to bed with him.

His door was still bolted next morning, and the servant who brought his breakfast gave him no chance to slip past, though indeed he had no intention of trying it, since he knew he would not get far, and his role now was to continue to be docile and disarm suspicion. When his grandmother drew the bolt and came in to him it was old familiar habit, rather than guile, that caused him to rise at her entrance, as he had been taught, and lift up his face for her kiss. And the kiss was no chillier than it had always been, and for a moment he felt the inescapable kindness of

157

the blood warm them both, something he had never questioned, though she had very seldom expressed it. The contact caused him to shake, and brought the sudden astonished sting of tears into his eyes just as inevitably as the surge of obstinate recoil into his mind. It did him no harm with her. She looked down at him from her erect and formidable height with a somewhat softened gaze.

'Well, sir, and how do you find yourself this morning? Are you minded to be a good, obedient boy, and do all you can to please me? If so, you shall find you and I will get on very well together. You have made a beginning, now go on as you began. And think shame that you defied and denied me so long.'

Richard drooped his long lashes and looked down at his feet. 'Yes, grandmother.' And then, in meek assay: 'May I go out today? I don't like being shut in here, as if it was night all the time.'

'We'll see,' she said, but to Richard the tone clearly meant: 'No!' She would not reason nor bargain, only lay down the law to him. 'But not yet, you have not deserved it. First prove that you've learned where your duty lies, and then you shall have your freedom again. You are not ill done to, you have everything you need here, be content until you have earned more and better.'

'But I *have*!' he flashed. 'I did what you wanted, you ought to do what I want. It's unfair to shut me up here, unfair and unkind. I don't even know what you've done with my pony.'

'Your pony is safe in the stable,' said Dionisia sharply, 'and well cared for, as you are. And you had best mind your manners with me, sir, or you'll have cause to regret it. They've taught you at that abbey school to be saucy to your elders, but it's a lesson you had better unlearn as quickly as you can, for your own sake.'

'I'm not being saucy,' he pleaded, relapsing into sullenness. 'I only want to be in daylight, I want to go out, not sit here without even being able to see the trees and the grass. It's wretched in here, without any company ...'

'You shall have company,' she promised, seizing on one complaint to which she could provide a complaisant answer. 'I'll send your bride to keep you company. I want you to get to know her better now, for after today she'll return to Wroxeter with her father, and you, Richard,' she said warningly and with a sharpening eye on him, 'will return with me to your own manor, to take your proper place. And I shall expect you to conduct yourself properly there, and not go hankering after that school, now that you're married and a man of substance. Eaton is yours, and that is where you should be, and I expect you to maintain that, if anyone – *anyone* – should call it in question. Do you understand me, sir?'

He understood her very well. He was to be cajoled, intimidated, bullied into declaring, even to Brother Paul and Father Abbot if need be, that he had run home to his grandmother of his own will, and of his own will submitted to the marriage they had planned for him. He hugged his secret knowledge gleefully to his heart as he said submissively: 'Yes, madam!'

'Good! And now I'll send in Hiltrude to you, and see that you behave well to her. You will have to get used to her, and she to you, so you may as well begin now.' And she relented so far as to kiss him again on leaving him, though it resembled a slap as much as a kiss. She went out in a dusty swirl of long green skirts, and he heard the bolt shot again after her.

And what had he got out of all that, except the fact that his pony was in the stable here, and if only he could get to it he might make his escape even now. But presently in came Hiltrude, as his grandmother had threatened, and all his resentment and dislike of the girl, undeserved though it was, boiled up within him into childish anger. She still seemed to him to belong at least to the generation of the mother he could hardly remember, but she was not really utterly plain, she had a clear, pale skin

159

and large, guarded brown eyes, and if her hair was straight and of a mousey brown colour, she had a great mass of it, plaited in a thick braid that hung to her waist. She did not look ill-natured, but she did look bitterly resigned and wretched. She stood for a moment with her back to the door, staring thoughtfully at the boy curled up glumly on his bed.

'So they've sent you to be my guard dog,' said Richard unpleasantly.

Hiltrude crossed the room and sat down on the sill of the shuttered window, and looked at him without favour. 'I know you don't like me,' she said, not sadly but with quite unexpected vigour. 'Small reason why you should, and for that matter, I don't like you. But it seems we're both bound, no help for it now. Why, *why* did you ever give way? I only said I would, at last, because I was so sure *you* were safe enough there at the abbey, and they'd never let it come to this. And then you have to fall into their hands like a fool, and let them break you down. And here we both are, and may God help us!' She relented of the note of exasperation in her own voice, and ended with weary kindness: 'It's not your fault, you're only a child, what could you do? And it isn't that I dislike you, I don't even know you, it's just that I didn't want you, I don't want you, any more than you want me.'

Richard was staring at her, by this time, with mouth and eyes wide open, struck dumb with astonishment at finding her, as it were, not a token embarrassment, a millstone round his neck, but a real person with a great deal to say for herself, and by no means a fool. Slowly he uncoiled his slim legs and set his feet to the floor, to feel solid substance under him. Slowly he repeated, in a small, shocked voice: 'You never wanted to marry me?'

'A baby like you?' she said, careless of offence. 'No, I never did.'

'Then why did you ever agree to do it?' He was too indignant over her capitulation to resent the reflection on his years. 'If you'd said no, and kept saying it, we should both have been saved.'

'Because my father is a man very hard to say no to, and had begun to tell me that I was getting too old to have another suitor, and if I didn't take you I should be forced to enter a sisterhood and stay a maid until I died. And that I wanted even less. And I thought the abbot would keep fast hold of you, and nothing would ever be allowed to come of it. And now here we are, and what are we to do about it?'

Himself surprised at feeling an almost sympathetic curiosity about this woman who had sloughed a skin before his eyes, and emerged as vivid and real as himself, Richard asked almost shyly: 'What *do* you want? If you could have your way, what would you like to have?'

'I would like,' said Hiltrude, her brown eyes suddenly burning with anger and loss, 'a young man named Evrard, who keeps my father's manor roll and is his steward at Wroxeter, and who likes me, too, whether you think that likely or not. But he's a younger son and has no land, and where there's no land to marry to his own my father has no interest. There's an uncle who may well leave his manor to Evrard, being fond of him and childless, but land now is what my father wants, not someday and maybe land.' The fire burned down. She turned her head aside. 'Why do I tell you this? You can't understand, and it's not your fault. There's nothing you can do to better it.'

Richard was beginning to think that there might be something very pertinent he could do for her, if she in her turn would do something for him. Cautiously he asked: 'What are they doing now, your father and my grand-mother? She said you'd be going back to Wroxeter after today. What are they planning? And has Father Abbot been looking for me all this time since I left?'

'You didn't know? Not only the abbot, but the sheriff and all his men are looking for you. They've searched

Eaton and Wroxeter, and are beating every bush in the forest. My father was afraid they might reach here by to-day, but she thought not. They were wondering whether to move you back to Eaton in the night, since it's been searched already, but Dame Dionisia felt sure the officers had several days' work left before they'd reach Leighton, and in any case, she said, if a proper watch was set there'd be ample time to put you over the river with an escort and send you down to shelter at Buildwas. Better, she said, than moving you back towards Shrewsbury yet.'

'Where are they now?' asked Richard intently. 'My grandmother?'

'She's ridden back to Eaton to have everything there looking just as it should. Her hermit went back to his cell in the night. It wouldn't do if anyone knew he'd been away.'

'And your father?'

'He's out and about among his tenants here, but he'll not be far away. He took his clerk with him. There'll be dues unpaid that he wants collected, I daresay.' She was indifferent to her father's movements, but she did feel some curiosity as to what was going on in this child's head, to sharpen his voice into such hopeful purpose, and brighten his disconsolate eye. 'Why? What is there in that for you? Or for me!' she added bitterly.

'There might,' said Richard, beginning to glitter, 'be something I can do for you, something good, if you'll do something for me in return. If they're both out of the house, help me to get away while they're gone. My pony's there in the stable, she told me as much. If I could get to him and slip away, you could bolt the door again, and no one would know I was gone until evening.'

She shook her head decisively. 'And who would get the blame? I wouldn't put it off on to one of the servants, and I've no great appetite for it myself. The troubles I already have are enough for me, I thank you!' But she added warily, seeing that his hopeful fire was by no means quenched: 'But I would be willing to think out the best means, if I thought it would solve anything for me. But how can it? For a fair deliverance I'd venture anything Father could say or do. But what's the use, when we're tied together as we are, and no way out?'

Richard bounded up from his bed and darted across the room to settle confidingly beside her on the broad sill. Close to her ear he said breathlessly: 'If I tell you a secret, will you swear to keep it until I'm safely away, and help me to get out of here? I promise you, I promise you it will be worth your while.'

'You are dreaming,' she said tolerantly, turning to look at him thus closely, and seeing his secret brightness undimmed by her disbelief. 'There's no way out of marriage unless you're a prince and have the Pope's ear, and who cares about lesser folk like us? True, we're not bedded, nor will be for years yet, but if you think your old dame and my father would ever let it come to an annulment, you waste your hopes. They've got their way, they'll never let go of their gains.'

'No, it's nothing like that,' he persisted, 'we need nothing from Pope or law. You must believe me. At least promise not to tell, and when you hear what it is, you'll be willing to help me, too.'

'Very well,' she said, humouring him, even half convinced now that he knew something she did not know, but still doubting if it would or could deliver them. 'Very well, I promise. What is this precious secret?'

Gleefully he advanced his lips to her ear, his cheek teased by the touch of a lock of her hair that curled loose there, and breathed his secret as though the very boards at their backs had ears. And after one incredulous instant of stillness and silence she began to laugh very softly, to shake with her laughter, and throwing her arms about Richard, hugged him briefly to her heart.

'For that you *shall* go free, whatever it cost me! You deserve it!'

Chapter Eleven

ONCE convinced, it was she who made the plans. She knew the house and the servants, and as long as there was no suspicion of her subservience she had the entry everywhere, and could give orders to grooms and maids as she pleased.

'Best wait until after they've brought your dinner and taken away the dish again. It will be a longer time then before anyone comes in to you again. There's a back gate through the pale, from the stable out into the paddock. I could tell Jehan to turn your pony out to grass, he's been shut in too long to be liking it. There are some bushes in the field there, round behind the stable, close to the wicket. I'll make shift to hide your saddle and harness there before noon. I can get you out of here through the undercroft, while they're all busy in hall and kitchens.'

'But your father will be home then,' protested Richard doubtfully.

'After his dinner my father will be snoring. If he does look in on you at all, it will be before he sits down to table, to make sure you're safe in your cage. Better for me, too, I shall have sat out my morning with you gallantly, who's to think I'll change my tune after that? It might even be good sport,' said Hiltrude, growing animated in contemplating her benevolent mischief, 'when they go to take you your supper, and find the window still shuttered and barred, and the bird flown.'

'But then everyone will be harried and cursed and blamed,' said Richard, 'because somebody must have drawn the bolt.'

'So then we all deny it, and whoever looks likeliest to be suspected I'll bring off safely, saying he's never been out of my sight and never touched the door since your dinner went in. If it comes to the worst,' said Hiltrude, with uncustomary resolution, 'I'll say I must have forgotten to shoot the bolt after leaving you the last time. What can he do? He'll still be thinking he has you trapped in marriage with me, wherever you run to. Better still,' she cried, clapping her hands, 'I'll be the one who brings you your dinner, and waits with you, and brings out the dish again – then no one else can be blamed for leaving the door unbolted. A wife should begin at once to wait on her husband, it will look well.'

'You're not afraid of your father?' ventured Richard, open-eyed with startled respect, even admiration, but reluctant to leave her to sustain so perilous a part.

'I am – I was! Now, whatever happens, it will be worth the pains. I must go, Richard, while there's no one in the stable. You wait and trust me, and keep up your heart. You've lifted mine!'

She was at the door when Richard, still thoughtfully following her light and buoyant passage, so changed from the subdued, embittered creature whose cold hand he had held in the night, said impulsively after her: 'Hiltrude – I think I might do worse than marry you, after all.' And added, with barely decent haste: 'But not yet!'

Everything that she had promised she performed. She brought his dinner, and sat with him and made desultory, awkward talk while he ate it, such talk as might be expected to a stranger, and a child at that, and one forced upon her and reluctantly accepted, so that however much he might be resented, there was no longer any point in being at odds with him. Less from guile than because he was hungry and busy eating, Richard responded with grunts rather than words. Had anyone been listening, they would certainly have found the exchanges depressingly appropriate.

Hiltrude carried the dish back to the kitchen, and returned to him as soon as she had made certain that everyone else about the house was occupied. The narrow wooden stair down into the undercroft was conveniently screened from the passage that led to the kitchen, they had no trouble in skipping hastily down it, and emerging from below ground by the deep doorway where Hyacinth had sheltered, and from there it was just one dangerous dart across open ground to the wicket in the fence, half hidden by the bulk of the stable. Saddle and bridle and all, she had left his harness concealed behind the bushes, and the sable pony came to him gladly. Close under the rear wall of the stable he saddled up in trembling haste, and led the pony out of the paddock and down towards the river, where the belt of trees offered cover, before he dared to tighten the girth and mount. Now, if all went well, he had until early evening before he would be missed.

Hiltrude went back up the stairs from the undercroft, and took care to spend her afternoon blamelessly among the women of the household, within sight every moment, and occupied with the proper affairs of the lady of the manor. She had bolted Richard's door, since clearly if it had been inadvertently left unfastened, and the prisoner taken advantage of the fact, even a ten-year-old boy would have the sense to shoot the bolt again and preserve the appearances. When the flight was discovered she could very well protest that she had no recollection of forgetting to fasten it, though admitting at last that she must have done so. But by then, if all went well, Richard would be back in the abbey enclave, and taking belated

166

thought how to present himself as the blameless victim, and bury all recollection of the guilty truant who had run off without permission and caused all this turmoil and anxiety. Well, that was Richard's affair. She had done her part.

It was a pity that the groom who had turned Richard's pony into the paddock should have occasion to fetch in one of the other beasts out to graze, about the middle of the afternoon, since he had noticed that it was slightly lame. He could hardly fail to observe that the pony was gone. Seizing on the first and obvious, if none too likely, possibility, he was halfway across the court crying that there had been thieves in the paddock before it occurred to him to go back and look in the stable for the saddle and harness. That put a somewhat different complexion on the loss. And besides, why take the least valuable beast in sight? And why risk theft in daylight? Good dark nights were more favourable.

So he arrived in hall announcing loudly and breathlessly that the young bridegroom's pony was gone, saddle and all, and my lord had better look to see if he still had the boy safe under lock and key. Fulke went himself, in haste, hardly believing the news, and found the door securely bolted as before, but the room within empty. He let out a bellow of rage that made Hiltrude flinch over her embroidery frame, but she kept her eyes lowered to her work, and went on demurely stitching until the storm erupted in the doorway and swelled to fill the hall.

'Which of you was it? Who waited on him last? Which fool among you, fools every one as you are, left the door unbarred? Or has one of you loosed him deliberately, in my despite? I'll have the hide of the traitorous wretch, whoever he may be. Speak up! Who took the slippery imp his dinner?'

The menservants held off out of his immediate reach, every one babbling out his own innocence. The maids fluttered and looked sidelong at one another, but hesitated to say a word against their mistress. But Hiltrude, her courage fast in both hands and bulking encouragingly solid now that it came to the test, laid her work aside and said boldly, not yet sounding defensive: 'But, Father, you know I did that myself. You saw me bring out the dish afterwards. Certainly I bolted the door again – I feel sure I did. No one else has been in to him since, unless you have visited him yourself, sir. Who else would, unless he was sent? And *I*'ve sent nobody.'

'Are you so certain, madam?' roared Fulke. 'You'll tell me next the lad's not gone at all, but sitting there where he should be. If you were the last to go in there, then you're to blame for letting him slip out and take to his heels. You must have left the door unbolted, how else could he get out? How could you be such a fool?'

'I did not leave it unbolted,' she repeated, but with less certainty this time. 'Or even if I may have forgotten,' she conceded defensively, 'though I don't believe I did – but if I did, does it matter so much now? He can't alter what's done, nor can anyone else. I don't see why it should cause such a flurry.'

'You don't see, you don't see – you don't see beyond the end of your nose, madam! And he to go running back to his abbot, with the tales he can tell?'

'But he has to come back into the light sooner or later,' she said meekly. 'You couldn't keep him shut up for ever.'

'So he has, we all know it, but not yet, not until we've got his mark – no, for he can sign his name, which is better! – on the marriage settlements, and made him see he may as well fit his story to ours, and accept what's done. A few days and it could all have been done our way, the proper way. But I'll not let him get away without a race for it,' swore Fulke vengefully, and turned to roar at his petrified grooms: 'Saddle my horse, and make haste about it! I'm going after him. He'll make straight for the abbey, and keep well clear of Eaton, surely. I'll have him back by the ear yet!'

In the full light of afternoon Richard did not dare take to the road, even by skirting the village widely. There he could have made better speed, but might all too easily attract the attention of tenants or retainers who would serve Astley's ends for their own sakes, and drag him back to his captivity. Moreover, the road would take him far too close to Eaton. He kept to the belt of woodland that stretched westward for half a mile or so above the river, thinning as it went until it was no more than a belt of single oaks spaced out beside the water. Beyond that, emerald water meadows filled a great bend in the Severn, open and treeless. There he kept inland far enough to have some cover from the few bushes that grew along the headlands of the Leighton fields. Upstream, where he must go, the valley widened into a great green level of flood meadows, with only a few isolated trees on the higher spots, but the northern bank where he rode rose within another mile into the low ridge of Eyton forest, where he could go in thick cover for more than half the distance to Wroxeter. It would mean going more slowly, but it was not pursuit he feared then, it was being recognised and intercepted on the way. Wroxeter he must avoid at all costs, and the only way he knew was by fording the Severn there, short of the village and out of sight of the manor, to reach the road on the southern side, and then ride full tilt for the town.

He made a little too much haste in the forest, where his familiarity with the land had led him to take a short cut between paths, and paid for it with a fall when his pony stepped in the soft edge of a badger's sett. But he dropped lightly enough into the thick cushioning of leaves, and escaped with a few bruises, and the pony, startled and skittish but docile, came back to him readily once the first fright was over. After that he bore in mind that haste was not necessarily another word for speed, and took more care until he came to the more open ways. He had not reasoned about his flight, but set off bent on getting back to the abbey and making his peace there, whatever scoldings and punishments might be waiting for him, once all anxiety on his behalf was banished. He knew enough about grown-up people, however various they might seem in all other ways, to understand that they all shared the same instinct when a child in their charge was recovered out of danger, to hug him first, and clout him immediately afterwards. If, indeed, the clout did not come first! He would not mind that. Now that he had been dragged forcibly away from the schoolroom, and Brother Paul, and his fellow pupils, and even the awesome face of Father Abbot, all he wanted was to get back to them, to have the safe walls and the even safer horarium of the monastic day wrapped round him like a warm cloak. He could, had he even thought of it, have ridden to the mill by the river at Eyton, or the forester's cottage, any dwelling on this soil held by the abbey, and been received into safe shelter, but that possibility never entered his head. He made for the abbey like a bird to its nest. At this moment he had no other home, lord of Eaton though he might be.

Once out of the forest there was a good and open track almost to the ford, which lay on the southern side of Wroxeter village. Over these two miles he went briskly, but not so fast as to call attention to himself, for here there were other people to be met with occasionally, about their daily business in the fields or travelling the path between villages. He saw none that he knew, and answered such casual greetings as they gave him as briefly as they were given, and did not loiter.

The belt of trees on the near side of the ford came into view, the few willows dipping to the water, and the top of the tower of the collegiate church just showed among the branches, with one corner of a roof. The rest of the village and the demesne lay beyond. Richard approached the shelter of the trees cautiously, and dismounted in cover to peer through at the shallow spread of the water round a small island, and the path that came down from the village to the ford. He heard the voices before he reached a clear view, and halted to listen acutely, hoping the speakers would pass towards the village and leave his path clear. Two women, chattering and laughing, and an accompanying light splashing in the edge of the water, and then a man's voice, equally idle and easy, teasing and chaffing the girls. Richard ventured closer, until he could see the speakers clearly, and halted with an indrawn breath of exasperation and dismay.

The women had been washing linen, and had it spread on the low bushes to dry, and since the day was not cold, and since they had been joined by a young and not unattractive companion, they were in no hurry to leave the shore. Richard did not know the women, but the man he knew only too well, though not his name. This big, red-haired, strutting young gamecock was Astley's foreman on the demesne farm, and one of the two who had encountered and recognised Richard in the woods, trotting home to the abbey in haste, and taken advantage of the hour and the solitude to do their lord a favour. Those same muscular arms which were now making free with one of the giggling laundresses had hoisted Richard ignominiously out of the saddle, and held him kicking and raging over a thick shoulder that might have been made of oak for all the effect his belabouring fists had on it, until the other miscreant had stopped the boy's mouth with his own capuchon, and pinioned his arms with his own reins. That same night, when it was fully dark, past midnight and all honest folk in their beds, the same trusted pair had bundled him away to the more distant manor for safekeeping. Richard remembered these indignities bitterly. And now here was this very fellow getting in his way once again, for he could not ride out of cover and make for the ford without passing close and being recognised, and almost certainly recaptured.

There was nothing to be done but draw back into deeper cover and wait for them all to go away, back to the village and the manor. No hope of circling Wroxeter by a wider way and continuing on this north bank of the river, he was already too close to the edge of the village and all the approaches were open to view. And he was losing time, and without reasoning why, he felt that time was vital. He lost an hour there, gnawing his knuckles in desperate frustration and watching for the first move. Even when the women did decide to take up their washing and make for home they were in no hurry about it, but dawdled away up the path still bantering and laughing with the young man who strode between them. Only when their voices had faded into silence, and no other soul stirred about the ford, did Richard venture out from cover and spur his pony splashing down into the shallows.

The ford was smooth going in the first stretch, sandy and shallow, then the path trod dry-shod over the tip of the island, and again plunged into the long passage beyond, a wide archipelago of small, sandy shoals, dimpling and gleaming with the soft, circuitous motion of the water. In mid-passage Richard drew rein for a moment to look back, for the broad, innocent expanse of green meadows oppressed him with a feeling of nakedness and apprehension. Here he could be seen from a mile or more away, a small dark figure on horseback, defenceless and vulnerable, against a landscape all moist, pearly light and pale colours.

And there, riding at a gallop towards the ford, on the same path by which he had come, distant and small still but all too purposefully riding after him, came a single horseman on a big, light-grey horse, Fulke Astley in determined pursuit of his truant son-in-law.

Richard shot through the shallows in a flurry of spray,

and was off in a desperate hurry through the wet meadows, heading west for the track that would bring him in somewhat over four miles to Saint Giles, and the last straight run to the abbey gatehouse. Over a mile to go before he could find cover in the undulating ground and the scattered groves of trees, but even then he could not hope to shake off the pursuit now that he had been sighted, as surely he must have been. And his pony was no match for that raking dappled beast behind him. But speed was the only hope he had. He still had a fair start, even if he had lost the best of it waiting to cross the ford. He dug in his heels and set his teeth and made for Shrewsbury as if wolves were at his heels.

The ground rose, folded in low hills, dotted with trees and slopes of bushes, hiding hunted and hunter from each other, but the distance between them must be shortening, and where the track ran level and unsheltered for a while Richard stole an uneasy glance over his shoulder, glimpsed his enemy again, nearer than before, and paid for his momentary inattention with another fall, though this time he clung to the reins and saved himself both the worst of the shock and the effort of catching his pony again. Muddied and bruised and furious with himself, he scrambled headlong back into the saddle and rode wildly on, feeling Astley's fixed stare as a dagger in his back. It was fortunate that the pony was Welsh-bred and sturdy, and had been some days spoiling for exercise, and that the weight he carried was so light, but even so the pace was unkind, and Richard knew it and fretted over it, but could not slacken it. By the time the fence of Saint Giles came in sight, and the track broadened into a road, he could hear the hooves pounding somewhere behind him. But for that he might have turned in there for refuge, since the leper hospice was manned and served by the abbey, and Brother Oswin would not have surrendered him to anyone unless on the abbot's orders. But by then there was no time to halt or turn aside.

Richard crouched low and galloped on along the Foregate, every moment expecting to see Fulke Astley's massive shadow cast across his quarter, and a big hand stretching out to grasp his bridle. Round the corner of the abbey wall now, and pounding along the straight stretch to the gatehouse, scattering the craftsmen and cottagers just ending their day's work and turning homeward, and the children and dogs playing in the highway.

There was barely five yards between them when Richard swung recklessly in at the gatehouse.

At Vespers that evening there were several worshippers from the guest hall, as Cadfael noted from his place in the choir. Rafe of Coventry was present, taciturn and unobtrusive as ever, and even Aymer Bosiet, after his day's activities in pursuit of his elusive property, had put in a morose and grim appearance, possibly to pray for a reliable lead from heaven. By the look of him he had weighty matters on his mind, since he was frowning over them all through Vespers, like a man trying to make up his mind. Perhaps the necessity to remain on good terms with his mother's powerful kin was urging him to hasten home at once with Drogo's body, and show some signs of family piety. Perhaps the thought of a subtle younger brother, there on the spot and fully capable of mischief for his own advancement, might also be arguing for the abandonment of a wild-goose chase in favour of a certain inheritance.

Whatever his preoccupations, he provided one more witness to the scene that confronted brothers and guests when the office was over, and they emerged by the south door and passed along the west range of the cloister into the great court, to disperse there to their various preparations for supper. Abbot Radulfus was just stepping out into the court, with Prior Robert and the whole procession of the brothers following, when the evening quiet was broken by the headlong thud of hooves along the beaten earth of the roadway outside the gatehouse, turning abruptly to a steely clatter on the cobbles within, as a stout black pony hurtled in past the gatehouse without stopping, slithering and stamping on the stones, closely followed by a tall grey horse. The rider on the grey was a big, fleshy, bearded man, crimson-faced with anger or haste, or both together, leaning forward to snatch at the bridle of the boy who rode the pony. The two of them had shot a matter of twenty yards or so into the centre of the court when his outstretched hand reached the rein, and hauled both mounts to a sliding, snorting halt, lathered and trembling. He had secured the pony, but not the boy, who let out a yell of alarm, and abandoning his reins, rather fell than dismounted on the other side, and fled like a homing bird to the abbot's feet, where he stumbled and fell flat on his face, and winding his arms desperately round the abbot's ankles, wailed out an indistinguishable appeal into the skirts of the black habit and hung on tightly, half expecting to be plucked away by force, and certain no one could prevent it, if the attempt was made, except for this erect and stable rock to which he clung.

The quiet which had been so roughly shattered had settled again with startling suddenness on the great court. Radulfus raised his intent and austere stare from the small figure hugging his ankles to the stout and confident man who had left the quivering horses sweating side by side, and advanced some paces to meet him, by no means abashed before the monastic authority.

'My lord, this is somewhat unceremonious. We are not accustomed to such abrupt visitations,' said Radulfus.

'My lord abbot, I regret being forced to disturb you. If our entry was unmannerly, I ask your pardon. For Richard rather than for myself,' said Fulke with conscious and confident challenge. 'His foolishness is the cause. I hoped to spare you this silly upheaval by overtaking him earlier and seeing him safely back home.

Where I will take him now, and see that he does not trouble you so again.'

It seemed that he was quite sure of himself, though he did not advance another step or reach out a hand to grasp the boy by the collar. He met the abbot's gaze eye to eye, unblinking. Behind Prior Robert's back the brothers broke ranks to come forth into the open and gather round in a discreet half-circle, to peer in awe at the crouching boy, who had begun to gasp out muffled protests and pleas, still incoherent, since he would not raise his head or relax the frantic grasp of his arms. After the brothers came the guests, no less interested in so unusual a spectacle. Cadfael, moving methodically round to a position from which he had a clear view, caught the detached but attentive eye of Rafe of Coventry, and saw the fleeting passage of a smile brush the falconer's bearded lips.

Instead of answering Astley, the abbot looked down again with a frowning face at the boy at his feet, and said crisply: 'Stop your noise, child, and leave go of me. You are in no danger. Get up!'

Richard slackened his hold reluctantly, and raised a face smudged with mud and the green of leaves from his falls, the sweat of his haste and fear, and a few frantic tears of relief from a terror seen now to be none too reasonable. 'Father, don't let him take me! I don't want to go back, I want to be here, I want to stay with Brother Paul, I want to learn. Don't send me away! I never meant to stay away, never! I was on my way back when they stopped me. I was on my way home, truly I was!'

'It would seem,' said the abbot drily, 'that there is some dispute here as to where your home is, since the lord Fulke is offering you safe-conduct there, whereas you are of the opinion that you are already arrived. What account you have to give of yourself can wait another occasion. Where you belong, it seems, cannot. Get up, Richard, at once, and stand erect as you should.' And he reached down a lean and muscular hand to take Richard by the forearm and hoist him briskly to his feet.

For the first time Richard looked about him, uncomfortably aware of many eyes upon him, and a little galled at having to cut so dishevelled and soiled a figure before all the assembled brothers, let alone the indignant shame he felt at the stiffening snail-trails of tears on his cheeks. He straightened his back, and scrubbed hurriedly with a sleeve at his dirty face. He looked briefly for Brother Paul among the habited circle, and found him, and was a little comforted. And Brother Paul, who had been hard put to it not to run to his strayed lamb, put his trust in Abbot Radulfus, and kept his mouth shut.

'You have heard, sir,' said the abbot, 'what Richard's preference is. No doubt you know that his father placed him here in my care, and wished him to remain here and study until he came of age. I have a claim to the custody of this boy by charter, duly witnessed, and it was from my care he disappeared some days ago. I have not so far heard what substance there may be in your claim on him.'

'Richard changes his mind daily,' said Fulke, confidently loud, 'for only last night he went willingly in quite another direction. Nor do I hold that such a child should be left to choose by his own liking, when his elders are better judges of what's good for him. And as for *my* claim on the charge of him, you shall know it. Richard is my son by law, with his grandmother's full knowledge and consent. Last night he was married to my daughter.'

The shiver of consternation that went round the circle of awestricken watchers subsided into absolute stillness. Abbot Radulfus was not shaken outwardly, but Cadfael saw the lines of his gaunt face tighten, and knew that the shaft had gone home. Such a consummation had been plotted long since by Dionisia, this self-important neighbour was little more than her instrument in the affair. What he announced could very well be true, if they had

177

had the boy in their hands all this time that he had been missing. And Richard, who had stiffened and jerked up his head, open-mouthed to cry that it was false, met the abbot's stern eyes fixed steadily upon him, and was utterly confounded. He was afraid to lie to that judicial countenance, indeed he admired as much as he feared, and he did not wish to lie, and confronted with this flat declaration he found himself at a loss to know what was truth. For they *had* married him to Hiltrude, and simple denial was not enough. A last bolt of fright went through him and took his breath away, for how if Hyacinth was himself deceived, and the vows he had tamely repeated had bound him for life?

'Is this true, Richard?' asked Radulfus.

His voice was level and quiet, but in the circumstances seemed to Richard terrible. He gulped down words that would not do, and Fulke, impatient, answered for him: 'It is true, and he cannot deny it. Do you doubt my word, my lord?'

'Silence!' said the abbot peremptorily, but still quietly. 'I require Richard's answer. Speak up, boy! Did this marriage indeed take place?'

'Yes, Father,' faltered Richard, 'but it is not —'

'Where? With what other witnesses?'

'At Leighton, Father, last night, that is true, but still I am not —'

He was cut off again, and submitted with a sob, frustrated and growing indignant.

'And you spoke the words of the sacrament freely, of your own will? You were not forced? Beaten? Threatened?'

'No, Father, not beaten, but I was afraid. They did so hammer at me —'

'He has been reasoned with, and he was persuaded,' said Fulke shortly. 'Now he takes back what he granted yesterday. He spoke his part without hand being laid on him. Of his own will!'

'And your priest undertook this marriage willingly? Assured that the consent of both was freely given? A good man, of honest repute?'

'A man of known holiness, my lord abbot,' said Fulke triumphantly. 'The country folk call him a saint. The holy hermit Cuthred!'

'But, Father,' Richard cried with the courage of desperation, determined to get out at last the plain, untangled truth of it, 'I did what I did so that they'd let me go free, and I could get back to you. I did say the vows, but only because I knew they could not be binding. I am *not* married! It was *not* a marriage, because —'

Both the abbot and Fulke broke into speech, sternly overriding his outburst and ordering his silence, but Richard's blood was up. If it must out here before everyone, then it must. He clenched his fists, and shouted loudly enough to fetch a stony echo from the walls of the cloister: '— because *Cuthred is not a priest!*'

Chapter Twelve

IN THE general ripple and stir of astonishment, doubt and outrage that passed like a sudden gust of wind through the entire assembly, from Prior Robert's indignant snort to the inquisitive and half-gleeful whisperings and shiftings among the novices, the thing that was clearest of all to Cadfael was that Fulke Astley stood utterly confounded. Never had he had the least notion what was coming, it had taken his breath away. He stood dangling his arms in curious helplessness, as though something of his own being had slipped from his grasp and left him lame and mute. When he had recovered breath enough to speak at all he said what would have been expected of him, but without the confidence of conviction, rather forcibly thrusting the very suggestion away from him in panic.

'My lord abbot, this is madness! The boy is lying. He'll say anything to serve his turn. Of course Father Cuthred is a priest! The brothers of Savigny from Buildwas brought him to us, ask them, they have no doubts. There has never been any question. This is wickedness, so to slander a holy man.'

'Such slander would indeed be wickedness,' agreed Radulfus, fixing his deep-set eyes and lowered brows formidably upon Richard. 'Think well, sir, before you repeat it. If this is a device to get your way and remain here with us, think better of it now and confess it. You shall not be punished for it. Whatever else, it would seem that you have been misused, abducted and intimidated, and that shall excuse you. I would remind Sir Fulke of these circumstances. But if you do not tell truth now, Richard, then you do incur punishment.'

'I have told truth,' said Richard stoutly, jutting his very respectable chin and meeting the awesome eyes without blinking. 'I am telling truth. I swear it! I did what they demanded of me because I knew then that the hermit is not a priest, and a marriage made by him would be no marriage.'

'How did you know?' cried Fulke furiously, stirring out of his confusion. 'Who told you so? My lord, this is all a childish ruse, and a spiteful one. He *is* lying!'

'Well? You may answer those questions,' said Radulfus, never taking his eyes from Richard's. 'How did you know? Who told you?'

But these were the very questions Richard could not answer without betraying Hyacinth, and bringing the hunt on to his trail with renewed vigour. He said with wincing gallantry: 'Father, I will tell you, but not here, only to you. Please believe me, I am not lying.'

'I do believe you,' said the abbot, abruptly releasing him from the scrutiny which had made him tremble. 'I believe you are saying what you have been told, and what you believe to be true. But this is a more serious matter than you can understand, and it must be cleared up. A man against whom such an accusation has been made has the right to speak up for himself, and prove his good faith. I shall go myself, tomorrow early, and ask the hermit whether he is or is not a priest, and who ordained him, and where, and when. These things can be proven, and should be. You will surely have an equal interest, my lord, in finding out, once for all, whether this was indeed a marriage. Though I must warn you,' he added firmly, 'that even if it is it can be annulled, seeing it cannot have been consummated.'

'Make the attempt,' retorted Astley, somewhat recovering his composure, 'and it will be contested to the limit. But I acknowledge that truth must out. We cannot have such doubts lingering.'

'Then will you not meet with me at the hermitage, as early as may be after Prime? It is fair we should both hear what Cuthred has to say. I am well sure,' he said with truth, having seen the effect of Richard's outburst, 'that you believed implicitly the man was a priest, with full rights to marry and bury. That is not in dispute. Richard has cause to hold to the contrary. Let us put it to the test.'

There was nothing Astley could object to in that, nor, thought Cadfael, had he any wish to avoid the issue. He had certainly been profoundly shocked by the suggestion of deceit, and wanted the damaging doubt removed. But he did make one more attempt to regain his hold meantime on the boy. He advanced a hand to Richard's shoulder. 'I will come to that meeting,' he said, 'and see this deluded child proved wrong. But for this night I still hold he stands as my son, and should go with me.'

The hand closed on Richard's arm, and the boy started and tore himself away. Brother Paul could no longer restrain himself, he hurried forward out of the staring ranks and drew the truant close to his side.

'Richard stays here,' said Radulfus firmly. 'His father entrusted him to me, and I set no limit on his stay with us. But whose son by law and whose husband the child is we must and will examine.'

Fulke was growing purple in the face again with suppressed anger. He had come so near to capturing the imp, and now to be thwarted, and the whole structure of his and Dionisia's territorial plans put in jeopardy. He would not give up so easily.

'You take much upon yourself, my lord abbot,' he began, 'in denying rights to his kin, you who have no blood claim upon him. And I think you are not without designs upon his lands and goods in keeping him here. You want no marriage for the boy, but rather to school him here until he knows no other world, and will enter tamely into his novitiate, and your house into his inheritance …'

He was so intent on his accusations, and all those about him so stricken into wonder at his daring, that no one had yet observed the new arrival at the gatehouse. All eyes were on Astley, and all mouths agape in amazement, and Hugh had tethered his horse at the gate and entered on foot, making no noise. He had taken but ten paces into the court when his eye fell first on the grey horse and the black pony, crusted with the drying lather of their hasty ride, and held now by a groom, who stood gaping at the group framed in the archway of the cloister. Hugh followed the man's fascinated stare, and took in at a glance the same arresting spectacle, the abbot and Fulke Astley face to face in obvious confrontation, and Brother Paul with an arm protectively about the shoulders of a small, wiry, grubby and dishevelled boy, who lifted to the evening light the wide-eyed face, half-frightened, half-defiant, of Richard Ludel.

Radulfus, standing disdainfully silent under abuse, was the first to notice the new arrival on the scene. Looking clean over his adversary's head, as with his height he could very well do, he said distinctly: 'No doubt the lord sheriff will pay the attention due to your charges. As he may also be interested in how Richard came to be in your care at Leighton as late as last night. You should address your complaints to him.' Fulke span upon one heel so precipitately that he all but lost his balance; and there was Hugh coming briskly down the court to join them, one quirky eyebrow tilted into his black hair, and the eye beneath it bright and sharply knowing, and levelled upon Fulke.

'Well, well, my lord!' said Hugh amiably. 'I see you

have made shift to discover and restore the truant I have just failed to find in your manor of Leighton. Here am I newly come from there to report failure to the lord abbot as Richard's guardian, and here I find you have been doing my work for me while I was wild-goose chasing. I take that very kindly of you. I'll bear it in mind when it comes to considering the little matter of abduction and forcible imprisonment. It seems the woodland bird that whispered in my ear Richard was at Leighton told simple truth, for all I found no trace of him when I put it to the proof, and no one to admit he'd ever been there. You can have been out of the house barely half an hour by some other path when I reached it by the road.' His observant eye roved over Richard's taut figure and wary face, and came to rest on the abbot. 'Do you find him in good heart, and none the worse for being caged, my lord? He's come to no harm?'

'None to his body, certainly,' said Radulfus. 'But there is another matter unresolved. It seems a form of marriage took place last night at Leighton between Richard and Sir Fulke's daughter. To that Richard agrees, but he says that it was no real marriage, since the hermit Cuthred, who conducted it, is not a priest.'

'Do you tell me so?' Hugh pursed his lips in a soundless whistle, and swung round upon Fulke, who stood mute but watchful, all too aware of the need to step warily, and think now before he spoke. 'And what do you say to that, my lord?'

'I say it is an absurd charge that will never stand. He came to us with the good will of the brothers of Buildwas. I never heard word against him, and do not believe it now. We have dealt with him in good faith.'

'That, I am sure, is true,' said the abbot fairly. 'If there is anything in this charge, those who desired this marriage did not know of it.'

'But Richard, I think, did not desire it,' said Hugh,

184

with a somewhat grim smile. 'This cannot rest so, we must have out the truth.'

'So we are all agreed,' said Radulfus, 'and Sir Fulke has contracted to meet with me tomorrow after Prime at the hermitage, and hear what the man himself has to say. I was about to send to you, my lord sheriff, and tell you how this thing stands, and ask you to ride with me tomorrow. This scene,' he said, casting an authoritative glance round at his all too attentive flock, 'need not be prolonged, I think. If you will sup with me, Hugh, you shall hear all that has happened. Robert, have the brothers proceed. I am sorry our evening should have been so rudely disrupted. And, Paul ...' He looked down at Richard, who had one fist tightly clenched on a fold of Paul's habit, ready to hold fast had his tenure been threatened. 'Take him away, Paul, clean him up, feed him, and bring him to me after supper. He has a great deal to tell us that has not been told yet. There, you may disperse, all, there is no more here to see.'

The brothers edged aside obediently, and moved away somewhat raggedly to resume the interrupted order of the evening, though there would be furtive whispering even in the frater, and a great deal of excited talk afterwards in the leisured hour before Collations. Brother Paul marched his restored lamb away to be washed and made presentable before abbot and sheriff after supper. Aymer Bosiet, who had looked on with a certain malevolent satisfaction at someone else's crisis and confusion as a relief from his own, detached himself moodily and went across the court to the guest hall. But Cadfael, suddenly moved to look back, missed the one figure he was seeking. Rafe of Coventry was nowhere to be seen, and now that Cadfael came to think of it, he must have taken himself off quietly some time before the intriguing scene ended. Because he had no interest in it, and was quite capable of detaching himself from a spectacle which held most men spellbound? Or because he had found something in it that interested him deeply and urgently?

Fulke Astley was left hesitant, eye to eye with Hugh, and unsure whether it would serve him better to attempt explanations and justification, or to withdraw – if he was allowed to withdraw – in dignified silence, or at least with as few words as possible, and no concessions.

'Tomorrow, then, my lord,' he said, settling upon brevity, 'I shall be at Cuthred's hermitage as I have promised.'

'Good! And you might do well,' said Hugh, 'to acquaint the hermit's patroness with what's mooted against him. She may wish to be present herself. As at this time, my lord, I have no more immediate need of you. And should I have need in the future, I know where to find you. You may have good reason to be glad that Richard slipped his collar. Mischief undone is best forgotten. Provided, of course, there's no further mischief in contemplation.'

Of that Fulke made the best he could. With a curt reverence to the abbot he turned to reclaim his horse, mounted, and rode out at the gatehouse at a deliberate and stately walking pace.

Brother Cadfael, summoned to join the colloquy in the abbot's lodging after supper, turned aside on his way, on a sudden impulse, and went into the stable yard. Richard's black pony was contented and easy in his stall after his strenuous ride, groomed and watered and placidly feeding. But the big chestnut with the white blaze down his forehead was gone from his place, saddle and harness and all. Whatever the occasion for his silent departure, Rafe of Coventry had ridden forth on some local errand of his own.

Richard sat on a low stool at the abbot's knee, washed and brushed and meekly grateful to be home, and told his story, or as much of it as he felt justified in telling. He had an interested audience. There were present, besides the abbot, Hugh Beringar, Brother Cadfael at Hugh's accepted request, and Brother Paul, still reluctant to let the returned prodigal out of his sight. Richard had tolerated, even enjoyed, being shaken, slapped, scrubbed and made much of, the whole chaotic process which had produced this neat, shining schoolboy for the abbot's inspection. There were gaps in his story, and he knew they would be questioned, but Radulfus was of noble family, and would understand that a nobleman cannot betray those who have helped him, or even certain underlings who at the instance of their masters have injured him.

'Would you know them again, the two who captured you and took you into Wroxeter?' asked Hugh.

Richard considered the tempting prospect of revenge on the strapping young fellow who had laughed at his struggles and hindered him at the ford, but rejected it reluctantly as unworthy of his nobility.

'I couldn't be sure of them. It was getting dark.'

They did not press him. Instead, the abbot asked: 'Had you help in escaping from Leighton? You could hardly have broken out on your own, or you would have done it earlier.'

Answering that presented something of a problem. If he told the truth it would certainly do Hiltrude no harm here among his friends, but if ever it reached her father it could do her harm enough. Better stick to the story as she must have told it, that the door had been mistakenly left unbolted, and he had made his own way out. Cadfael observed the slight flush that mantled in the boy's well-scrubbed cheeks as he recounted that part of his adventures, with notable brevity and modesty. If it had been true he would have been exulting in it.

'He should have known what a slippery fish he had caught,' said Hugh, smiling. 'But you still have not told us why you rode out from the abbey in the first place, nor who told you that the hermit is not the priest he purports to be.'

This was the crux, and Richard had been thinking about it with unaccustomed labour and pain while he submitted to Brother Paul's affectionate homily on obedience and order, and the evil consequences to be expected from transgressing their rules. He looked up warily into the abbot's face, shot an uneasy glance at Hugh, whose reactions as the secular authority were less calculable, and said earnestly: 'Father, I said I would tell you, but I did not say I would tell any other. There is someone who might be harmed if I told what I know of him, and I know he has not deserved it. I can't bring him into danger.'

'I would not wish to make you break faith with any man,' said Radulfus gravely. 'Tomorrow I'll hear your confession myself, and you shall tell me then, and rest happy that you've done right, and your confidence is sacred. Now you'd best get to your bed, for I fancy you need it. Take him away, Paul!'

Richard made his ceremonial reverences, glad to have got off so lightly; but as he passed where Hugh sat he hesitated and stopped, plainly with something still on his mind.

'My lord, you said everyone at Leighton said I had never been there, of course they'd be afraid to say anything else. But did Hiltrude say so?'

Hugh could make connections perhaps faster than most men, but if he instantly made this one he gave no sign of it. With respectful gravity and a blank countenance he said: 'That's Astley's daughter? I never spoke with her, she was not in the house.'

Not there! So she did not have to lie. She must have slipped out discreetly as soon as her father was gone. Richard said a relieved and grateful goodnight, and went away to his bed with a lightened heart.

'She let him out, of course,' said Hugh as soon as the door had closed after the boy. 'She was a victim no less than he. Now I begin to see a pattern. Richard is seized as he rides back through Eyton forest, and what is there in Eyton forest and along that path but Eilmund's cottage and the hermitage? And to the hermitage we know he did not go. And who should walk into Shrewsbury about noon this day and send me off hotfoot to Leighton, which otherwise I should not have reached before tomorrow, but Eilmund's girl? And where she got the news she never clearly said, but some passing villager had said he'd seen a boy there who might well be Richard. And Richard, more forthrightly, *will not* say why he went off there alone, nor who told him the hermit is no true priest. Father, it seems to me that someone – let's not go so far as to name him! – has very good friends among our acquaintance. I hope they are as good judges! Well, tomorrow, at any rate, there'll be no hunting. Richard is safely home with you. And to tell truth, I doubt the other quarry will ever be flushed out of cover. Tomorrow our morning business is laid down for us. Let's first see that resolved.'

As soon as Prime was over they mounted and rode, Abbot Radulfus, Hugh Beringar and Brother Cadfael, who in any case was bound for Eilmund's cottage that day, to see how the forester was progressing. It was by no means the first time he had adjusted his legitimate visits to accommodate his reasoned curiosity. That he could count on Hugh to abet his plans was an added advantage, and an additional witness with a sharp eye for the infinitesimal changes by which the human countenance betrays itself might be invaluable in this encounter.

The morning was clearer of mist than in recent days, there had arisen a steady, drying wind that was crisping the fallen leaves in the forest rides, and colouring in muted gold those that still hung on the trees. The first frost would set the crowns of the forest blazing in russets and browns and flame. Another week or two, thought Cadfael, and there'd be no shelter for Hyacinth in the trees when inconvenient visitors came to the cottage, even the oaks would be half-naked. But in a few more days, God willing, Aymer would have abandoned his revenge, cut his losses, and made off in haste to secure his gains at home. His father's body was safely coffined, and though he had only two grooms with him, there was also Drogo's good horse as a remount for a new master in a hurry, and he would find no difficulty in hiring litter bearers at every way-stage on his journey. He had already scoured the whole region without success, and showed distinct signs of fretting between two desired ends, of which surely the more profitable would win in the end. Hyacinth's freedom might be nearer than he knew. And he had already served and deserved well, for who else could have got word to Richard that the hermit was not all he claimed to be? Hyacinth had travelled with him, known him well before he ever set foot in Buildwas. Hyacinth might well know things about his reverend master that were known to no one else.

The thick woodland hid the hermitage from them until they were very near. The sudden parting of the trees before them came always as a mild surprise, unveiling in an instant the small green clearing, the low pales that made a mere token fence about the garden, and the squat cell of grey stone, patched with the newer and paler grey of its recent repairs. The door of the house was open, as Cuthred had said it always was, to all who came. There was no one at work in the half-cleared garden, no sound from the interior of the cell, as they dismounted at the gateless gateway and tethered their horses. Cuthred must be within, by the silence perhaps at his prayers.

'Go first, Father,' said Hugh. 'This is more within your writ than mine.'

The abbot had to stoop his head to pass through the

stone doorway, and stood motionless for a moment within, until his eyes grew accustomed to the dimness. The single narrow window let in a subdued light at this hour by reason of the overhanging trees, and the shapes within the bare room took on substance only gradually, the narrow pallet against the wall, the small table and bench, the few vessels, plate and cup and pottery bowl. The doorless opening into the chapel revealed the stone block of the altar by the tiny glow of the lamp on it, but left all below in obscurity. The lamp had burned very low, was no more than a spark.

'Cuthred!' called Radulfus into the silence. 'Are you within? The abbot of Shrewsbury greets you in the name and grace of God!'

There was no answer but the small, stony echo. Hugh stepped past and advanced into the chapel doorway, and there halted abruptly, drawing in hissing breath.

Cuthred was indeed within, but not at his prayers. He lay sprawled on his back beneath the altar, head and shoulders propped against the stone, as though he had fallen or been hurled backwards while facing the doorway. His habit billowed in dark folds round him, exposing sinewy feet and ankles, and the breast of the gown was matted and blackened by a long stain, where he had bled from the stab that killed him. His face, between the tangled dark fell of hair and beard, was contorted in a grimace which might have been of agony or of rage, the lips drawn back from strong teeth, the eyes glaring half-open. His arms were flung wide, and beside his right hand, as though released in the moment of falling, a long dagger lay spilled on the stone floor.

Priest or no, Cuthred was never going to testify in his own defence. There was no need to question or touch to see that he was some hours dead, and dead by violence.

'Christ aid!' said the abbot in a harsh whisper, and stood

191

like stone over the body. 'God have mercy on a murdered man! Who can have done this thing?'

Hugh was on his knees beside the dead man, touching flesh already grown chill and waxen in texture. There was nothing to be demanded now of the hermit Cuthred, and nothing to be done for him in this world, short of the final balance of justice. 'Dead some hours at least. A second man struck down within my shire, and no requital yet for the first! For God's sake, what is it let loose in these woods to such devilish effect?'

'Can this possibly have any bearing,' wondered the abbot heavily, 'on what the boy has told us? Has someone struck first to prevent him ever answering in his own defence? To bury the proof with the man? There has been such resolute plotting over this marriage, all for greed of land, but surely it could not be carried so far as murder?'

'If this is murder,' said Brother Cadfael, rather to himself than to any other, but aloud. He had remained still and silent in the doorway all this time, looking round him intently at the room he remembered well from a single visit, a room so sparsely furnished that every detail was memorable. The chapel was larger than the living room of the cell, there was room here for free movement, even for a struggle. Only the eastern wall was built up beneath its tiny square window with the great fashioned stone of the altar, and atop that the small carved reliquary on which stood the silver cross, and on either side a silver candlestick holding a tall candle, unlighted. On the stone before the reliquary, the lamp, and laid neatly in front of it — But there was nothing laid in front of it. Strange to have the man thrown down in disordered and disregarded death, but the altar so trim and undisturbed. And only one thing missing from the picture Cadfael carried in his mind's eye. The breviary in the leather binding fit for a prince, tooled in intricate scrolls and leaves and gilded ornament, was gone.

Hugh rose from his knees and stood back to view the room as Cadfael was viewing it. They had seen it together, by rights their memories should match. He shot a sharp glance at Cadfael. 'You see cause to doubt it?'

'I see that he was armed.' Hugh was already looking down at the long dagger that lay so close to Cuthred's half-open hand. He had not touched it. He stood back and touched nothing, now that he knew the discarded flesh before him was cold. 'He loosed his hold as he fell. That dagger is his. It was used. There is blood on it – not his blood. Whatever happened here, it was no furtive stabbing in the back.'

That was certain. The wound was over his heart, the stiffening patch of blood from it had reached his middle. The dagger that killed this man had been withdrawn and let out his lifeblood. Its fellow here on the floor was stained for only a thumb's length from its tip, and had barely shed one drop upon the stone where it lay.

'You are saying,' said the abbot, stirring out of his horrified stillness, 'that this was a fight? But how should a holy hermit keep sword or dagger about him? Even for his own defence against thieves and vagabonds such a man should not resort to arms, but put his trust in God.'

'And if this was a thief,' said Cadfael, 'he was a most strange one. Here are cross and candlesticks of silver, and they are not taken, not even shaken from their places in the struggle. Or else they were set right afterwards.'

'That is truth,' said the abbot, and shook his head over so inexplicable a mystery. 'This was not done for robbery. But what, then? Why should any man attack a solitary religious, one without possessions by choice, one whose only valuables are the furnishings of his altar? He has lived unmolested and serviceable among us, by all accounts open and accessible to all who came with their needs and troubles. Why should anyone wish to harm him? Can this be the same hand that killed the lord of

Bosiet, Hugh? Or must we fear we have two murderers loose among us?'

'There is still this lad of his,' said Hugh, frowning over the thought but unable quite to discard it. 'We have not found him, and I had begun to think that he had made off westward and got clean away into Wales. But it's still possible that he has remained close here. There may well be those who are sheltering him and believe in him. We have grounds for thinking so. If he is indeed the villein who ran from Bosiet, he had some cause to rid himself of his master. And say that Cuthred, who disowned him on hearing he had been deceived in him, found out his hiding place now – yes, then he might also have cause to kill Cuthred. All of which is mere matter for conjecture. And yet cannot be quite rejected.'

No, thought Cadfael, not until Aymer Bosiet has gone his way back to Northamptonshire, and Hyacinth can come out of hiding and speak for himself, and Eilmund and Annet, yes, and Richard, can speak for him. For between the three of them I'm sure it can be proved exactly where Hyacinth has been at all times, and he has not been here. No, we need not trouble about Hyacinth. But I wish, he thought regretfully, I wish they had let me confide in Hugh long ago.

The sun was higher in the sky by now, and found a better angle through the leafage of the trees, to shed more light upon the distorted and lamentable body. The skirts of the rusty black habit were gathered together at one side, as if a large fist had drawn them into its grasp, and there the woollen cloth was clotted with a sticky dark stain. Cadfael kneeled and drew the folds apart, and they separated with a faint, rustling reluctance.

'Here he wiped his dagger,' said Cadfael, 'before sheathing it again.'

'Twice,' said Hugh, peering, for there was a second such smear, barely perceptible. Coolly and efficiently, a methodical man cleaning his tools after finishing his work! 'And see here, this casket on the altar.' He had stepped carefully round the body to look closely at the carved wooden box, and draw a finger along the edge of the lid, above the lock. The flaw was no longer than a thumbnail, but showed where the point of a dagger had been thrust in to prise the box open. He lifted down the cross and raised the lid, which gave readily. The lock was sprung and broken, and the casket was empty. Only the faint aromatic scent of the wood stirred upon the air. There was not even a filming of dust within; the box had been well made.

'So something was taken, after all,' said Cadfael. He did not mention the breviary, though he could not doubt that Hugh had noticed its absence as readily as he.

'But not the silver. What could a hermit have about him of greater value than Dame Dionisia's silver? He came to Buildwas on foot, carrying only a scrip like any other pilgrim, though to be sure his boy Hyacinth also carried a pack for him. Now I wonder,' said Hugh, 'whether this casket was also the lady's gift, or whether he brought it with him?'

They had been so intent on what they were observing within that they had failed to pay attention to what was happening without, and there had been no sound to warn them. And in the shock of what they had discovered they had almost forgotten that at least one more witness was expected at this meeting. But it was a woman's voice, not Fulke's, that suddenly spoke in the doorway behind them, high and confidently, and with arrogant disapproval in its tone.

'No need to wonder, my lord. It would be simple and civil to ask me.'

All three of them swung round in dismayed alarm to stare at Dame Dionisia, tall and erect and defiant between them and the brightening daylight from which she had come, and which left her half-blind at stepping into this relative obscurity. They were between her and the body, and there was nothing else to startle or alarm her but the very fact that Hugh stood with his hand on the open casket, and the cross had been lifted down. This she saw clearly, while the dying lamp lit nothing else so well. And she was outraged.

'My lord, what is this? What are you doing with these sacred things? And where is Cuthred? Have you dared to meddle in his absence?'

The abbot moved to place himself more solidly between her and the dead man, and advanced to persuade her out of the chapel.

'Madam, you shall know all, but I beg you, come out into the other room and be seated, and wait but a moment until we set all in order here. Here is no irreverence, I promise you.'

The light from without was still further darkened by the bulk of Astley looming at her shoulder, blocking the retreat the abbot was urging. She stood her ground, imperious and indignant.

'Where is Cuthred? Does he know you are here? How is it he has left his cell? He never does so —' The lie ended on her lips in a sharp indrawn breath. Beyond the abbot's robe she had seen one small pallor jutting from the huddle of dark skirts, a foot that had shaken loose its sandal. Her vision was clearer now. She evaded the abbot's restraining hand and thrust strongly past him. All her questions were answered in one shattering glance. Cuthred was indeed there, and on this occasion at least had not left his cell.

The long, patrician composure of her face turned waxen grey and seemed to disintegrate, its sharp lines fallen slack. She uttered a great wail, rather of terror than of grief, and half-sprang, half-fell backwards into the arms of Fulke Astley.

Chapter Thirteen

HE neither swooned nor wept. She was a woman who did not lightly do either. But she sat for a long while bolt upright on Cuthred's bed in the living room, rigid and pale and staring straight before her, clean through the stone wall before her face, and a long way beyond. It was doubtful if she heard any of the abbot's carefully measured words, or the uneasy blusterings of Astley, alternately offering her gallantries of comfort she did not value or need, and recalling feverishly that this crime left all questions unanswered, and in some none too logical way went to prove that the hermit had indeed been a priest, and the marriage he had solemnized still a marriage. At least she paid no attention to either. She had gone far beyond any such considerations. All her old plans had become irrelevant. She had looked closely on sudden death, unconfessed, unshriven, and she wanted no part of it. Cadfael saw it in her eyes as he came out from the chapel, having done what he could to lay Cuthred's body straight and seemly, now that he had read all it had to tell him. Through that death she was confronting her own, and she had no intention of meeting it with all her sins upon her. Or for many years yet, but she had had warning that if she was willing to wait, death might not be.

At last she asked, in a perfectly ordinary voice, perhaps milder than any she normally used to her household or tenants, but without moving, or withdrawing her eyes from her ultimate enemy: 'Where is the lord sheriff?'

'He's gone to get hold of a party to carry the hermit away from here,' said the abbot. 'To Eaton, if you so wish, to be cared for there, since you were his patroness. Or, if it will spare you painful reminders, to the abbey. He shall be properly received there.'

'It would be a kindness,' she said slowly, 'if you would take him. I no longer know what to think. Fulke has told me what my grandson says. The hermit cannot answer for himself now, nor can I for him. I believed without question that he was a priest.'

'That, madam,' said Radulfus, 'I never doubted.'

The focus of her stare had shortened, a little colour had come back into her waxen face. She was on her way back, soon she would stir and brace herself, and turn to look at the real world about her, instead of the bleak distances of judgement day. And she would face whatever she had to face with the same ferocious courage and obstinacy with which she had formerly conducted her battles.

'Father,' she said, turning towards him with abrupt resolution, 'if I come to the abbey tonight, will you yourself hear my confession? I shall sleep the better when I have shed my sins.'

'I will,' said the abbot.

She was ready then to be taken home, and Fulke was all too anxious to escort her. No doubt he, who had very little to say here in company, would be voluble enough in private with her. He had not her intelligence, nor nearly so acute an imagination. If Cuthred's death had cast any shadow on him, it was merely the vexation of not being able to claim proof of his daughter's marriage, not at all a bony hand on his shoulder. So at any rate thought Brother Cadfael, watching him arm Dionisia to where

198

her jennet was tethered, in haste to have her away and be free of the abbot's daunting presence.

At the last moment, with the reins gathered in her hand, she suddenly turned back. Her face had regained all its proud tension and force, she was herself again.

'I have only now remembered,' she said, 'that the lord sheriff was wondering about the casket in there on the altar. That was Cuthred's. He brought it with him.'

When the abbot and the litter-bearers and Hugh were all on their slow and sombre way back to the abbey, Cadfael took a last look round the deserted chapel, the more attentively because he was alone and without distractions. There was not a single stain of blood on the flags of the floor where the body had lain, only the drop or two left by the point of Cuthred's own dagger. He had certainly wounded his adversary, though the wound could not be deep. Cadfael sighted a course from the altar to the doorway, and followed it with a newly lighted candle in his hand. In the chapel he found nothing more, and in the outer room the floor was of beaten earth, and such faint traces would be hard to find after the passage of hours. But on the doorstone he found three drops shaken, dried now but plain to be seen, and on the new and unstained timber with which the left jamb of the doorway had been repaired there was a blurred smear of blood at the level of his own shoulder, where a gashed and bloodied sleeve had brushed past.

A man no taller than himself, then, and Cuthred's dagger had taken him in the shoulder or upper arm on the left side, as a stroke aimed at his heart might well do.

Cadfael had intended to ride on to Eilmund's cottage, but on impulse he changed his mind, for it seemed to him that after all he could not afford to miss whatever might follow when Cuthred's body was brought into the court at the abbey, to the consternation of most, the relief, perhaps, of some, and the possible peril of one in particular. Instead of cutting through the forest rides, he mounted and rode back in haste towards Shrewsbury, to overtake the funeral procession.

They had a curious audience as soon as they entered the Foregate, and the camp-following of inquisitive boys and attendant dogs followed at their heels all along the highroad, and even the respectable citizens came after them at a more discreet distance, wary of abbot and sheriff but avid for information, and breeding rumours as fast as flies breed on summer middens. Even when the cortège turned in at the gatehouse the good folk from market and smithy and tavern gathered outside to peer expectantly within, and continued their speculations with relish.

And there in the great court, as they carried one bier in from the world, was another funeral party busy assembling to leave. Drogo Bosiet's sealed coffin was mounted on a low, light cart, hired in the town with its driver for this first day's travelling, which would be on a good road. Warin stood holding two of the saddled horses, while the younger groom was busy adjusting a full saddle-roll to get the weight properly balanced before loading it. At sight of all this activity Cadfael drew a deep breath of gratitude, sensible that one danger, at least, was being lifted away even earlier than he had dared to hope. Aymer had finally made up his mind. He was bound for home, to make sure of his inheritance.

The attendants on one death could not forbear from stopping what they were doing to stare at the attendants on the other. And Aymer, coming out from the guest hall with Brother Denis beside him to wish the departing train godspeed, halted at the top of the steps to take in the scene with surprise and sharp speculation, his eyes dwelling longest on the covered form and face. He came striding down to cross purposefully to where Hugh was just dismounting.

'What's this, my lord? Another death? Has your hunt brought down my quarry at last? But dead?' He hardly knew whether to be glad or sorry if the corpse was that of his lost villein. The money and favour Hyacinth's skills brought in were valuable, but revenge would also be a satisfying gain, and just when he had despaired of winning either, and made up his mind to go home.

Abbot Radulfus, too, had dismounted, and stood looking on with an uncommunicative face, for the two groups carried a curious and disturbing suggestion of a mirror image, gathered about the arriving and departing dead. The abbey grooms who had come to take the bridles of abbot and sheriff hung upon the fringes of the assembly, reluctant to move away.

'No,' said Hugh, 'this is no man of yours. If the boy we've been hunting is yours. Of him we've seen no sign, whether he is or no. You're bound for home, then?'

'I've wasted time and effort enough, I'll waste no more, though I grudge letting him go free. Yes, we're away now. I'm needed at home, there's work waiting for me. Who is this one you've brought back?'

'The hermit who was set up no long time ago in Eyton forest. Your father went to visit him,' said Hugh, 'thinking the servant he kept might be the fellow you were looking for, but the youngster had already taken to his heels, so it's never been put to the test.'

'I remember, so the lord abbot told me. So this is the man! I never went to him again, what use if the lad he kept was gone?' He looked curiously down at the shrouded figure. The bearers had laid down their burden, awaiting orders where to take the dead. Aymer stooped and turned back the brychan from Cuthred's face. They had drawn back the wild fell of hair from his temples, and brushed down his bushy beard into order, and the full light of noon shone over the lean countenance, the deep-set eyes, the lofty lids a little bruised and bluish now, the long, straight, patrician nose and full lips within the dark beard. The glare of the half-open eyes was now veiled, the snarl on the drawn-back lips carefully smoothed out to restore his harsh comeliness. Aymer leaned closer, startled and disbelieving.

'But I know this man! No, that's to say too much, he never said his name. But I've seen him and talked with him. A hermit – he? I never saw sign of it then! He wore his hair trimmed Norman fashion, and had a short, clipped beard, not this untended bush, and he was well clothed in good riding gear, boots and all, not this drab habit and sandals. And he wore sword and dagger into the bargain,' said Aymer positively, 'and as if he was well accustomed to the use of them, too.'

Until he looked up again he was not fully aware of the significance of what he had said, but Hugh's intent face and instant question made it plain he had touched on something more vital than he knew.

'You are sure?' said Hugh.

'Certain, my lord. It was only one night's lodging, but I diced with him for the dinner, and watched my father play a game of chess with him. I'm certain!'

'Where was this? And when?'

'At Thame, when we were looking towards London for Brand. We lodged overnight with the white monks at their new abbey there. This man was there before us, we came well into the evening, and went on south next day. I can't say the exact day, but it was towards the end of September.'

'Then if you know him again,' said Hugh, 'changed as his condition is, would your father also have recognised him at sight?'

'Surely he would, my lord. His eyes were sharper than mine. He'd sat over a chessboard with the man, eye to eye. He'd know him again.'

And so he had, thought Cadfael, when he went man-hunting to the cell in the forest, and came face to face with the hermit Cuthred who had been no hermit a month or so earlier. And he had not lived to return to the abbey and let out to any man what he knew. And what if he knew no great evil of this transformed being? He might still let fall to other ears the casual word that would mean more to them than ever it had to him, and bring to the cell in Eyton forest someone in search of more than a runaway villein, and worse, surely, than a spurious priest. But he had not lived to get further on his return journey than a close forest thicket, sufficiently far from the hermitage to remove suspicion from a local saint reputed never to leave his cell.

The evidence of circumstances is not positive proof, yet Cadfael had no doubts left. There before them the coffined body and the new corpse rested for a few moments side by side, before Prior Robert directed the bearers to the mortuary chapel, and Aymer Bosiet covered Cuthred's face again, and turned afresh to his own preparations for departure. His mind was on other things, why distract and detain him now? But Cadfael did suddenly take thought to ask one curious question.

'What manner of horse was he riding when he halted overnight at Thame?'

Aymer turned from fastening the straps of his saddle-bags in detached surprise, opened his mouth to answer, and found himself at a loss, frowning thoughtfully over his recollections of that night.

'He was there before us. There were two horses in the priory stables when we came. And he'd left before us next morning. But now you come to ask, when we got to horse, the same two beasts we saw there the night before were still in their stalls. That's strange! What would such a well-found man, knightly by the look of him and his arms – what would he be doing without a horse?'

'Ah, well, he may have stabled it somewhere else,' said Cadfael, abandoning the puzzle as trivial.

But it was not trivial, it was the key to open a very strange door in the mind. There before so many eyes lay the slayer and the slain, side by side, justice already done.

But who, then, had slain the slayer?

They were gone, all of them, Aymer on his father's handsome light roan horse, Warin with the horse Aymer had ridden on the outward journey now on a leading rein, the young groom with the carter and the cart. After the first day-stages Aymer would probably be off at speed, leaving the grooms to bring the coffin after at their slower pace, and most likely sending other retainers back along the way to relieve them, once he reached home. In the mortuary chapel Cadfael had seen Cuthred's body laid out in seemly fashion, hair and beard trimmed, not, perhaps, so closely as the knight at Thame had worn them, but enough to display, in the fixed and austere tranquillity of death, a face appropriate enough to a dignified religious. Unfair that a murderer should look as noble in death as any of the empress's paladins.

Hugh was closeted with the abbot, and as yet had said no word to Cadfael of what he made of Aymer's witness, but by the very questions he had asked it was clear he had made the same connections Cadfael had made, and could not have failed to arrive at the same conclusion. He would speak of it first with Radulfus. My part now, thought Cadfael, is to bring Hyacinth out of hiding, and let him shake himself loose from all suspicion of wrong-doing. Barring, of course, the occasional theft to fill his belly while he lived wild, and a lie or two by way of preserving himself alive at all. And Hugh won't grudge him those. And that should settle the matter of Cuthred's ordination once for all, if there's still any lingering question about it. A sudden conversion can turn a soldier into a hermit, yes, but it takes much longer than that to make a priest.

He waited for Hugh in his workshop in the herb garden, where Hugh would certainly come looking for him as soon as he left the abbot. It was quiet and aromatic and homely within there, and Cadfael had been too much away from it of late. He would have to be thinking of replenishing his stocks of the regular winter needs very soon, before the coughs and colds began, and the elder joints started to creak and groan. Brother Winfrid could be trusted to take excellent care of all the work in the garden, the digging and weeding and planting, but here within he had much to learn. One more ride, thought Cadfael, to see how Eilmund does, and let Hyacinth know he can and should come forward and speak up for himself, and then I shall be glad to settle down to work here at home.

Hugh came in through the gardens and sat down beside his friend with a brief, preoccupied smile, and was silent for some moments. 'What I do not understand,' he said then, 'is why? Whatever he was, whatever he has done, aforetime, here he seems to have lived blameless. What can there have been, perilous enough to make him want to stop Bosiet's mouth? It may be a suspect thing to change one's dress and appearance and way of life, but it is not a crime. What was there, more than that, to justify murder? What is there of that enormity, except murder itself?'

'Ah!' said Cadfael with a relieved sigh. 'Yes, I thought you had seen it all as I saw it. But no, I do not think it was murder he had to hide in the obscurity of a hermit's gown and a forest cell. That was my first thought. But it is not so simple.'

'As so often,' said Hugh with his sudden, crooked smile, 'I think you know something that I do not. And what was that about his horse, down there in Thame? What has his horse to do with it?'

'Not his horse, but the fact that he had none. What's a soldier or a knight doing travelling on foot? But a pilgrim may, and never be noticed. But as to knowing something I would have told you long ago if I had been let – yes, Hugh, I do. I know where Hyacinth is. Against my will I promised to say nothing until Aymer Bosiet had given up the pursuit and taken himself off home. As now he has, and now the boy can come forward and speak for himself, as, trust me, he's well able to do.'

'So that's it,' said Hugh, eyeing his friend without any great surprise. 'Well, who can blame him for being wary, what does he know of me? And for all that I knew, he could well have been Bosiet's murderer, we knew of no other with as good a cause. Now he need say no word on that score, the debt is known and paid. And as for his freedom, he need fear nothing from me on that head. I have enough to do without playing the errand boy for Northamptonshire. Bring him forth whenever you like, he may yet shed light on some things we do not know.'

So Cadfael thought, too, reflecting how little Hyacinth had had to say about his relations with his sometime master. Candid enough, among friends, about his own vagabondage and the mischief done in Eilmund's coppice, he had scrupulously refrained from casting any aspersions against Cuthred. But now that Cuthred was dead and known for a murderer Hyacinth might be willing to extend his candour, though surely he had known no great harm of his fellow traveller, and certainly nothing of murder.

'Where is he?' asked Hugh. 'Not far, I fancy, if it was he who got word to young Richard that he could safely go through that marriage service. Who would be more likely to know Cuthred for an impostor?'

'No further,' said Cadfael, 'than Eilmund's cottage, and welcome there to father and daughter alike. And I'm bound there now to see how Eilmund's faring. Shall I bring the boy back with me?'

'Better than that,' said Hugh heartily, 'I'll ride with you. Better not hale him out of cover until I've called off the hunt by official order, and made it known he has nothing to answer, and is free to walk the town and look for work like any other man.'

*　　*　　*

In the stable yard, when he went to saddle up, Cadfael found the bright chestnut horse with the white brow standing like a glossy statue under his master's affectionate hands, content and trusting after easy exercise, and being polished to a rippling copper sheen. Rafe of Coventry turned to see who came, and smiled the guarded, calm smile with which Cadfael was becoming familiar.

'Bound out again, Brother? This must be a wearing day you've had.'

'For all of us,' said Cadfael, hoisting down his saddle, 'but we may hope the worst is over. And you? Have you prospered in your errand?'

'Well, I thank you! Very well! Tomorrow morning, after Prime,' he said, turning to face Cadfael fully, and his voice as always measured and composed, 'I shall be leaving. I have already told Brother Denis so.'

Cadfael went on with his preparations for a minute or two in silence. Converse with Rafe of Coventry found silences acceptable. 'If you'll be riding far the first day,' he said then simply, 'I think you may need my services before you set out. He drew blood,' he said briefly, by way of adequate explanation. And when Rafe was slow to answer: 'A part of my function is to tend illness and injury. There is no seal of confession in my art, but there is a decent reticence.'

'I have bled before,' said Rafe, but he smiled, a degree beyond his common smile.

'As you choose. But I am here. If you need me, come to me. It is not wise to neglect a wound, nor to try it too far in the saddle.' He tested the girth, and gathered the reins to mount. The horse sidled and shifted playfully, eager for action.

'I'll bear it in mind,' said Rafe, 'and I thank you. You will not stop me leaving,' he said in amiable but solemn warning.

'Have I tried?' said Cadfael, and swung himself up into the saddle and rode out into the court.

'I never told all the truth,' said Hyacinth, seated beside the hearth in Eilmund's cottage, with the firelight like a copper gloss on cheekbones and jaw and brow, 'not even here to Annet. As to myself I did, she knows the worst I could tell. But not of Cuthred. I knew he was a rogue and a vagabond, but so was I, and I knew nothing worse of him than that, so I kept my mouth shut. One rogue in hiding doesn't betray another. But now you tell me he's a murderer. And dead!'

'And out of further harm,' said Hugh reasonably, 'at least in this world. I need to know all you can tell. Where did you join fortunes with him?'

'At Northampton, at the Cluniac priory, as I told Annet and Eilmund, though not quite as I told it. He was no habited pilgrim then, he was in good dark clothes, with cloak and capuchon, and armed, though he kept his sword out of sight. It was almost by chance we got into talk, or I thought so. But I fancy he guessed I was running from something, and he made no secret he was, too, and suggested we might be safer and pass unnoticed together. We were both heading north and west. The pilgrim was his notion, he had the face and bearing for it. Well, you've seen him, you know. I stole the habit for him from the priory store. The scallop shell came easy. The medal of Saint James he had – it may even have been his by right, who knows? By the time we got to Buildwas he had his part by rote, and his hair and beard were well grown. And he came very apt to the dame at Eaton, for her own ends. Oh, she knew no worse of him than that he was willing to earn his keep with her. He said he was a priest, and she believed it. I knew he was none, he owned as much when we were alone. He laughed about it. But he had the gift of tongues, he could carry it off. She gave him the hermitage, so close and handy to the abbey's woods, to do all the mischief he could in the abbot's despite. I said that was my part, and he knew nothing of it, but I lied for him. He'd never blabbed on me, no more would I on him.'

'He abandoned you,' said Hugh flatly, 'as soon as he knew the hunt was up for you. You need not scruple to speak out on his account.'

'Well – I live, and he's dead,' said Hyacinth. 'No call now for me to bear him any grudge. You know about Richard? I'd talked with him only once, but he took me so for a true man he'd hear no wrong of me, nor have me run to earth and dragged back into villeinage. That set me up again in my own respect. I never knew till afterwards that he'd been seized like that on his way back, but I was forced to run or hide, and chose to hide till I could make shift to find him. If it hadn't been for Eilmund's goodness to me, and after I'd been a thorn in his flesh, too, your men might have had me a dozen times over. But now you know I never laid hand on Bosiet. And Eilmund and Annet can tell you I've not been a step away from here since I came back from Leighton. What can have happened to Cuthred I know no more than you.'

'Less, I daresay,' said Hugh mildly, and looked across the fire at Cadfael, smiling. 'Well, after all you may call yourself a lucky lad. From tomorrow you'll be in no peril at the hands of any of my people, you can be off into the town and find yourself a master. And which of your names do you choose to keep for a new life? Best have but one, that we may all know with whom we have to deal.'

'Whichever is pleasing to Annet,' said Hyacinth. 'It's she will be calling me by it from this on lifelong.'

'I might have something to say to that,' grunted Eilmund from his corner on the other side of the hearth. 'You mind your impudence, or I'll make you sweat for my good will.' But he sounded remarkably complacent about it, as though they had already arrived at an understanding to which this admonitory growl was merely a gruff counterpoint.

'It was Hyacinth first pleased me,' said Annet. She had kept herself out of the circle until now, like a dutiful daughter, attentive with cup and pitcher, but wanting and needing no voice in the men's affairs. Not from modesty or submission Cadfael judged, but because she already had what she wanted, and was assured no one, sheriff nor father nor overlord, had either the power or the will to wrest it from her. 'You stay Hyacinth,' she said serenely, 'and let Brand go.'

She was wise, there was no sense in going back, none even in looking back. Brand had been a villein and landless in Northamptonshire, Hyacinth would be a craftsman and free in Shrewsbury.

'In a year and a day,' said Hyacinth, 'from the day I find a master to take me, I'll come and ask for your good will, Master Eilmund. Not before!'

'And if I think you've earned it,' said Eilmund, 'you shall have it.'

They rode home together in the deepening dusk, as they had so often ridden together since first they encountered in wary contention, wit against wit, and came to a gratifying stand at the end of the match, fast friends. The night was still and mild, the morning would be misty again, the lush valley fields a translucent blue sea. The forest smelled of autumn, ripe, moist earth, bursting fungus, the sweet, rich rot of leaves.

'I have transgressed against my vocation,' said Cadfael, at once solaced and saddened by the season and the hour. 'I know it. I undertook the monastic life, but now I am not sure I could support it without you, without these stolen excursions outside the walls. For so they are. True, I am often sent upon legitimate labours here without, but also I steal, I take more than is my due by right. Worse, Hugh, I do not repent me! Do you suppose there is room within the bounds of grace for one who has set his hand to the plough, and every little while abandons his furrow to turn back among the sheep and lambs?'

'I think the sheep and lambs might think so,' said Hugh, gravely smiling. 'He would have their prayers. Even the black sheep and the grey, like some you've argued for against God and me in your time.'

'There are very few all black,' said Cadfael. 'Dappled, perhaps, like this great rangy beast you choose to ride. Most of us have a few mottles about us. As well, maybe, it makes for a more tolerant judgement of the rest of God's creatures. But I have sinned, and most of all in relishing my sin. I shall do penance by biding dutifully within the walls through the winter, unless I'm sent forth, and then I'll make haste with my task and hurry back.'

'Until the next waif stumbles across your path. And when is this penance to begin?'

'As soon as this matter is fittingly ended.'

'Why, these are oracular utterances!' said Hugh, laughing. 'And when will that be?'

'Tomorrow,' said Cadfael. 'If God wills, tomorrow.'

Chapter Fourteen

ON HIS way down the court to the stables, leading his horse, and with the better part of an hour left before Compline, Cadfael saw Dame Dionisia coming from the abbot's lodging, and walking with sober step and decorously covered head towards the guest hall. Her back was as erect as ever, her gait as firm and proud, but somewhat slower than was her wont, and the draped head was lowered, with eyes on the ground rather than fixed challengingly into the distance before her. Not a word would ever be said concerning her confession, but Cadfael doubted if she had left anything out. She was not one to do things by halves. There would be no more attempts to extract Richard from the abbot's care. Dionisia had suffered too profound a reverse to take any such risks again until time had dimmed the recollection of sudden unshriven death coming to meet her.

It seemed she meant to stay overnight, perhaps to make her peace tomorrow, in her own arbitrary fashion, with a grandson by this time fast asleep in his bed, blessedly unmarried still, and back where he preferred to be. The boys would sleep well tonight, absolved of their sins and with their lost member restored. Matter for devout thanksgiving. And as for the dead man in the mortuary chapel, bearing a name which it seemed could hardly be

212

his name, he cast no shadow on the world of the children.

Cadfael led his horse into the stable yard, lighted by two torches at the gate, unsaddled him and rubbed him down. There was no sound within there but a small sighing of the breeze that had sprung up with evening, and the occasional easy shift and stir of hooves in the stalls. He stabled his beast and hung up his harness, and turned to depart.

There was someone standing in the gateway, compact and still. 'Good even, Brother!' said Rafe of Coventry.

'Is it you?' said Cadfael. 'And were you looking for me? I'm sorry to have kept you up late, and you with a journey to make in the morning.'

'I saw you come down the court. You made an offer,' said the quiet voice. 'If it is still open I should like to take advantage of it. I find it is not so easy to dress a wound neatly with one hand.'

'Come!' said Cadfael. 'Let's go to my hut in the garden, we can be private there.'

It was deep dusk, but not yet dark. The late roses in the garden loomed spikily on overgrown stems, half their leaves shed, ghostly floating pallors in the dimness. Within the walls of the herb garden, high and sheltering, warmth lingered. 'Wait,' said Cadfael, 'till I make light.'

It took him a few minutes to get a spark he could blow gently into flame, and set to the wick of his lamp. Rafe waited without murmur or movement until the light burned up steadily, and then came into the hut and looked about him with interest at the array of jars and flasks, the scales and mortars, and the rustling bunches of herbs overhead, stirring headily in the draught from the doorway. Silently he stripped off his coat, and drew down his shirt from the shoulder until he could withdraw his arm from the sleeve. Cadfael brought the lamp, and set it where the light would best illuminate the stained and crumpled bandage that covered the wound. Rafe sat patient and attentive on the bench against the wall, steadily eyeing the weathered face that stooped over him.

'Brother,' he said deliberately, 'I think I owe you a name.'

'I have a name for you,' said Cadfael. 'Rafe is enough.'

'For you, perhaps. Not for me. Where I take help, generously given, there I repay with truth. My name is Rafe de Genville . . .'

'Hold still now,' said Cadfael. 'This is stuck fast, and will hurt.'

The soiled dressing came away with a wrench, but if it did indeed hurt, de Genville suffered it as indifferently as he did the foregoing pain. The gash was long, running down from the shoulder into the upper arm, but not deep; but the flesh was so sliced that the lips gaped, and a single hand had not been able to clamp them together. 'Keep still! We can better this, you'll have an ugly scar else. But you'll need help when it's dressed again.'

'Once away from here I can get help, and who's to know how I got the gash? But you do know, Brother. He drew blood, you said. There is not very much you do not know, but perhaps a little I can still tell you. My name is Rafe de Genville, I am a vassal, and God knows a friend to Brian FitzCount, and a liege man to my overlord's lady, the empress. I will not suffer gross wrong to be done to either, while I have my life. Well, he'll draw no more blood, neither from any of the king's party nor oversea, in the service of Geoffrey of Anjou – which I think was his final intent, when the time seemed right.'

Cadfael folded a new dressing closely about the long gash. 'Lend your right hand here, and hold this firmly, it shuts the wound fast. You'll get no more bleeding, or very little, and it should heal closed. But rest it as best you can on the road.'

'I will so.' The bandage rolled firmly over the shoulder and round the arm, flat and neat. 'You have a skilled hand, Brother. If I could I would take you with me as a prize of war.'

'They'll have need of all the surgeons and physicians they can get in Oxford, I fear,' Cadfael acknowledged ruefully.

'Ah, not there, not this tide. There'll be no breaking into Oxford until the earl brings up his army. I doubt it even then. No, I go back to Brian at Wallingford first, to restore him what is his.'

Cadfael secured the bandage above the elbow, and held the sleeve of the shirt carefully as Rafe thrust his arm back into it. It was done. Cadfael sat down beside him, face to face, eye to eye. The silence that came down upon them was like the night, mild, tranquil, gently melancholy.

'It was a fair fight,' said Rafe after a long pause, looking into and through Cadfael's eyes to see again the bare stony chapel in the forest. 'I laid by my sword, seeing he had none. His dagger he'd kept.'

'And used,' said Cadfael, 'on the man who had seen him in his own shape at Thame, and might have called his vocation in question. As the son did, after Cuthred was dead, and never knew he was looking at his father's murderer.'

'Ah, so that was it! I wondered.'

'And did you find what you came for?'

'I came for him,' said Rafe grimly. 'But, yes, I understand you. Yes, I found it, in the reliquary on the altar. Not all in coin. Gems go into a small compass, and are easily carried. Her own jewels, that she valued. And valued even more the man to whom she sent them.'

'They said that there was also a letter.'

'There is a letter. I have it. You saw the breviary?'

'I saw it. A prince's book.'

'An empress's. There is a secret fold in the binding, where a fine, small leaf can be hidden. When they were apart, the breviary went back and forth between them by trusted messenger. God he knows what she may not have written to him now, at the lowest ebb of fortune, separated from him by a few miles that might as well be

215

the width of the world, and with the king's army gripping her and her few to strangulation. In the extreme of despair, who regards wisdom, who puts a guard on tongue or pen? I have not sought to know. He shall have it and read it for whose heart's consolation it was meant. One other has read it, and might have made use of it,' said Rafe harshly, 'but he is of no account now.'

His voice had gathered a great tide of passion that yet could not disrupt its steely control, though it caused his disciplined body to quiver like an arrow in flight, vibrating to the force of his devoted love and implacable hate. The letter he carried, with its broken seal as testimony to a cold and loathsome treachery, he would never unfold, the matter within was sacred as the confessional, between the woman who had written and the man to whom it was written. Cuthred had trespassed even into this holy ground, but Cuthred was dead. It did not seem to Cadfael that the penalty was too great for the wrong committed.

'Tell me, Brother,' said Rafe de Genville, the wave of passion subsiding into his customary calm, 'was this sin?'

'What do you need from me?' said Cadfael. 'Ask your confessor when you come safely to Wallingford. All I know is, time has been when I would have done as you have done.'

Whether de Genville's secret would be preserved inviolate was a question never asked, the answer being already clearly understood between them. 'This is better than by morning,' said Rafe, rising. 'Your order of hours tomorrow need not be broken, and I can be away early, and leave my place cleansed and furbished and ready for another guest, and travel the lighter because I do not go without a fair witness. I'll say my farewell here. God be with you, Brother!'

'And go with you,' said Cadfael.

He was gone, out into the gathering darkness, his step firm and even on the gravel path, silent when he reached the grass beyond. And sharp upon the last slight sound of his going, the bell rang distantly for Compline.

Cadfael went down into the stables before Prime, in a morning dry and sunny but chill, a good day for riding. The bright chestnut with the white brow was gone from his stall. It seemed empty and quiet there, but for the cheerful chirpings of chatter and laughter from the last stall, where Richard had come down early to pet and make much of his pony for carrying him so bravely, with Edwin, happily restored to grace and to the company of his playmate, in loyal attendance. They were making a merry noise like a brood of young swallows, until they heard Cadfael come, and then they fell to a very prim and seemly quietness until they peeped out and saw that he was neither Brother Jerome nor Prior Robert. By way of apology they favoured him with broad and bountiful smiles, and went back to the pony's stall to caress and admire him.

Cadfael could not but wonder if Dame Dionisia had already visited her grandson, and gone as far as such a matriarch could be expected to go to re-establish her standing with him. There would certainly be no self-abasement. Something of a self-justifying homily, rather: 'Richard, I have been considering your future with the abbot, and I have consented to leave you in his care for the present. I was grossly deceived in Cuthred, he was not a priest, as he pretended. That episode is over, we had all better forget it.' And she would surely end with something like: 'If I let you remain here, sir, take care that I get good reports of you. Be obedient to your masters and attend to your books . . .' And on leaving him, a kiss perhaps a little kinder than usual, or at least a little more warily respectful, seeing all he could relate against her if he cared to. But Richard triumphant, released from all anxieties for himself and others who mattered to him, bore no grudge against anyone in the world.

By this hour Rafe de Genville, vassal and friend of Brian FitzCount and loyal servitor of the Empress Maud, must be well away from Shrewsbury on his long ride south. So quiet, unobtrusive and unremarkable a man, he had hardly been noticed even while he remained here, his stay would soon be forgotten.

'He is gone,' said Cadfael. 'I would not slough off the burden of choice on to you, though I think I know what you would have done. But I have done it for you. He is gone, and I let him go.'

They were sitting together, as so often they had sat at the last ebb of a crisis, weary but eased, on the seat against the north wall of the herbarium, where the warmth of noonday lingered and the light wind was shut out. In another week or two it would be too cold and bleak for comfort here. This prolonged mild autumn could not last much longer, the weather-wise were beginning to sniff the air and foretell the first hard frost, and plentiful snow to come in December.

'I have not forgotten,' said Hugh, 'that this is the tomorrow when you promised me a fitting ending. So *he* is gone! And you let him go! Another he, not Bosiet. You were aching for him to tire of his vengeance and depart, more likely to urge him away than try to prevent. Say on, I'm listening.'

He was always a good listener, not given to exclamation or needless questions, he could sit gazing meditatively across the dishevelled garden in receptive silence, and never trouble his companion with a glance, and never miss a word, nor need many of them for understanding.

'I am in need of the confessional, if you will be my priest,' said Cadfael.

'And keep your confidences as tightly sealed – I know! My answer is yes. I never yet found you in need of absolution from me. Who is this he who is gone?'

'His name,' said Cadfael, 'is Rafe de Genville, though here he called himself Rafe of Coventry, a falconer to the earl of Warwick.'

'The quiet elder with the chestnut horse? I never saw him but the once, I think,' said Hugh. 'He was one guest here who had nothing to ask of me, and I was grateful for it, having my hands full of Bosiets. And what had Rafe of Coventry done, that either you or I should hesitate to let him go?'

'He had killed Cuthred. In fair fight. He laid his sword by, because Cuthred had none. Dagger against dagger he fought and killed him.' Hugh had said no word, only turned his head towards his friend for a moment, studied with penetrating attention the set of Cadfael's face, and waited. 'For good reason,' said Cadfael. 'You'll not have forgotten the tale we heard of the empress's messenger sent out of Oxford, just as King Stephen shut his iron ring round the castle. Sent forth with money and jewels and a letter for Brian FitzCount, cut off from her in Wallingford. And how they found his horse straying in the woods along the road, with blood-stained harness and empty saddlebags. The body they never found. The Thames runs close. There's room in the woods for a grave. So the lord of Wallingford was robbed of the empress's treasure. He has beggared himself for her long ago, ungrudging, and his garrison must eat. And the letter meant for him was stolen along with all the rest. And Rafe de Genville is vassal and devoted friend to Brian FitzCount, and loyal liegeman to the empress, and was not minded to let that crime go unavenged.

'What traces he found along the way to bring him into these parts I never asked, and he never told me, but bring him they did. The day he came I met with him in the stables, and by chance it came out that we had Drogo Bosiet lying dead in the mortuary chapel. I recall that I had not mentioned the name, but perhaps if I had he would still have done what he did, since names can be changed. He went straightway to look at this dead man, but at a glance he lost all interest in him. He was looking for someone, a guest here, a stranger, a traveller, but it was not Bosiet. In a young fellow of twenty, like Hyacinth, he had no interest at all. It was a man of his own years and estate he was seeking. Dame Dionisia's holy man he must surely have heard about, but dismissed him as priest and pilgrim, vouched for and above suspicion. Until he heard, as we all did, young Richard bellow that the hermit was no priest but a cheat. I looked for Rafe afterwards, and he and his horse were gone. It was an impostor and cheat he was looking for. And he found him, Hugh, that night at the hermitage. Found him, fought him, killed him. And took back all that he had stolen, jewels and coin from the casket on the altar, and the breviary that belonged to the empress, and was used to carry letters between her and FitzCount when they were apart. You'll recall that Cuthred's dagger was bloodied. I have dressed Rafe de Genville's wound, I have received his confidence as I have now delivered you mine, and I have wished him godspeed back to Wallingford.'

Cadfael sat back with a deep and grateful sigh, and leaned his head against the rough stones of the wall, and there was a long but tranquil silence between them. Hugh stirred at last, and asked: 'How did you come to know what he was about? There must have been more than that first encounter, to draw you into his secrets. He said little, he hunted alone. What more happened, to bring you so close to him?'

'I was with him when he dropped some coins into our alms box. One of them fell to the flags, and I picked it up. A silver penny of the empress, minted recently in Oxford. He made no secret of it. Did I not wonder, he said, what the empress's liegeman was doing so far from the battle? And I drew a bow at a very long venture, and said he might well be looking for the murderer who robbed and slew Renaud Bourchier on the road to Wallingford.'

'And he owned it?' said Hugh.

'No. He said no, it was not so. It was a good thought, he said, almost he wished it had been true, but it was not so. And he told truth. Every word he ever said to me was truth, and I knew it. No, Cuthred was not a murderer, not then, never until Drogo Bosiet walked into his cell to enquire after a runaway villein, and came face to face with a man he had seen, talked with, played chess with, at Thame some weeks before, in a very different guise. A man who bore arms and showed knightly, but went the roads on foot, for there was no horse belonging to him in the stable at Thame, none that came with him, none that departed with him. And this was early in October. All this Aymer told us, after his father had been silenced.'

'I begin,' said Hugh slowly, 'to read your riddle.' He narrowed his eyes upon distance, through the half-naked branches of the trees that showed above the southern wall of the garden. 'When did you ever question so far astray without a purpose? I should have known when you asked about the horse. A rider without a horse at Thame and a horse without a rider wandering the woods by the Wallingford road make sense when put together. No!' he said in shocked and outraged protest, staring aghast at the image he had raised. 'Where have you brought me? Is this truth, or have I shot wild? *Bourchier himself?*'

The first tremor of the evening chill shook the harvested and sleepy herbs with a colder wind, and Hugh shook with them in a convulsion of incredulous distaste. 'What could be worth so monstrous a treason? This was fouler than murder.'

'So thought Rafe de Genville. And he has taken vengeance for it in measure accordingly. And he is gone, and I wished him godspeed in his going.'

'So would I have done. So I do!' said Hugh, and stared across the garden with lips curled in fastidious disdain, contemplating the enormity of the chosen and deliberate dishonour. 'There is nothing, there can be nothing, worth purchasing at such a price.'

'Renaud Bourchier thought otherwise, having other values. He gained his life and liberty first,' said Cadfael, checking off the score on his fingers, and shaking his head over every item. 'By sending him out of Oxford before the ring of steel shut fast, she released him to make off into safer pastures. Not that I believe he had even the excuse of being a simple coward. Quite coldly, I fancy, he preferred to remove himself from the risk of death or capture, which have come closer to her armies there in Oxford than ever they came before. Coldly and practically he severed all his ties of fealty, and retired into obscurity to look round for the next opportunity. Second, with the theft of the treasure she entrusted to him he had ample means to live, wherever he might go. And third, and worst of all, he had a powerful weapon, one which could be used to secure him new soldier service, and lands, and favour, a new and profitable career to replace the one he had discarded. The letter the empress had written to Brian FitzCount.'

'In the breviary that vanished,' said Hugh. 'I knew no way of accounting for that, though the book had a value even for itself.'

'It had a greater value for what was in it. Rafe told me. A fine leaf of vellum can be folded into the binding. Only consider, Hugh, her situation when she wrote. The town lost, only the castle left, and the king's armies closing round her. And Brian who had been her right hand, her shield and sword, second only to her brother, separated from her by those few miles that could as well have been an ocean. God knows if those gossips are right,' said Cadfael, 'who declare that those two are lovers, but surely it is truth that they love! And now at this extreme, in peril of starvation, failure, imprisonment, loss, even death, perhaps never to meet again, may she not have

222

cried out to him the last truth, without conceal, things that should not be set down, things no other on earth should ever see? Such a letter might be of immense value to a man without scruples, who had a new career to make, and needed the favour of princes. She has a husband years younger than herself, who has no great love for her, nor she for him, one who would not spare a man to come to her aid this summer. Suppose that some day it should be convenient to Geoffrey to repudiate his older wife, and make a second profitable marriage? In the hands of such as Bourchier her letter, her own hand, might provide him the pretext, and for princes the means can always be found. The informer might stand to gain place, command, even lands in Normandy. Geoffrey has castles newly conquered there to bestow on those who prove useful to him. I don't say the count of Anjou *is* such a man, but I do say so calculating a traitor as Bourchier would reckon it a possibility, and keep the letter to be used as chance offered. What knowledge, what suspicion, brought Rafe de Genville to doubt that death by the Wallingford road I do not know, I never asked. Certain it is that once the spark was lit, nothing would have prevented him from pursuing and exacting the penalty due, not from some supposed murderer – he told me truth there – but from the thief and traitor, Renaud Bourchier himself.'

The wind was rising now, the sky clearing, the broken fragments of cloud that remained scudding away before the wind. For the first time the prolonged autumn hinted at winter.

'I would have done as Rafe did,' said Hugh with finality, and rose abruptly to shake off the residue of loathing.

'When I bore arms, so would I. It grows chilly,' said Cadfael, rising after him. 'Shall we go in?'

Late November would soon be tearing away with frost and gales the rest of the quivering leaves. The